T0128862

TEACUPS AND SANDSTORMS

A Novel

Susan Yorke

TEACUPS AND SANDSTORMS
A NOVEL

iUniverse books may be ordered through booksellers or by contacting:

iUniverse
1663 Liberty Drive
Bloomington, IN 47403
www.iuniverse.com
1-800-Authors (1-800-288-4677)

Because of the dynamic nature of the Internet, any web addresses or links contained in this book may have changed since publication and may no longer be valid. The views expressed in this work are solely those of the author and do not necessarily reflect the views of the publisher, and the publisher hereby disclaims any responsibility for them.

Any people depicted in stock imagery provided by Thinkstock are models, and such images are being used for illustrative purposes only. Certain stock imagery © Thinkstock.

ISBN: 978-1-4917-6930-0 (sc)
ISBN: 978-1-4917-6929-4 (e)

Library of Congress Control Number: 2015908855

Print information available on the last page.

iUniverse rev. date: 07/28/2015

For all the toilets that have been violated with my Death Ray Stench, including those at Marshalls and Walmart where staff and customers alike thought the sewer had backed up. To all the nurses on the 7th floor of St. Anthony's hospital who allowed me to release my gases and "blend in" with all the sick people.

CHAPTER 1

"Do you know you have your t-shirt on backwards again, Herman?" Alfred nods at me over his cup of afternoon tea. For the better part of thirty years, give or take, Alfred is the reason I hang on for dear life when shit starts flaring up. He reminds me of an overdressed starship navigator every time I get the urge to vomit; the quizzical stare at me over his trifocals when my stomach makes those impressive gurgling sounds like a Klingon in heat. And the way his daily uniform of Ralph Lauren, Calvin Klein and Dockers all fit together like a Ken doll making its debut on Star Trek. Only rounder. "Did you wonk your head on the door again?" Alfred asks in his usual Vulcan-like manner. I scrutinize him for a moment before answering.

"No, I did not wonk my head on anything. And no, I don't care if it bothers you that I have my shirt on backwards, yet again." I respond. "Why, does it bother you how I wear this or any other shirt?"

I sit my over-sized teacup down on the antique oak table, and relax against the arm of my recent find: thrift chair a-la-king. A vintage masterpiece, handcrafted spiral inlays, oak and cherry married into a throne wherein I can relish at my leisure, a bar of rich Irish chocolate. The chair purchased a week earlier and Alfred gets to enjoy it first before I am able get anywhere close to enjoying anything from my throne. Except for today. Today, I sit in my chair and enjoy the way the wood hugs my body against its sultry curves and aging varnish. The arm rests are precise as I settle in against the chiseled decorations; I feel like a marionette waiting to dance a barynya on the holodeck.

The ominous low-hanging grey-white skies of Denver grumble as the wind picks up a leaf and drags it along the front walk. The kitchen wall clock murmurs with a tick and tock as I sip my tea. My Spidy sense twitches as a tree branch taps at the window: Danger! Danger! We sit opposite each other this cheerless Tuesday afternoon, biting at each other like a pair of old roosters. I take out my spiral notebook and begin to scratch away on the first line. Alfred clears his throat before summing up his usual cursory edits of dressing.

"Yes, it bothers me. It bothers me that the tag is in the front and located under your chin where the wash and care instructions are in plain view. I would rather not read the tour dates of Korn first. The cemetery of zombies and god-knows what else should be facing me. Not this tombstone stretched between your man-tits. You dress as though you are five and not in your seventies." Alfred takes another chocolate chip muffin and peels its wrapper off. I frown at the much shorter version of myself.

"Do you know what annoys me, Alfred?" I stare at my friend as he continues to pick apart the muffin.

"No, what?" Alfred muffles through a mouthful of dough and chips. He ignores the annoyance on my face as he continues to picks out all the chocolate.

"You dissect your food as though it's Biology 101 all over again. First, you eat the top of the muffin followed by picking out the chocolate chips and leaving the rest of the muffin in a heap on the table. You do the same thing with a Reese's, too; eat all the chocolate off the sides, peel off the top and this hunk of peanut butter is sitting between your fingers, then you proceed to eat it as though you have all the time in the world. Why not just eat a jar of peanut butter and save us all the horrors of your eating habits?" Al's despicable eating give me an idea.

I scribble my usual unreadable (only to others) script: *In his younger days, he (Professor Etiquette) would have been slapped upside the head for dismantling food at the table the way a mechanic tears down an engine. His behavior, grounds for instant admission to boarding school. A refined man, Professor Etiquette married an equally refined and proper woman. They had four proper children who all became doctors and lawyers and left the refined and proper nest to start their own refined and equally proper nest of dysfunctional and overwhelmingly boring offspring. Tremont, another Ken doll replica and the youngest son to leave the nest, bid his refined parents fair* well as he blazed a trail of his own away from his parents. Professor Etiquette and his beloved Brittany Lucille Parker, the swan-like debutante of a wealthy family in the Polo Grounds, and heir to a house big enough to accommodate all the glamour and elegance from the Confederate and Colonial Armies, separate and ride the wings of a different wind. Alfred never notices Brittany's appearance; devastating, thin and hollow after the last of their young left the nest. Her only lot in life: germinate and nurture replicas of herself. P.E.'s refined and proper mate left him in the middle of the night; her death leaving a barren and empty hole sitting in the core of a man unsure and confused; the silence came to him in such a flurry that he unwittingly turned to me for companionship. I attended the funeral at his request, refusing to begrudge him any argument of the no-contact imposed by his mate. I view P.E. the same way I do the guys feeding pigeons in Washington Park day in and day out. Their lives no longer crystal and sparkling; gone are the dances and parties until dawn, gone like stars in the morning sky. Gone are the days of the business meetings, luncheons, pretty secretaries, office gossip, the shuffle of papers from one box to another, nagging phones and nagging wives. He is by accounts a surrealistic dinosaur walking the earth in search of a place to rest his ass. P.E., the savvy business guy with a knowledge that rules in the business world. And there is me, the college professor. The laid back geek-nerd all the kids adore. The guy who lives and breathes Sci-Fi, history, rock-n-roll. Romance is my nemesis; love the ladies. Unlike P.E., with the one and only on my deck, I have few ex-wives waiting for me to die so they can split my fortune. (Just the other day I had the overwhelming idea to donate a rather generous portion of my wealth to a group of kids just starting their own band. My exes are going to have a field day wiggling out any money from a group called the Beastie Boys.)

I look up from writing and see Alfred stripping down another muffin. My inspiration vanishes. The chips fall like star fleet officers in an episode of Star Trek the onto the plate. He laps the chips up like an animal and I wonder what Brittany or even what his parents would say if they could see this over-grown Ken doll behave in such a way. I shake

3

my head, close my eyes, and seek help from whomever is watching the same horror I am.

"Alfred, for the love of the Immortals, please stop!" I glare at Al whose face is a messy, childish chocolate smile.

"But you always wear your shirts backwards!" Alfred whines.

"And you always pick apart your food and I never say anything, until now. What would Brittany say?"

"She would …." Alfred thinks for a moment. "I guess she would get fussy with me and just prance about the place, screaming to high heaven about my eating."

"Exactly. So please, if you value your man parts, please stop! Besides, I find your habits profoundly grueling and characteristic of a man in dire need of retraining."

"Is that so? So we are going to go down this road again!" Alfred begins to relinquish his hold on the muffin.

"No, I am pointing out your horrific eating practices. I swear, it's getting worse. You do this every afternoon just like you have since college. Etiquette classes would behoove you right now. You know the ones that those fancy, hot to trot debutants in distress took in order to get hitched, cinched and ….." Alfred interrupts me with his not so cheerful retort.

"Watch it." Alfred cautions. His finger waves in the air like a flag.

"You remind me of a sandstorm" I begin. "One moment it's not there and the next it's like a vulture swooping down to kick my ass. You turn a perfectly groovy day into one of the most wretched ones, ever." I take a sip of tea and settle against the back of my chair. The afternoon grows colder and the clouds huddle overhead like dirty cotton balls.

"What do you mean I remind you of a sandstorm? Is this your way of being rude?" Alfred cocks his head at me, taking another muffin and proceeds to dissect it chip by melting chip.

"One minute I am walking along minding my own business, you walk in and get things all tumbling about and I can't see shit out of my glasses because of all the crap flying around." I am dying for a joint right now; my ass hurts from the stern beating in the chair and my stomach keeps jumping about as though I am on a trampoline.

"That's not a sandstorm Herman, that's a shit storm." Alfred stands up and walks over to the window. "There's a storm brewing."

"No shit! You think?" I shift in my seat. I am stiff and every part of me screams a Klingon battle cry. "We go through this same thing every day and it's the same shit that causes us to reach a point where we fuss at each other. You leave and slam the door behind you, return the next day and we start all over again. Our friendship is like being aboard the Jefferson Starship with ELO at the helm, and Pink Floyd is first mate!" I rub my temples. A headache begins its ascent; it's going to be a nasty one. Alfred blinks at me and clears his throat.

"Let's take a Journey with Queensryche and see if Fleetwood Mac is any closer to Rolling over Beethoven." Alfred's look said it all; our old game was afoot.

"You are one sorry, Twisted Sister, and your White Zombie girlfriend can get her Whitesnake out of my Backstreet Boys. Now are we N'YSNC?" I sneer back.

"Carry on my Wayward Son, the Foo Fighters game is now Smashing Pumpkins. I hear your Celtic Woman and her Dead Girl are tasty morsels for Dracula! You don't even have enough Guns n Roses for Lynryd Skynryd in your Paradise City! You better have a lot more Rolling Stones tucked under your Black-eyed Peas before you try that Ozzy Osbourne crap with me!" Alfred smiles while cracking his knuckles. He chomps down on a handful of neglected chips before he continues. I am behind by a few zingers but not by much. It's time to send out the torpedoes.

"So, you want a little Green Day with that Nox Arcana? Well, Meticalla. Hold onto your STYX because the Beach Boys will trample your Red Hot Chili Peppers to the ground. Matter of fact, it Smells Like Teen Spirit on your end. Better step it up a notch before I take my Nine Inch Nails and use it like a Supertramp revival. And when I'm done Breaking Benjamin up your Steely Dan, you will be exposed to The Doors and Pearl Jam will be dancing around you like Ambrosia Korn. So stick that Rob Zombie in your Papa Roach and rotate on it, you deranged Genesis Queen. Now, I've Got My Mojo Working." I am out of breath and feeling like I did when we were in college.

"Wow, Herman! Pulling out all the Monkees aren't you? I was beginning to wonder where all the Beetles were hiding and why you had been like The Byrds when it comes to bringing out Def Leppard from the Jackson 5. You have caused me to Rush to Boston. I can almost KISS you in Kansas but not without R.E.M sitting next to me holding my White Lion in her hand." Alfred giggles.

"You're funny and disgusting, Bluegrass Momma. One of these days you will wind up on Skid Row and then you will be AC/DC for sure. Cinderella I am not. I plan on putting up a Quiet Riot just to Poison your sick little XTC. I'm going to dance with the Hooters like a Motorhead and then U2 can see just how Great White I am." I snicker as my friend searches for a comeback. The good times are back and rolling.

"Judas Priest, Iron Maiden. All that Tesla you put up and not one Dio or Ratt in the mix? Why I am the Survivor of this Kix? Rage against the Machine will be present when I put my Warrant up your Living Colour and psychedelic Bee Gees!"

"You found that in Europe didn't you old Blondie? I put all my Blood and Sweat and Tears into this and all you give me is a Blue Oyster Cult which doesn't even amount to The Carpenters. You are nothing but a Cheap Trick. You are like the Climax Blues Band; always in Dire Straits with Dust settling on The Emotions of your Earth, Wind and Fire. You are so lame that not even The Cars will be able to free your Heart or your Hotlegs from the MC 5. As a matter of fact, that Eruption you're feeling right now in the pit of your Meat Loaf and Nazareth is doing a Point Blank all over your MC Hammer. All those Pretty Things you used to know are mere Raspberries and Scorpions mocking you like Donna Summer. No Pentagram to help you get out of this one. Triumph is a Three Dog Night all over your Parliament, and Toto and his UFO are like the Village People at this point; Wizzard, Zoot, and Sweet. The Talking Heads have spoken and that just leaves Stevie Wonder to ponder whether the Simple Minds are more like The Runaways or The Outlaws. Time for you to sing The Moody Blues because you are all Humble Pie." I am the warrior of my ship and the captain of my voyage as I take the helm and steer yet another whammy to my friend.

"Gees get me some Cream will you? I'm feeling a bit Thin Lizzy here. My Rainbow and The Who are like the Eagles right now. Uriah Heep better than I expected and my Foo Fighters and I are going to Aerosmith out of here like Foreigner. YES, I'm going to get the T-Rex out of here before you get all Bay City Rollers on me and Badfinger me like a Grand Funk Railroad going after Stevie Nicks." Alfred winks at me over another muffin.

"Good-bye Tom Petty and the Heartbreakers. Take your Iron Butterfly home and get a good night's Focus. You're going to need it, Isis. And Foo Fighters have already been taken, can't use it. No points this round. Now What You Gonna Do?" Alfred looks at me the way a dog looks when you are eating a hamburger in front of it: doe-eyed.

"Alright Firefall, you may have just won The First Edition after all." Alfred picks up another muffin and marvels at the chocolate decadence.

"You bet your Creedence Clearwater Revival I have, Cactus!" I about yell, puffing out my chest like a peacock.

"So, Rosemary, want some Tarragon to go with that Cinnamon you have stashed with Bad Company?" Al sachets over to the couch with two more muffins. *Note to self: next time hide my muffins from P.E. Handleman.*

"Stay out of my spice rack Vanilla Bean or I'll Tabasco you all over the minced onions!" I struggle to get out of the chair like some invalid. Everything screams from my hips to my big toe. *Phasers set to stun, commander.*

"Keep your Nutmeg on, Allspice, we don't need your Baking Soda flouring the halls of Mustard Seed." Tears spill from my friend's eyes. His laughter infectious.

"Worcestershire do you come up with all these sprinkles? I thought you had No More Tears for Fears left in your repertoire."

"Guess it's thyme for celery, fennel and cardamom to head home and evaluate the situation in the icebox. Some damn bagel head ate all my beer, brauts, and beans and then had the nerve to leave an empty box of Fruit Loops on the stove. Damn cereal killer." Al shakes his head, downing the rest of his muffin and tea.

"I have something for you, Al. Something from the old days. A reminder of when the stress was less and food was aplenty." I walk across the room to one of the many bookshelves that line the walls of my house.

Where is Bones when you need him; intruder alert on decks 7 through 11. I open the book box of Gulliver's Travel and take out a baggie of weed left by a friend. *This should liven things up.* I walk over to the couch.

Journal entry: P.E. is the Sunday afternoon driver-type that people honk at, he's sight-seeing, fiddling with the radio, and trying to forget the real reason he is still alive. He never goes any faster than he needs to, never speeds, never swears, and he never masturbates.

Alfred is wound up so tight that he needs to have all his screws loosened, get blind-stinking stoned, drunk and laid. Joan and the Blackhearts are singing, "I Love Rock and Roll" on the radio. A commercial for Trojans follows... *as if we need that at our age!* "Here you go, Al." I hand my friend a joint and I swear he thought I was giving him a stick of dynamite with the intent of blowing up the cereal-killing-bagel-headed-monkey that left his icebox barren.

"What the hell is this? A death warrant? Can you see me getting caught with this stuff? Can you see me behind bars? Can you see us at our age behind bars?" Al shoves the joint away.

"Dude, this is legal now. The law passed and it's all good!" I take the joint from Alfred and light it. I hold the drug for a moment before exhaling. My misery begins fades. I take another hit and feel the tension lesson. "Wow! What a rush!" I hand the joint to Al.

"You'll think it's a rush when the cops come banging on the front door and take you to the tank and lock you up with the rest of the fools. Those guys will be using you like you were a mop, wiping the floor with a man who should've have known better but didn't have the sense enough to be a Back Street Boy and leave the stage when the applause was over!" Alfred glares at me like I am twelve. I take another hit and kick back in my recliner. I am listening to the sermon but I am not following the preacher. I reach for my spiral notebook, writing is my outlet when high.

"What the hell are you doing, Herman?" He asks in his usual interrogation manner.

"I'm writing a proposal for dog shit to be used in the cultivation of sugar cane in Napa Valley. The process will utilize all pooper scooper receptacles, wherein the poop will be broken down and used to fertilize the sugar cane. I have this great antique meat grinder that I use for it...."

cuts up all the chunks and puts them into pellets for easier application. When I'm done with that one, I've got a brilliant idea about legalizing catnip. What does it look like I'm doing?" I mutter as my pen flies across the page.

"Gawd, you are just so ….gross. You better be writing your will, you're going to need one." He taps his finger on the coffee table like the Velociraptor did while taking a stroll through the kitchen looking for kiddy snacks in Jurassic Park. It is annoying, even in my current mild stoned condition.

"Know what, Al? I'm going to write a letter to Brittany and then find one of those unicorns and hot glue the sum-bitch to its ass and see if I get a response back. I wanna know if she's chasing unicorns and tossing glitter on the muffin killer who keeps pissing down my rainbow and spreading water bubble farts in the shower!"

"I don't fart in the shower." Al mutters taking the joint and assessing it before inhaling.

"And I ain't Marilyn Manson either but I sure as hell know when I fart in the shower; the dog next door barks."

"You're disgusting, do you know that Herman? You are so disgusting that…my god man, you are in your seventies. Act like it!"

"Where's the fun in that? You know what your problem is Alfred P. Handleman? You need to get loose, stoned, laid, drunk, and rode hard, put away with a hard on that rocks the underworld. Everyone living there will sing the Devil Went Down to Colorado, Smoking Dope!" I cross my arms and wait for the counter attack.

CHAPTER 2

"I see your sense of sarcasm is still alive and screaming. Don't be a dope and drop the soap!" Alfred walks over and looks down my writing. "How the hell am I supposed to read that scribbling you call writing. Your penmanship hasn't improved, that's for sure." Al hands me the joint.

"You are a Devils Reject. But I'm not jumping on your ass about it nor am I ripping out your throat for eating all my food now am I?" I take the joint, consider the pain smoldering in my rear end, and take another hit. The writing bug is underway.

"You're impossible, Herman. Why did your parents call you that tragic name in the first place? Relative have it?" Al reaches over and takes the joint from me before I am able to get another hit. He inhales several times before passing it back to me. *His eyes are glossing over.....the surfer is riding his wave.*

"For the same reason your parents gave you an equally tragic name. All the good stuff was taken. The P is for prick: see that works though, Alfred's Prick is his Handle, Man!" I bust out laughing. I am laughing so hard that I fall out of the recliner, rack my balls on the arm and land on my knees. The pain spreads through my groin like a speeding meteor. Tears spill down my face like Niagara Falls but I don't care. I am stoned and everything and everyone is hilarious.

Journal entry: *Even though he fumes like a frigging volcano, P.E. is damn entertaining.*

"The P stands for Peter." Alfred huffs. I laugh even harder.

"Alfred's Peter is his Handle, Man!" I am rolling on the floor holding my aching sides. "You are frigging insane, Al. That P has gone straight to your head." I snicker and belt out another series of laughs.

"Your Peter has a head!" The pain in my sides moves to my groin. I cannot stop laughing.

"So disgusting, you ancient old, smelly pothead!" Alfred bellows at me. "You belong in an asylum for the mentally stoned!"

"Will you come visit me after you remove your head from the Skittle bag? I saw you picking them out and then stuffing them down your pants. Did Peter, Skittle around too much while playing with his Fruit Loops?" I state in a sarcastic, little boy voice. I laugh so hard that a snort escapes.

Journal entry: The nose-snort comes from nowhere pretty much like all the old man sounds do when you reach a certain age. Like old people smells arrive after one starts cruising into their forties; the farts smell worse, the armpits need sponging five times a day, and the crotch tends to smell like oysters accompanied by an onion and garlic waltz. The friction cascades between the thighs until the cotton begins to pucker up and thin out. That's the where the stench lies, in the seams of the unsuspecting old guy. The dormant alien unleashes its hold on the crotch and begins the hot air balloon assent to the nose and to surrounding territories. Its smell spreading like the mushroom cloud over the room. Old people smells sneak up on you like the snort does. The body does strange and peculiar things as we age. Things get worse by fifty. Everything is like a Starburst; sweet and bitter all in one bite. Old age has its perks, but damn, I snort!

I roll over on my back and look up at Alfred. He misses the chair and lands on his ass on the carpeted floor. He is laughing so hard that he pisses in his favorite pair of slacks. "Alfred's Peter had an accident!" I snort out again.

"I know!" Alfred says laughing. "I know!" He reaches for a napkin to wipe the tears from his face only to find that he is wiping his face with the muffin wrapper of crumbs. This sends Alfred in to a furry of unfettered laughter.

Journal entry: I witness the long lost P.E. from Northeastern. Cowboy U. Suitcase College. The agricultural college with its Rocky Mountain Oyster Fries, farm-fed gals, buck-riding boys, red neck professors that swoon over outstanding grades and curse the grades that damage their egos. We hear it all week long until Friday. Most of the kids head home to do laundry. P.E. and I stay behind to conquer damsels and pitchers of beer in distress. After a few drunken stints at Cowboy U, P.E.'s parents yank him out of junior college, send him to Harvard and that is the last I hear of him until he and Brittany hook up like a pair of tribbles stuck in a food replicator.

From time to time, P.E.'s name pops up like a Jack in the Box inside the business section of the Rocky Mountain Post. Sometimes his name is listed in advertisements, dark and looming. P.E. made his mark in life. Carpe Diem, he did. My mark, my moment is different. Teaching creative writing to kids that have yet to figure out the difference between the noun, verb, or subject. They believe that "really" and "seriously" are the only two words in the English language that are able to sum up their feelings. They can barely speak coherently, another battle I add to my list of accolades. I have no business plan or marketing strategy other than making it to the john in time to puke my guts up or lavish the john with a round of defecting aliens from the torpedo area. I can heave from both ends at the same time without hesitation. The endless battle of not knowing what I have bothers me. Without notice, my back spasms and this most intense pain hold me hostage until my hands cramp up for no apparent reason. I never let anyone hear me scream or cry. Joints keep me sane, keep me mellow, functioning at a level where I can operate at minimal thrusters. Teaching occupies my mind. High school kids, college kids, they are all the same.......they don't take anything seriously.

* * * * * * *

"Great things are done by a series of small things
brought together."
--Van Gogh—

Journal entry: I find a temporary docking post at Classen High School for a decade. I meet students that I will not want to meet outside the classroom. They are vicious misfits and they all belong to the same gang named" I don't give a fuck." Half of the kids I flunk, a quarter of the remaining students drop out or transfer out of my class or the district all together, leaving a quarter of students that have to finish high school. They walk across a stage to receive a piece of paper that they can wave at the world. That small piece of paper, given to a few brave souls in exchange for 12 years of education. Proof that something is accomplished, a stepping stone to college if they are lucky. The last bunch of graduating seniors are my last. I resign my post and run like hell to some other tower of teaching. When one door closes, sometimes the overwhelming need for a hammer and nails is needed to make sure that bitch stays shut. I was hammering that door closed when a letter from Metro State flew in the window. I took flight in a new direction but not before my body does a tapioca dance and a succession of stomach cramps cause me to wish I was dying. So much pain. I call Dr. Haggel; he looks like a pedophile, strides in as though he has a rod crammed up his anus; all you have to do is lick him to know he is not cherry flavored pot grown in my home state. His ginger hair is fluffed up and matches his high collar stripes and swirl shirt. The crease in his slacks indicates that someone from the dry cleaners is meticulous; an urge to puke all over his freckles quickly backs down the moment he hands me a script for pain meds. I smoke pot, the last thing I need is some bullshit doctor with wall of degrees issuing me more narcotics. I want answers but he can't help. I recall our conversation as though it just happened.

"What do you mean you can't help me? I'm tossing cookies, have the squirts, I sleep all fucking weekend. I ache all over. I feel like someone stuck a hemorrhoid sticker up my ass overnight and you tell me that you can't help me?" I am yelling at this person who stands before me with a pad of paper, a pad of blank prescriptions and mocks me with his chevron eyes. He stands as clueless as a dodo with a watermelon at the beginning of the ice age. I am missing a class room of writing-challenged students to speak with a doctor who is probably the first one in the can of stupid to escape.

"Well, I can call around to a few specialists in the area and see if any of them can help. Beyond that, all I can do is give you some pain medication. I will give you one refill and then you have to come back and see me." He scrawls his notes, changes pens and issues a note for drugs. "The nurse will be in to draw some blood....to make sure you aren't, you know, diabetic." He leaves the room. I stare at the wall of degrees and wonder if all doctors are this stupid or just this one. *More fucking drugs, I don't need those, you gawd damn motherfuckingasshole!* The door opens and a young Hispanic nurse waddles in. She looks as though she is ready to pop out a mini version of herself at any moment.

"Mr. Strickland, I'm going to take your temperature again and your blood pressure. Then I am going to draw a few vials of blood for the lab." She announces her lines with precision. She is as friendly a piranha in a pool of blood. A thermometer grazes the underneath side of my tongue. Her cool hand grips my left wrist, counting off the beats of life under her tips. A beep goes off and she removes the stick from my mouth. "Your temperature is 98.4. A bit low, but not bad. Now roll up your sleeve for me." She places the cup around my arm, pumping the cuff until it bulges. Her name tag is askew; Mildred. I notice the fine lines of grey starting to splay around her temples. Not unattractive until I see her eyebrows; I am not fully versed on cosmetics but, Queen Nefertiti did a better job painting hers on. "Your blood pressure is 130 over 98, Mr. Strickland." *That's because I'm here where stupid meets the painted piranha.* I smile. Mildred wraps a rubber tube around my arm and begin searching for a vein. A needle the size of a whaling harpoon is unsheathed. I turn my head away and look at the wall of stupid degrees, again. *Are those damn things multiplying? Seems like there were three the last time I counted.* It's not a poke nor a prod, but a ram into my arm that makes me wince. "Okay, you are done." She says putting the last vial on the counter. I roll my sleeve down and I'm ready to get off the table when Mildred announces her best kept surprise. "You need to collect a sample of your feces for these containers and then bring them back as soon as they are full." She is not joking as she hands me the bag with the plastic containers.

"You're kidding, right?" I look like the deer in the headlights with a sucker punch from my ex-wife.

"No. We will send the samples off to the lab to see if there is something we are missing."

"And what are we hoping to find? Gold or rubies?" I look inside the bag and feel a slight nausea forming.

"Neither."

"How do you propose I collect my shit in these containers, Mildred?" My curiosity gets the best of me.

"You cannot go in the toilet. You have to collect it and bring it back. Good day, Mr. Strickland." She turns and leaves me sitting on the table. *How in blue blazes do you collect shit without crapping in the crapper? On paper like some damn puppy?* I am at a loss for words as I leave Haggel's little shop of piranhas. *I miss a half a day of teaching to be told that my shit…. I am not making this up, am I?*

The conversation still makes me wonder what the hell I thought I was doing asking Dr. Stupid for help. I drive home in shock, park in the driveway and open the bag of goodies Dr. Stupid gives me. Two plastic containers with pop off lids; a spoon and two labels. *Enter thing one and thing two.* Inside the safety of my house, I take a joint out and proceed to light it, letting the drug do its job. I hurt like I have never hurt before. I am holding the bag of crap catchers wondering in the depths of my saturated brain how creative I have to be to catch my own crap.

The next morning phase one of crap catching begins. I was not successful. I place a plastic trash bag over the commode to catch my droppings. The bag falls into the blue waters and I lose my shit. A mouthful of colorful expletives races out into the silence. I hang my head, still swearing and cursing up a storm when a wave of nausea hits….now my shit is covered in macaroni and cheese leftovers. I call the University….the House of Herman is sick for what appears … I have lost track. As soon as I lay down, I'm out for the count. I wake up the following morning, feeling tons better than the day before. My stomach screams and I race for the head only not fast enough. My bowels drop the bomb and it runs down my leg. A perfect start to the morning. I clean up and drag my tail to the University. I am not even at my office before the Dean shows up and sees me looking like something out of a horror flick. He sends me home, no questions asked. I pass out as soon as I hit the couch.

I wake up to the grumblings of my stomach. I know the signs, the fury of the Titans on the brink of battle. I quickly gather another trash bag and lay it on the floor of the bathroom, drop my drawers and there she blows. My shit hits the bag….fresh, fuming, and ready for scooping. I fill both the containers, cap them off, label them and drop them in the paper bag. A dirty job, but someone has to do it. I arrive at Dr. Stupid's office just before five, hand over my shit and leave without so much as a cursory howdy-do. Now I wait.

The weekend is here. No phone calls, no P.E., just me, the weed, and an office full of student paper in boxes. I slowly go through the collected papers of high school students. I don't know why I saved their papers. Their personal statements, stories, and hidden moments belong to me. I peruse the papers, remember each and every student like a parent remembers the time when their own offspring does something worth remembering. I remember them:

"'Cuz I don't want no one knowing how smart I is." They confess.

"You don't want anyone knowing how smart you are." I correct them.

"Yeah, that's what I said." They say. I sigh and smile.

By the time the kids made it to twelfth grade, their language leaves a lot to be desired and their grammar is quite alarming. I tutor and mentor several students once the final bell rings for the day. Only a handful of students are left to take on the world. But I remember them, each and every one of them as I write about them in spiral notebooks. I have more than sixty journals; the pages curl, barely hanging onto the metal that keeps them in place. Every pimpled-faced kid, every freckle smile, hung-over stare, Mohawk and fro-hawk, bangs and curls, tattoo and piercing, those who sneak out of class via the back door and never return, the kids with sick parents and unemployed parents collecting welfare, gifted kids, pregnant teens, the kids that are tardy or absent more than the allotted fifteen absences in a school year, and the kids that confess things to me that a school counselor should be helping them with and don't because they are too busy with their own lives to worry about those that are struggling to make it to class every day. These kids are the ones I remember long after others have shoved them out the door to face the world. The characteristics of each kid is engraved on my memory like a tattoo. Even if I want to forget them down the road, I won't because I will still see them and I cannot escape what I already know.

* * * * * *

Alfred is still sitting on the floor busting a gut. He is so high, I leave him be.

Journal entry: I remember every detail of all the stuff P.E. and I do in college. Stringing up girl's lace panties on the flagpole is the highlight of our freshman year. The wet t-shirt contests at the Wooden Kegg Saloon, and the courtship of wife number one begins.

Kathy Fey Richards of Sterling, Colorado. A farm girl straight out from one of those Harlequin Romance crap novels. She is a pulchritudinous baby; big breasts, blue-eyed-blond-babe-bombshell, with strawberry lips and an ass tight enough to pry off pop bottle caps without any effort. She wants me to be the lawyer, wealth pouring from my pockets as I defend the guilty that prey on defenseless old women and neglected children. She is a smooth talker and gets me all hard for a dream that is strictly hers. I fall hard for Kathy, never see the bottom drop out of my wallet until four months after we are married.

We marry on a crisp Monday morning at the Sterling Courthouse in October and four months later, I stand in front of the same judge with papers voiding my contract with Kathy. A law school student friend of mine gives me the low down on Kathy Fey Richards, exposing her as a vial little fraud. My wife is one of those "oh-shit-has-brought-you-home" girls. At the time of our divorce, I'm out fifty thousand, my car gone, and everything I own in the world.....all pawned, stolen, or misplaced by Kathy. The judge does not let Kathy walk. Everything she has on her at the time of her arrest is given back to me along with a divorce. A month later, the so-called "parents" are arrested for passing counterfeit twenty's and hundred's around Yuma. Seems the fresh ink on one of the bills is too fresh and someone squeals and causes quite a scene. I collect the remnants of my belongings and self-esteem and hi-tail it away before the judge changes his mind.

Mondays always come too fast after a weekend of beer-drinking-keg-partying festivals. The Wooden Kegg is closed Sunday through Tuesday, probably for good reason, college kids wear them out too fast. The first drinks of the week come on Wednesday nights, known

17

as "Drown night." We drink beer through a funnel, eat peanuts and toss shells on the floor, barf in the stud's room and come back and do it all over again, closing the bar down at midnight. By Thursday morning P.E. and I are so hung-over that the whites of our eyes are used as geological maps for our Earth Science class. We smell of vomit, stale cigarettes, and cheap perfume. That doesn't stop us from repeating the adventure Thursday night for wet t-shirt contests. Chicks with tit's the size of grapefruits get pitchers of ice water thrown on them and then we hoot and holler at them like a bunch of inbred heathens. And so the process repeats itself; close the bar down at midnight, stagger up three flights of stairs to our room, then pass out until the alarm scares us at seven forty, twenty minutes before class. Friday mornings are far worse than Thursday's because we are not the only ones hung-over and every professor on campus knows this. Half of every class smells like a swamp and fresh linen over-lays, which is rather interesting especially if you study the effects of toxic waste on the human body.

The last Friday before spring break Is brutal as this is my chemistry final. Mr. Hoofmyer stands at the front of the class as I skulk in through the back door. I carefully lay my stack of books on my work area and offer a sheepish smile at my lab partner, Verna Marple Cook. I notice for the first time that Verna is well endowed and she catches me. I stare at her ample breasts in amazement.

"Drunken vagrant" Verna hisses.

"Thank you. May the camels of a thousand flies land on your ass and carry you away." I exclaim, aware that I am still a bit hazy. I never notice Mr. Hoofmyer as he stands in front of our table. I look up at him and grin. "Morning sire." I mutter. I mean to say "sir" but "sire pops out like the joint sticking out from my tennis shoe. Mr. Hoofmyer surveys me before turning around and walking back to the front of the room.

"Mr. Strickland, were you by any chance at all, out late last night?" I nod my head up and down. "Are you aware that you smell like a rotting corpse this morning, Mr. Strickland?" Again I nod like one of those damn bobble heads my mother has perched on the dashboard of the Buick. "So it is safe to say Mr. Strickland that you are not dead, is that correct?" I nod again and this time whatever has been in my stomach suddenly erupts from me like something from The Exorcist. It lands all over Verna. Troy Masters, the chemistry nerd, gets a blast in the face. A few cursory swear bombs drop. I look up at Mr. Hoofmyer, a sheepish grin appears on my face as he yanks my hung over ass out of that seat and escorts me out of class. I do not finish chemistry or apologize to those wearing my new cologne, nor do I complete the remainder of the term or am allowed back on campus until I figure out which is more important to me; partying or studying.

Alfred is still flopping around on my front room floor laughing his ass off. I reach over and hand him a joint. At first, he pushes my hand away, shakes his head sideways and then decides he wants another hit. A few minutes later, he is thumping the floor like a Van Halen drummer and laughing until the tears run down his face.

P.E. is like all those journals I keep. At any point I can open one up like I do my underwear drawer, leave it open just to see what I find lying in wait as I sort through the endless boxers and briefs. Each boxer labeled with questions: What do they do with their lives after high school? After the tragedy or jail time? What does P.E. do in his spare time, when he's not with me? Often times I see the same acne faced-kids in each of my college English students and wonder if......
Each journal is a picture of a year that brings kids from other parts of the city and world together. And then the tapioca dance begins, I race to the john holding my butt checks as tight as I can, praying for the shit not to crawl down my legs and collect in my sandals. Or I vomit and then a rash appears. I am so exhausted from my day that I drop asleep the moment I sit on the couch. I have no real appetite. A few bites of a hamburger and I'm done.

CHAPTER 3

Journal entry:

Dr. Stupid calls me a week after the shit sample is delivered.

"Mr. Strickland, this is Lucie from Dr. Haggel's office. The samples you gave are negative."

"What does this mean, negative?" I ask.

"It means the lab can't find nothing. Your blood work is back though. You need a blood transfusion right away. You need to go to the emergency room, tell Dr. Haggel sent you for the procedure."

"Why do I need a transfusion?" My heart is thumping in my ears, something I have grown use to over the months.

"Your blood count is dangerously low. Your white blood cells are higher than your red ones. Your blood count is 6.42. You need a transfusion." She continues to dictate the message.

"Does this mean I am dying?"

"Well, you will if you don't get this transfusion."

"How long do I have?"

"Not long. Maybe a few days." She sounds more scared than I am. I thank her and hang up. I call Nutritional Health Foods and ask what I can take to build up my blood.

"You need to take some chlorophyll." The raspy-voice advises. "You need to take it once in the morning and again in the afternoon. It works but it takes a few days before your blood starts getting where it needs to."

"What is the normal blood count for humans" I inquire.

"Around 10." Heavy breathing greets my silence.

"Thank you." I hang up and stare out the window. "What the fuck do I have?" I say to no one in particular. I get the chlorophyll. It is cheaper than a needle. It tastes like bloody syrup so I mix it with water. I drink green water twice a day for several weeks before Dr. Stupid calls me.

"Herman, how come you didn't go get the transfusion like you are supposed to?" Lucie asks. She is chewing gum and it smacks against my ear. "All you had to do was go to the hospital and tell them that we sent you for a transfusion."

"I am trying a different method. I feel better. I'm taking chlorophyll."

"Dr. Haggel wants to check your blood. Can you come in tomorrow morning around eight?"

"Sure. I will be there. Do you want another shit sample, too?" I snicker into the phone. I hear the click of the other line. *Bitch hung up on me.* So I play it safe and appear at Dr. Stupid's place just before eight the next morning. My blood is drawn and I am sent away.

"So, I see Godsmack did a number on you didn't he, Al?"

"Herm, you are the Beastie Boys in Linkin Park, you know that?" Alfred falls back against the couch with a new joint hanging between his lips. He takes a long toke and slowly lets the smoke out like the caterpillar in Alice in Wonderland. Although Al isn't speaking like the caterpillar, he appears to be one right then and there.

"You are one Stone Temple Pilot, Al. "I giggle at the joke and then snort again. Since picking up my pen and writing, I notice Al is silent. I look up to see him watching me, watching him.

"Why do you care, my little Devo man?"

"The Eagles are going to invest in Hotel California. I will be back after checking out the real estate." Al gets up. I watch him the way I watch a drunk maneuver his way through a crowded alley of empty boxes and trashcans. The only thing missing are stray dogs and empty liquor bottles lining his path to the bathroom. I hear the steady stream of Al's ship clear into the front room. He forgot to close the bathroom door, another damning trait that Brittany would piss and moan about.

"You okay in there Green Day or do I have to come rescue you from Three Dog Night?" I snicker. I take another hit from the joint Al left in the ashtray next to me. I nearly smoke the entire joint before hearing Al bellow from the bathroom.

"You my man, are a lunatic! You have some weird shit in your medicine box you know that? ABBA gonna be coming here just to see why the Flintstones are so popular and why you have Michael Jackson written all over your walls!" Al is so stoned that he doesn't make any sense.

"I'm the lunatic? Al you are the veggie egg roll, and it's high time we Scooby Do you home so you can sleep this off." I get a firm grip on Al before he falls over the coffee table.

"Herm?" He begins.

"What?" The look on Al's face concerns me. We are both higher than Fruit Loops in space, but I know this look on his face.

"You got any food in your Yellow Submarine?"

"We can order out okay. What do you feel like?"

"I feel like a Trojan horse hiding shit that a man my age shouldn't hide at all."

"Such as what?" I ask sitting next to Al. I take out my cell phone and call for Chinese takeout.

"I'm hiding shit from everyone, Herm. Why did your parents name you Herman?"

"I told you. All the good names were taken but this one. Herman Melville… a guy who has a thing for a white whale got the best name." I look at my friend who is quiet. "How about Chinese tonight?"

"We foo yung to be this old." Al blurts out. "We foo yung to be stoned, chopstick." Al finds this to be hysterical and we both laugh.

"Wonton Chinese it is, grasshopper. No more shrimping for us!" I giggle as I take another drag from the roach. "You can bet your Collective Soul, Al, that you are going to dine well in Chicago even if you are Three Faces to riding around on your own Rainbow. So, what sort of shit are you hiding Al?"

"So you think that you are going to Steppenwolf all over me like The Ramones? Well, Santana, get your joint ready because Cat Stevens is here to stay and be your Candy Stryper like the Three Stooges are after a UFO lands on your Velvet Underground." Al snaps back, he takes the last remaining hit from the roach. He forgets about whatever it is that he hiding. I let it drop.

"I declare War on you X. You better get to Counting Crows because the Cornershop of this Candlebox is Everclear; you have Faith No More on this Cracker because I'm sending you my Fastball to Filter out all the Garbage that The Flaming Lips have been hiding in The Lemonheads. Furthermore my Incubus, this isn't one of your Marcy Playground type games, this is a Meat Puppets, Primal Scream, Red Kross, Sister Hazel, Soul Asylum ass-kicking! So now you know what I have in my Sound Garden, you can take your little Toadies and your Urge to Overkill and get the Weezer out of here! Now that's a dare you can take to the Stone Temple Pilots any day of the week, Radiohead." I smirk at Alfred, he weaves his head back and forth like a cobra. Al is dazed and speechless. A rapping like an SOS distress signal sounds at the door.

"You gonna get that, Butthole Surfers, or do I have to?"

"Keep your Eels in your pockets, you don't have any money, Dishwalla. You spent it all on Eve 6, remember? She took you for a ride in her Bush, and all you have to show for it is Ash in your Kula Shaker." My sides were beginning to hurt from laughing so much.

"I did not." Al scoffs. "Spent it on Mudhoney!"

"Oh, that's just wrong! High five My Bloody Valentine, now we know who The Offspring are!" I open the door and the Chinese delivery guy stands in front of me smelling of noodles. "Hey Al, Shellac him if he wants a Sponge to go with the Muppets?"

"Nope, give him one of The Smashing Pumpkins, I'm sure he'll enjoy that immensely." Al's laughter is so infectious, that the delivery kid starts laughing. So much for the no doubles on the group titles.

"Is he high?" The delivery guy asks. I take the large bag of food and hand the kid the fee plus a sizable tip. The bowl hair cut sits cutely on top of a head that is too small for the frame. The bobble head bounces up and down as the body scurries down the front walk. "Thanks!" He yells over his shoulder.

I pull out white boxes of food and line them up like Starfleet officers. The smell from each of the eight boxes lingers momentarily in a cloud until the spell is released and food is dumped onto a plate.

"In light of my current condition, Crosby, Stills, and Nash, I believe I will just take mine without the plate and proceed to pillaging the contents next to Back in Black." Al ambles back to the couch, bowing neatly to the cushions as though asking for permission to rest his backside on its lap. I am almost positive that the conversation Al is having with my couch is borderline insane. I pick up my journal and began to write. He is oblivious to what I am doing; his face buried in a box of chow Mein and chicken. I shake my head, snicker at the chaos and grab another joint from Gulliver's Travels. I stand in the doorway and inhale the drug, letting it carry my mind to where no one ever has gone been before. Al smokes it to forget and I smoke it to fight a monster that some ancestral bastard sent down through the ages, whatever it may be.

I swear that when I die or rather when my body decides it is fed up with crapping half a dozen times a day, I am going spend the rest of eternity searching for the bastard that gave me this fucking bug and stick my size twelve foot up his or her ass. I have not told P.E. that I am sick. How do I tell my friend this, while he is stoned?

Dr. Stupid's office calls. My blood work is still in the red zone. I need a blood transfusion. They find a hematologist by the name of Parker. My appointment is for the following day. I also have an appointment for another doctor, a specialist that deals with hemorrhoids. I will miss an entire day of teaching just to attend my appointments. I hope they are not like Dr. Stupid; the next idiots that escape from the can of stupid.

Dr. Parker is a guy that is right up my alley. Well-dressed dapper fellow in a grey pin-stripe suit complete with vest and handkerchief in the pocket. He smells of Old Spice. It comforts me as he takes a listen to my heart.

"Your heart knows your body is anemic, Herman. You need blood. We will test you here and see how bad it is. Have you been bleeding anywhere?"

"No. Why?" I ask.

"You are bleeding from somewhere to be this anemic."

24

"I can hear my heart in my ears. I have back spasms and they hurt like hell. They practically knock the wind out of me."

"The bone marrow in your spine is pushing the blood through your body. It's trying to keep you alive. And hearing your heart beat in your ears is not uncommon for one being anemic. We will get you squared away, don't worry." Parker stands next to me and pats my shoulder. The House of Herman is shaking.

I get to the lab, blood drawn and I'm sent home to wait for the results. I feel shitty, and call to reschedule my hemorrhoid visit. The following morning I walk into the office of Dr. Morgan. It's too sterile for my liking. Everything is like chalk on chalk, bunch of flakes in jackets. I walk into the exam room and go through the usual body checks before Morgan steps across the threshold. He's a tall, lanky guy with a white coat and binocular glasses. He smells of bleach and I shrink away from him, aware that I want nothing to do with him.

"I understand you have a hemorrhoid giving you grief." He sits in the chair across from me.

"Yes. Hurts like you would not believe." I confess. "I hate to say this, but the damn thing makes me cry."

"Yup. Those boogers are nasty. They can bring a grown man down to his knees, as you are well aware. So let's take a look shall we." He hands me a gown and asks me to disrobe from the waist down. He returns with his assistant and they have me go over to the exam table. "Okay, bend over so I can see what's going on."

"Keep in mind doc that I am leaking back there so it may be kind of gross."

"When did this start?"

"It comes and goes. Maybe a few months now or so." I indicate. I have my ass cocked up in the air like some acrobat. He pokes around, spreads my butt cheeks and finds the culprit.

"You have a rather nasty guest up there. We can schedule you for surgery in a few weeks. In the meantime, make sure to keep taking the pain meds as needed, alright?" He flips my gown over my exposed ass and leaves. This guest in my ass is not the reason why I am not feeling spunky. I dress, get the paperwork and wait, yet again for answers.

25

CHAPTER 4

Alfred Peter Handleman, aka Professor Etiquette, is the primary reason why I keep writing. One day, when I can no longer hold a pencil or pen because of the nagging hand cramps, he will be able to read what I am going through. He will know why I give him the gory details of my less than perky existence.

It is my first day teaching and I have the attention of all my students. Scared to death to step foot into a classroom full of kids, I smoke an entire joint prior to walking on campus. I am in the zone. I walk into my classroom, my knees buckle and I trip over some unseen object. Right away the entire class is rolling on the floor with me. I pull myself up from my primal stance and stand in front of the class with a shit-eating grin.

"Talk about an entrance, right?" I chuckle. Students laugh, some clap but I have their attention. "Take out your journals and write about the most embarrassing moment you have ever had. We already know what mine is…." I hear students chuckle. They hide their amusement behind fresh journals and unbroken spines; the pages wait for stories and journeys by the traveler. "I am Herman Strickland, your guide into this term's English creative writing trek."

The years roll into each other. My collection of journal entries grows and so does the convictions and confessions of my students. I take on teaching high school English (I'm sure I was stoned when I agreed to this), in addition to my college commitments and find high school students suffering in creative misery.

I admit that after a while, I am bored with the countless number of students and their lame excuses as to why they cannot put pen to paper and write an essay. On a clear, Friday afternoon in late September, I get a visit from my friend, P.E.

"Old man" he begins, "it's time to lay a little funk on them. Do a little Jefferson Starship and a Three Dog Night. Let the Blues Brothers do the rest." P.E. says, resting his backside in a chair. And that is how our little game begin. Then Brittany comes along and the good times come to a screeching halt. The Blues Brothers sing, Simon and Garfunkel split up and I stare into the empty seat of P.E. It is all very proper, but it's for shit.

During the July 4th holiday break, I go through box after box of collected writings and start browsing through the pages. I realize that hidden in the thousand or so pages I have penned in my off time, are characters and stories that are pleading to be let free into space. The pages yellow and bent with remnants of caffeine and spearmint glossing each edge. There is a faint smell of herbs brewing between the pages; the trip to the Rockies. Wild marijuana growing near a river. I pick some and place it with care between notes regarding identification of flowers and close the cover. At some point later I open that journal and take out the weed, roll it, smoke it. It is the best high in the galaxy. I didn't want to come down off that high, but eventually work reels me back in. Ten pounds drops off and I can no longer wear my size 32 jeans. Another year rolls by. Another graduating class of seniors walks across the stage. Another class of college freshman greet me in August and the gerbil in the wheel never stops running.

By the time P.E. and Brittany celebrate two years of marriage, I wobble around with another wife of my very own. We divorce six months later. She doesn't like the hours that college professors keep. She likes the money and the sex, but the rest is for shit. So she leaves me for some derelict she finds on the street corner and they have a kid or two. I lose track of her until she knocks on my door asking for money.

"Hey, baby" she says as I answer the door. "You look good," She sizes me up in her usual, dick to head survey.

"Yes. Teaching suits me. Never your gig though, was it?" I ask her. I watch her shuffle from foot to foot sweeping her stringy brunet locks over her boney shoulders. She's lost the vigor in her baby blues, she is pale and smaller now that she is with the corner gigolo.

"Herm" she begins, "I'm real sorry I made a mess of things in our marriage. I ......left you for Riley. Do you think maybe you can spare me a few hundred so I can get some food for me and the kids?" Her makeup is a smeary mess under her eyes. Picasso is googling at me instead of the drop-dead-beauty-twenty-something I married.

"Lacie, I wish things were different and that you and I stayed together because we were good once. But you left for what's-his-face, the drummer, stole thousands of dollars in antiques from me, drop me a farewell letter with divorce papers not more than six months after we are wed. You stand before me smelling of sewer and dung, a monologue for a Zombie commercial, and you want a few dollars to buy you some baubles and food, isn't that right?" I watch Lacie shuffle back and forth from foot to foot, stuffing her hands in the pockets of her ratty shorts. Her t-shirt is torn from being in a fight; a fact that I am sure is the truth.

"C'mon, Herm. Don't be heartless. Cut me some slack, ok. Please." Lacie begs, a trait I loathe.

"Okay, I'll cut you a bit of slack. Get off my front porch and if you leave quietly, I won't release the hounds of hell on your boney ass."

"Herm, don't be hateful. You know you still love me."

"Yup, like a rogue great white likes a piece of human ass."

"That's not funny."

"Oh you want funny! Well then, I love you like a python loves a rat."

"Herman! Don't be such an asshole!" Lacie screams as loud as she can despite the smallness of her too-thin frame.

"Oh, you want asshole? Why didn't say so?" I slam the door in her face, blocking out the rest of her niceties with a long, long haul on a joint. I never again see or hear from Lacie. The thing about karma is that every once in a while we get to see her wrath as well as her revenge. Sometimes we get to read what karma does to others, and the fun isn't so funny, as Lacie well knows. I read in the papers days later that Riley picked up a DWAI with two small kids sitting in the back seat of his beat up ride. Human Services gets the kids. Few days later, the mom of the kids is found; shot twelve times and her estranged husband pleads guilty. He is later found dead in his jail cell, beaten to a pulp, his pants yanked down around the ankles and Riley junior is missing. Whereabouts unknown.

Dr. Parker's office calls. Lab says my white blood cells are not supposed to be the way they are. My current red cell blood count is 6.42. The chlorophyll remedy is not working to rebuild my blood. I need a blood transfusion, immediately. I need to be at the hospital in the morning by six.

I check into the Denver General just before six. A stack of papers later and I am walking to the cancer wing of the hospital. *Dr. Parker is a cancer doctor, do I have cancer?*

The nurse, a pudgy sort with a mole lodged alongside her nose, verifies my identity. She scans my wristband, scans the charts, scans another label and leaves the room. I stare at the ceiling. The room is stark white and cold. Another cheerless environment. *No wonder cancer patients hate it here. I'd want to die at home too if I had to look at this stark, innocuous death chamber every day.*

The nurse returns with a bag of blood. She scans my wrist tag, scans the label on my chart and scans the label on the blood. I remain quiet as nurse "pudgy mole" does her job.

"Whoops. You aren't Margaret Hathaway. I grabbed the wrong bag!" Nurse Pudgy Mole rushes out of the room, yakking about a mistake. I hear her call the blood bank for A- positive blood. Someone else tells her to toss the bag away. *Whoever Margaret is, she is going to be here a bit longer. I about got your blood, missy.*

Another nurse, taller than nurse pudgy mole, comes with a fresh bag. She scans my wristband, chart, and the label on the blood. She stares at me with intent while I get comfortable in the bed. She takes my arm, ties a rubber tourniquet on and slaps around for a vein.

I turn my head. I feel a poke and the tourniquet is removed. Blood begins to feed my starving body.

"So how long will this take?" I ask in the nicest, possible way.

"About two hours, give or take. You need two pints of blood, takes about an hour per pint." She hands me a pink and white pill, the size of a honey bee. "This is Benadryl. We give this just in case you develop an allergic reaction to the blood. The antibodies match yours, but sometimes there is something in the other person's blood that may cause a reaction." I swallow the pill with water. She turns the television on and leaves the room. I close my eyes. *Sleep, take me away.*

Four hours later I am back at home. I am groggy as hell. Thankfully I still have a job and I am at the mercy of doctor's. Doctor Morgan's office checks in, surgery is delayed as he is going to be out of town for a week to attend a seminar. My surgery will be rescheduled as soon as there is an opening in his schedule. And so I wait, again.

Since I just got two pints of blood, smoking a joint is sort of out of the question. Fortunately, the effects of the Benadryl are still coursing through my body as I slink under the blankets on my bed. Sleep greets me like a long lost friend. I slip in a dream wherein I see lights and beings walking down a ramp to greet me. They wave, I wave and we greet each other like long lost relatives. They are taller than I remember, thinner too. I squint to see their faces but their features are outlines of an existence I cannot remember.

I hear the phone. The voice message replays in my dream. Call Parker when you are able too.

Another call forces me to awake, my eyes struggle to focus but my eyelids keep closing over my elements of sight. Doctor Stupid calling. Test results are negative on the second blood draw. Will find another specialist in your area. Please return this call to......I doze off. My relatives are walking towards me.....

The phone breaks into my dream. Hernan, Its Luke Hamstein, from Farmers Insurance. Hey pal give me a call. You're getting older and your insurance is cheaper. Call me, okay! I doze off, again. They are closer now, these relatives from another dimension. They do not speak, but they smile and I am at ease in their presence.

What the fuck! The phone rings again. I turn it off and lower the volume on the machine. This time I am dead asleep, for the last time.

The next morning, dopey black clouds parade overhead. The news is brimming with warnings about a potential storm. It lurks over the Rockies like a thief. Oh my goonies... locks your doors and bolt the kiddos, it's going to be a rip-snorter for sure! It made me laugh the way people scoured the horizon in search of the storm.

But the storm came P.E. It rattled my house like a ball hitting a bowling pin. I didn't just dive to safety P.E. I found refuge the moment that first siren blared. I had just enough time to grab a few essentials and you know as well I as do, one cannot live with the storm essentials: Popsicles, lighter, radio and of course, my weed. Then of course I had to drag Lady out and that made things a bit weird, but I survived P.E. all because I was thinking of you. Hoping that you were right behind me as I dove into the fucking bathtub loaded with my surplus of survival amenities carefully prepared by yours truly.

CHAPTER 5

It is gloomy, crappy, shitty........stormy as hell, tornado alarms going off every few minutes and I curl up under my mattress in the bathtub riding out the most awful storm, ever. The wind howls and my house creaks. I'm eating popsicles until the storm blows over and until I can get to the store and stock up on munchies. Ever since the blood transfusion days earlier, I feel like my old spunky self again. I close my eyes and replay the events of the day; oversleep- check, two pots of coffee-check, grade the dreadful sophomore English essays-check, lunch with Darcie Beck-check, sex with Darcie-check, Junior class essays-check, meeting with Dean Hamilton-check, dinner with Mary Strauss-check, sex with Mary-check, drinks with Beth-check, threesome with Beth and Mary-check an check, run like Banshee to bathroom-yes and all accounted for, thank you very much. The wind continues to howl and the rains pelt the windows. I am not going to be sleeping in my bed tonight; bathtub, party of three, please! I close my eyes, listening to the storm whistle around my house. It's going to be a long night, according the distant rantings of news guy on the radio.

* * * * * *

In 1972 I met a young geeky girl with lofty ambitions; storm the castle and claim the world as hers. Her only stumbling blocks are her parents. To convince them that she is a natural born writer is like trying to convince King Arthur that he doesn't control the Knights of the Round Table.

Oftentimes I think I should have left well enough alone, but it was my job as a teacher, to help set students sail in their tiny raft until they reached the shores of their destiny. Young Marion Clemson showed potential; she had a passion and a desire to fill the world with treasures her young mind fashioned out of when's and what if's. Yarn and crochet hooks. Needles and darning socks. She was not my typical student…she was different, quiet, well-mannered and scared.

"Mr. Strickland, I want to be a writer" Marion said to me one day. "I want to be like Agatha Christie or Hemingway. I want to be great." Marion was an innocent girl whose desires were a whole lot bigger than she was. Her candor was refreshing and straightforward. Standing before me was a young girl of fourteen. Her strawberry blond hair was cut just above her ears. She dressed in a boy's t-shirt, dark blue polyester pants with a crease sewn down the front of each leg, and holey tennis shoes. Her glasses were more like pop-bottles balanced on the bridge of her nose, hi-lighting the numerous freckles on her face. One of the arms of the glasses had been taped to the frames, making them lop-sided as she adjusted them to keep them from falling off her nose. A small bruise above her right eye peeked out from behind those frames and a fresh cut punctured her lower lip. Either Marion was fighting or she had been beat up, either way, I tried not to ponder what had happened to her.

Marion's reading level was that of a high-school junior. She knew words and authors most kids in ninth grade had yet explored. She was by far, brighter than any star I had ever seen and I wanted her success to be fruitful. Her mother held the snifter over her head and snuffed out that bright light of possibilities each and every night. Mrs. Clemson was a stout woman of forty, black curly locks, and clearly as arrogant as any rich middle class woman I had ever met. Negative in every, possible way. Her plans for Marion were simple; become a secretary like her and play the violin until she found a man worthy of her father. Edgar Clemson, tall and broad, a well-built man of Iroquois and Sioux decent with a grip that was as strong as his opinion. The day I first met the Clemson's I wanted to crawl back under the rock of conception and wait for danger to pass. Evil clung to them like a cocoon and I was not the only one affected by their demeanor. They had the entire school on edge the moment they sauntered over the threshold of Merrill Junior High.

"My dad thinks that all I'm good for is to be barefoot and pregnant." Marion indicated one day after class. "He doesn't really like me, Mr.

Strickland. He has his bad days when he comes home from work and storms the house like some foot solider at Wounded Knee. If I don't have dinner ready when he gets home, I get beat up. If I burn any of the dinner, I get beat up and if dinner isn't on the table exactly at four-thirty, there is hell yet to pay." Marion folds her hands in her lap.

"Have you told the school counselor?" I questioned.

"Oh hell no" Marion said looking scared.

"The last time I said anything to a counselor or nurse was in sixth grade."

"What happened?" I pressed.

"Well" Marion began, "the cops showed up at the house that night and threatened to take me away because of all the marks on my body."

"What marks?" I inquired. Suddenly I felt a stone begin its decent into the pit of my stomach. It was the same feeling I had when Alfred told me he was marrying Brittany.

"Belt marks. My dad hit me with the buckle end of the belt."

"My god!" I was trying to keep calm.

"Dad always beats me. I get blamed for everything. I even get hit with a dowel about the size of a quarter. He beats us."

"Us?"

"Yes. My brothers and I get hit with it a lot. But it's mostly me. I am the oldest and he hates me the most." Marion squirmed a bit in her chair as she held her essay in her lap. She kept reading the notes I had written in red; I had made her paper bleed the way her lip must have. "I want to be a writer, Mr. Strickland." She implored again.

"Do you still live with your parents?"

"Yes, unfortunately."

"Have the police done anything to your dad or mom?"

"No."

"Why not?"

"Because my dad said, 'I will correct my daughter the way I see fit when she steals from me. So get your nigger ass out of my house, hear me'?"

"They were black cops?"

"Yes."

"Then what happened?" I didn't know if I could bare to hear any more from the girl sitting before me. I was already in too deep to turn back. She needed to tell someone, I wanted her to tell me so that I could help her, somehow. "What did you take?" If you don't mind me asking.

"The police and the social worker left. Dad slammed the door and started yelling at me and mom. Then dad took out the stick and began wailing on me. He hit me so hard that blood started coming out of my backside. I ran out of the way but he caught me and I got hit on the back of my legs, across my back and arms. I screamed for him to stop but he just kept beating me until he had taken out all of his anger on me." Marion was crying. "I'm sorry for stealing money from his wallet. I only took it so that I could buy candy and give to my friends at school. That was the only time they would talk to me or be my friend was when I had candy. They wouldn't talk to me any other time. I was always made fun of. I was fat and ugly and my mom would always yell at me for being that way. I stole money because I was sent to bed without food because I am a bad person. I stole because I could and they hate me because of it." The tears on Marion's face fell into a chin collection bowl. A big droplet fell against her t-shirt leaving a watermark stain just above her blooming womanhood. My heart had just been ripped out of my chest, stomped on by a child that had been beaten for being different, neglected and hungry. I wanted to hold her next to me and never let her go, to call the police and have her parents arrested for abuse. I wanted revenge for Marion, to make all the bad things disappear and fill her life with all the good that was out there. Of all the things I had wanted to say, I couldn't because my own tears were hot against my cheeks.

After I collected my thoughts, I told her that I would be happy to help her become the writer she yearned to be. Parent teacher conferences or not, I would never reveal again to Mr. and Mrs. Clemson my discussion with their daughter or that I knew what they had done to her. As I look back on that last Parent teacher conference, I wish I had said something, stopped the misery that tore Marion away from this world. I wish I could undo what happened, but it was already too late.

My own world was falling apart and the battle to make it through each day was painful. I had dropped 40 pounds, my appetite was minimal, and I slept more on the weekends than I ever had as a kid.

I ached all over and I found it necessary to take hot showers in the summer so that my joints wouldn't scream "foul" every time I attempted to climb the stairs. I was always cold so I wore sweaters in the summer, suffered from heat exhaustion. I suffered from dehydration and carrying around an unlimited supply of bottled water was my lifeline to surviving each day. During the winter, I fought to stay warm. I had shut out the voice to see the doctor and kept struggling to stay on my feet. The only solace I found was smoking my illegal stash of weed. One of the best comforts afforded to mankind since the Puritans began burning witches at the stake.

"Mr. and Mrs. Clemson, so good to see you again." I lied. "Marion is a blossoming writer. Her essays and story-telling are truly imaginative. I always look forward to her creative writing assignments."

"Well, that's a first." Mrs. Clemson spoke up. "She can't spell, so maybe you should be teaching her that instead of how to write a story."

"While we are on the topic of stories, maybe you could teach her how to stop making things up and tell about things that exist." Mr. Clemson added.

"Exist?" I had to ask.

"Yeah, stories that are not make-believe. She needs to tell true stories. Like those she hears in Sunday school. Like that does any good." Mr. Clemson stated.

"Bible stories?"

"Yes, bible stories" Mrs. Clemson said matter of factly.

"I understand your concern. However, the students are given a topic to write about. That's why it's called a creative essay." I felt uneasy as I conveyed this to the Clemson's. There was an awkward silence and the Clemson's left, dragging Marion out of the classroom by her ear. I heard her yell out in the hallway and I ran to the doorway to see Mr. Clemson kick his daughter in the rear end.

"Marion you better listen and listen well. Writers never prosper and they sure has hell never have a pot to piss in." Her mother snarled. That nigger teacher of yours needs to stop filling your head with nonsense and teach you something useful like how to use proper grammar and punctuation, spelling and things like that."

"No." Marion screamed. Her mother slaps the face and then proceeds to drag Marion out the front door. Her screams filled the gap between my feet and brain. I didn't know what to do except stand there and wish for the caterpillar to tell me that things were not as they looked, but there was no caterpillar and no words of wisdom.

The following morning, Marion sat sullen in her seat in the back of the classroom as I checked attendance. The days' assignment was to write down ten things my students would change about the world and to use those ten things in an essay. Marion sat motionless. Her blank stare was more of a dead stare I had often seen in old family photos. The kind where no one smiles, but sits stoic and waits for the gun powder light to go off before breaking the pose. Then they smile and pray 'Jesus' the torture of the picture taking is over. She picked up her pencil and began to write.

* * * * *

The end of the week drew to a close and my ninth graders in four classes all turned in essays. Saturday morning arrived like a detached whisper. Aspen were beginning to remove summer coats in exchange for fall ones. The Columbines were peeking through the underbrush of spruce and pine, a gentle reminder that the changing of the seasons were at hand. I had already consumed a sizeable pot of coffee and was brewing another when my stomach cramps began singing. Late morning clouds were creeping back and forth across the sky like demons in flight. I was about to the end of reading all the essays when I came across Marion Clemson's essay. I froze as I read her essay.

If I Had the Power to Change the World
Marion A. Clemson

1. Change the way parents treat their children. If you don't want me, then don't keep me. Don't stick me in a corner and expect me to be quiet and not tell someone what you have done to me. I can't keep this secret anymore, I don't want to keep the secret. I wish someone would listen.

2. Brothers don't need to repeat what my parents have already done. I don't need brothers to beat me up or call me stupid or make me feel

any less than I already do. I need them to understand that I should be protected, not continue to hurt me by kicking in my shins or calling me names that my parents already call me.

3. Whenever I am "bad" my mother makes me read the bible. I find this a complete waste of time simply because if there is a god, why would he allow me to get beat up all the time? Why would he allow my parents to keep me when they hate me as much as they do? My favorite part of the bible is Revelations; because I know that the end is coming, it's just not soon enough.

4. Math should be easier for people like me who don't think in a logical way. Every time I make a mistake in math, my dad hits me upside the head, yells at me, and then storms out of the room leaving me to wonder why I can't get simple equations. Both my brothers call me stupid. My mother sent me to Evelyn Woods Reading Center thinking that I can't read when in fact, I can read very well. So these people tutor me and find out that I have an advanced high school reading level but math seems to have missed me. The harder they work on my math skills, the worse I get. I don't know, but math is not just not my cup of tea. Math should be easier for people like me.

5. Bad words for people really make me angry. I had a best friend once in grade school named Dolores. She was my only black friend after they let them attend our school, Washington Park, which was all white. I once asked to touch her hair, and when I did, I found it kinky and not silky like mine. Because I talked to her, I got put in the corner of the classroom where other kids laughed at me. Then I got sent to the principal's office to wait for my mother, who further assaulted me for touching Dolores. "Niggers are no good. Leave them alone. Beaners and Chinks are the same; just because one has brown skin and the other is yellow, doesn't mean you have to touch them. The next time I have to come to school because you couldn't leave your hands to yourself, I will break your fingers before your father takes the belt to your fat ass."

6. Sweetened condensed milk and graham crackers should be their own food group. I have some of this hidden in the back of my closet behind my shoes. I keep it there just in case I get sent to bed without supper and for the beating I am about to receive.

7. Hershey's chocolate makers need to keep making cases of my favorite candy. Dad keeps this box of 24 candy bars next to his recliner. Sometimes it's Mr. Goodbar and sometimes it Hershey's plain or with almonds. Sometimes, it's even the crispy goodness of Krackel! When dad is not around, I sneak into the box and take a few bars to even out the row. Dad has never figured out that I am stealing food for later..... food for thought, I am getting away with it.

8. Grandma should be my real mom. My grandmother is the sweetest woman I know. She never hurts me and her hugs are like warm sunshine on a rainy day. She smells like the roses in her garden, the raspberries along the back fence, the fresh air through a window, and the cedar that I find lining the drawers in the den. I love going to grandma's house because I can be a kid and dance to the jukebox and pretend that I am in a castle with all the animals that keep me from danger. The 'Yellow Rose of Texas' is my theme song, and only grandma knows this.

9. Dogs should always be my friend, should be someone I talk to when no one else will. Samson was my first dog and then there was Mitzi. Samson was my toy collie and Mitzi a Great Dane, the runt of the litter. Samson was taken away from me while protecting me from dad. He stepped between dad and me when was I getting beat, and it was Samson that received the blow that killed him. Mitzi had a litter of puppies and dad gave them all away, including Pretzel, my most beloved. Dad said he gave Pretzel away to a road worker that was doing construction work on our street. I found Pretzel in the trash can the next day with his neck broken and Mitzi was sent away to live out the rest of her days in the country; or so my dad said.

The neighbor's cat also had a mishap as well. One day dad was cleaning out his truck and this Siamese cat jumped up into the front seat and proceeded to do its business there. Next thing I knew, the cat was flying across the alley and hit the neighbor's garage, landing in a heap on the cement. My dad only looked at me and said, "I hate cats, especially those sons of bitches." The neighbor found the dead cat when he came home from work; he is a Rear Admiral in the military. I watched the neighbor pick up the lifeless form of the cat and take it in the yard with him. He never asked what happened, but I think if he knew, he would stop being so nice to my dad. My dad said at supper that night, 'the neighbor's cat is gone. I broke its neck before sending it back across the alley.' I wonder if the Rear Admiral ever figured it out…… (Note to dad: Do not meddle in the affairs of cats, for they are cunning and you sleep with your mouth open!)

10. Today in my orchestra class I learned about knots not notes. I hate the violin and when I have the chance, I'm going to return this hateful thing to my mother and tell her that I hate it and her. I learned to tie a hangman's noose by using the strings of the blind by the music class window. I was watching Gerry tie knots and asked him to show me how he was doing it. While the teacher was playing 45s on the record player, I was learning all about the different kind of knots one can use to secure things and to tie things up with. Knots are like math; they are logical tools needed in our lives and they help fight boredom when we have reached that moment of nowhere else to turn. Knots are extensions of time; no matter how tangled the thread or yarn may get, it's only a matter of time before the solution presents itself. Math can be solved but it's the equation that is difficult to solve. I don't have the answer, and I don't know how to get the equation because I don't understand why the solution has to be this. I don't understand a great many things, but I want too. I want to be able to tie up loose ends and the only solution I see is the knot ….. It's not a good one.

The weekend was a blur and I don't remember any of it beyond Marion Clemson's essay. Monday was my antagonist, my enemy of all enemies and I was scared shitless of what I would find. I hadn't slept since Marion's essay laid in my hands. I never left a mark on her essay; it was perfect.

My third period class came and Marion Clemson wasn't in it. She never missed a day of school. I kept telling myself that she was just tardy, or maybe she was ditching like all the other kids do but she was at least safe. I was still convincing myself of these scenarios up until and including when the office aid came into my classroom with a pink message slip. I looked at the neatly scrawled message several times before the words finally registered in my brain.

Marion Clemson - withdrawn from class/school

It was some time before I was able to acknowledge my students or fellow faculty members. I can only conclude the worst had happened to Marion and that somewhere, somehow, justice would be served no matter how cold that dish would be delivered.

CHAPTER 6

"Good morning, class. I'm Professor Strickland. Welcome to Tenth grade English." I surveyed the class of geeky-looking high school students and wondered why I ever agreed to take the class in the first place. I was already teaching Creative Writing at the community college four afternoons a week and needed to fill up my mornings until I picked up more classes at the college. I had taken the summer off from teaching to get my bearings and to grieve the sudden disappearance of Marion Clemson, my bright and shiny ninth grader who wanted to conquer the world as a writer. I had gotten a call from Principle Meister at South High Academy asking if I would be interested in teaching a writing class for the year. I jumped at the chance, probably a bit too eager, but I plunged in and here I stand in front of twenty or so fresh young minds. "Okay guys here are the rules. We write essays. We don't converse with others, or skip class unless we are dead. And last but not least, I give points for attendance and participation on top of your grade. Anyone skipping class before the almighty bell rings, will not get points. Understand?" The class looked at me through glossy eyes.....a frightening and rather maddening position to be in. But here I was, damn it. "Okay, take out some paper and a pencil and I want you to write an essay telling me about your summer. Please use correct spelling, grammar, and punctuation. The assignment is due at the end of class." I was staring at each of my twenty or so students where the brain-wheels were beginning to shift and ignite into the on position. The hamster and guinea pigs looked as though they had already given up the ghost.

Class ended and this young kid comes sauntering up to the desk and flings his essay in the tray at the edge of my desk.

"C.J. Wester." I said boldly.

"Yuppers" The kid says.

"What does the C. J. stand for?" I asked him as I did a once over of his essay.

"Christ Jesus."

"Excuse me? Your parents named you Christ Jesus? Why on earth for?"

"Whenever my dad gets pissed off at me, which is nearly all the time, he calls me Christ Jesus."

"So, what's your real name? Or do you prefer CJ?"

"My mom calls me CJ, its short for Christofer Jason, spelled with an "F" not a "PH"."

"I see. Well, for the record, I will call you CJ. Your dad must be quite a piece of work." I stated while straightening the stack of essays.

"Yeah, he's a work of art all right. A working asshole caught in a loop of shit that seems to keep him in the shit all the time. As for the piece, I would have to say he needs to get a piece of reality and leave me the fuck alone! But that's not going to happen because assholes have a habit of never stepping aside from anything. They just keep on, keeping on." CJ takes a glance at the stack of papers in my hand.

"I see." I was doing my level best not to snicker at CJ's bluntness. It was refreshing, but also quite disturbing as well. "So, CJ, this is your essay." I was not going to get involved in another student/parent thing.

"So you can read. Well, at least you aren't blind!" He yawns.

"You are full of sarcasm, CJ."

"Really? You got that already? Can't pull a sheet over your face, now can I?" CJ crossed his arms against his chest and stood as though he was ready for a fight. His shoulder length brown hair was oily, the latest shipment of sludge keeping things in place. His faded jeans, ratty and torn in places, graffiti hi-lighted boredom on both legs, his tie-dyed shirt was badly faded and in need of a good bleaching or something. Finally, the toping to this kid: shoes with holes in the toes. He was in my opinion, the very definition of tatterdemalion and that was not a compliment. I glanced back at the single sheet of paper in front of me.

"Right. Okay. So, your essay is a bit short and maybe you should think of rewriting it from its current state. I don't think, 'I smoked pot all fucking summer' constitutes an essay. Perhaps you would care to elaborate on the topic?" I ask peering up at CJ.

"Why? I think it'd good enough as it is." CJ said almost in a mocking tone.

"Maybe, but I would like you to explore what you have written and we will go from there."

"You're kidding, right? Really?"

"Not kidding and really you need to rework this." I said handing back the paper to the oiled student.

"Why? Any other teacher would have just let me go on with my life and forget I exist."

"I'm not other teachers. I want to give you a letter grade worthy of your talent. Letters 'F' and 'D' are not among them." I smiled at CJ. "So Monday you will bring back an essay worthy of a grade better than failing, all right?"

"Well shit, I had plans this weekend." CJ blurted out.

"Really, and what would that be? Sleeping, eating, taking a dump, more sleeping, eating, taking a hit off a righteous joint, and yet another dump?" I had a tendency of being spiteful at times…..I found one of my moments.

CJ stormed out of the classroom with a sheet of paper bearing only one line. I found it wadded up outside in the hallway as I headed home. I had news for CJ, he was going to write the essay and he was going to earn a passing grade…I was banking on at least a C as in Christ. I laughed aloud at the thought and then walked briskly out to the parking lot. The weekend had officially begun.

* * * *

Monday afternoon reared its ugly head in style. The coffee in the faculty lounge was half sludge. A container of sugar and several cups of creamer did little to improve its taste. There was morning gridlock in my mouth and the roar of a dinosaur in my frontal lobe. Half my students managed to be missing in action; one in particular was CJ Wester.

"Anyone know the whereabouts of Mr. Wester?" I inquired.

"Did you check the boy's bathroom? He usually hides out there smoking his wad." One student said.

"Very funny." I said mocking him. "Fine, just so you know that I was serious about the essay, each and every one of you needs to redo your essay and find a way to spell; perhaps locating a dictionary would be a useful tool at this juncture. You're spelling sucks!" I uttered more to myself than to the class. My students suddenly felt a bit of annoyance in me and they grew very quiet. The remaining class period was silent as a cemetery. Only an occasional clearing of the throat could be heard as each student worked on the revision of his or her essay. The final bell of the day bellowed through the school. Students filed out one by one, each handing in their work. I stood like a statue in the front of the class; rigid, piercing, annoying and aware that I had made the class very uncomfortable.

I walked to the main office and asked for the address of CJ Wester. Ms. Hammond, a stout little woman with a pasty round pudgy face, rosy cheeks, grey hair and blaring red lipstick handed me a slip of paper with the address.

"Thank you." I said to her. Ms. Hammond nodded to me and then proceeded to waddle back to her post behind the desk. Her penmanship was perfect. Each letter dancing into the next like a waltz across the page. It was penmanship with perpetual perfection, just like Ms. Petunia Hammond. Positively perfect.

Adams Drive was on the other end of the school district, which made me wonder why CJ Wester was attending South High Academy and not East High School. I located 666 Adams Drive sitting near the end of the block. A small empty field separated the Wester house from the corner lot. The house next to the Wester place had been boarded up and the house across the street looked as though it had been hit by a wildfire. Charred remains stood where a house used to sit. All that was clearly visible were the front stairs and a few chalk figures tumbling along the sidewalk. I began to wonder what happened but that all went away when I looked over and saw CJ standing by the front door of his house. I waved to him and CJ just stood as he had in my classroom; arms crossed against his chest ready for a fight.

"I see you found me." CJ declared.

"Yes, it was the 666 that gave it away. Although sticking it next to the Adams Drive is a nice touch. Little demonic but nonetheless a nice touch." I said climbing two stairs. *Two fucking stairs. What is with people and stairs to their house? Can't the architectural geniuses build anything without stairs? Why not a ramp?*

"Now who's being sarcastic?"

"How come you didn't come to school today?"

"Are you writing a book or doing a documentary?" CJ replied rather cheaply.

"I thought of that but you know, I decided that I wanted to do a screen play based on pot-heads in high school and searched out the one student I knew that did it so that I could get a better perspective on the subject. I am speaking to such a person am I not?" I stood my ground.

"I'm not interested." CJ said.

"Indeed. Okay, let's try this. I'll give you a jellybean and you shit it out through your nostrils and we'll both get rich."

"You're an asshole."

"And you're an idiot, but let's not start opening that box of crackers, now shall we?" I waited for an invitation into the 666 realm of Christ Jesus.

"Why are you here?"

"I'm that little yellow caution light you see in your peripheral vision each and every day flashing on and off, hoping that you will get the message that if you fuck up this opportunity, the next light you will be staring at will be the red one in your jail cell."

"Oh we are so funny, aren't we Mr. Strickland."

"Yes I am. My parents thought so too, that's why they named me Herman, so that I could be funny and cool at the same time. Once again, why weren't you in school today?" I pressed on.

"Because."

"Finish the sentence please, Mr. Wester."

"I didn't want to see your ugly face or hear your nagging voice rattling about in my overloaded brain, that's why." CJ shouted.

"Okay then, why didn't you say so instead of starting out with because?"

"What the hell is your problem, you old faggot?"

"Faggot refers to a cigarette. You would do well to look up the word first before using it incorrectly." I kept pressing the button. My finger was not going to lay off until I got my point across.

"Are you mentally off?"

"Not since my last psychological evaluation, which was fourth grade. No."

"Then what is your problem?"

"You Mr. CJ Wester, are my problem."

"Fine. What do you want from me?"

"You owe me an essay. I want it tomorrow first thing. If I don't see it or you, then I'm coming back over here for round two. Understand?"

"Fine. I'll bring it tomorrow." CJ walked through the front door and closed it smartly behind him. It had a hallow sound which was rather creepy considering the late afternoon. I made a bet with the front door that CJ would grace my classroom. The front door said nothing.....like most of my students did when confronted with a challenge.

The following afternoon, CJ Wester walked in the classroom and tossed his essay on my desk. This time it was a half sheet of paper full of writing that I would need help in deciphering. CJ slept in class but at least he was there. When the bell rang, CJ popped out of that chair faster than toast in French. He was out the door before the bell stopped. I sighed. The battle had just begun.

I pulled out CJ's essay and begged for patience and a joint.

What I Did Over Summer

On Monday I smoked pot. I did the same thing on Tuesday and Wednesday. By Thursday I was doing the same thing as I had previously, only it was more entertaining than Monday. Friday I had the munchies so I raided the kitchen after mom came home from the store and stormed it like a robber. I smoke more pot, got high and that got me into Saturday. I don't remember much beyond that only that it was Sunday and I was about down to my last ounce when I hit up my mom for some green to buy weed. She gave me five and out I went. So

I smoked the pot by five and here I live to give back the fucking essay to Mr. Strickland. The End.

At first I was surprised by the attempt on CJ's part to contrive such an essay. I thought of writing a few notes at the bottom and then decided that my notes would be served in person. I arrived at the Wester residence shortly after six. I called prior to my arrival and informed Mrs. Wester that I needed to do some additional "tutoring" with CJ. The invitation to the 666 Christ Jesus realm loomed in front of me like a vulture on a dead carcass.

Mrs. Wester greeted me as I rang the bell. She is taller than I am. Her dark hair pulled tight against her head into a bun and held in place with pins. Topaz eyes seemed to peer into my soul as she leads me into her house. She was quite pale in her grey dress with the white collar and sash around her small waist. The darkness hit me like a shovel, it was like a tomb inside the two-story Victorian home. Once my eyes adjusted to the darkness, I was able to see a room full of boxes and other odds and ends piled in front of the windows. The curtains had been drawn to keep people out and the sun from coming in. Two lamps had been turned on to hi-light the corners, causing the shadows to flee elsewhere. A stone fire place loomed like a dead dog and I immediately thought of Pet Cemetery and what happens when you wish for the beloved to be returned from death. Chairs piled with stacks of aging newspapers sat off to one side and the smell of decay settled around me like a battlefield. This was not the most pleasant of homes I had ever been in and felt as if I was in a scene for Leather Face. CJ stood next to his mother, glaring at my ability to locate him on such short notice. Mr. Wester wasn't home from his job at the meat plant. I suspected that my presence would be upsetting so I made my visit short.

"My son needs all the help he can. He's slow somewhat. Don know how he goin to git a job when he done wit school." She said. I thought my ears were going to explode with her demolished version of the English language. I so wanted to correct her, but refrained.

"It's my pleasure, Mrs. Wester." I said. "Just doing the best I can to help him." That was a lie. I wanted CJ to excel, to succeed, to be the first one in his family to get the hell out of the place he lived in.

"CJ" I began. "While your essay is, shall we say inventive, I would like to see more effort in the process. I believe you are capable of so much more, don't you think?" I was soliciting an answer.

"No."

"Why not?"

"I don't like writing, and I don't like being nagged about it either." CJ was about to storm off when his mother caught him by the shoulder and pushed him back towards me.

"I understand your situation, but, perhaps you should give it another try. I think that if you try just bit harder, you will be happy with the result."

"Will you leave me alone if I do?"

"No." I said quite calmly. "I will keep after you until you do it the way it needs to be done." I waited for CJ to run out of the room in a rage but his mother blocked his exit.

"Fine. Gees. I don't need you coming over here again. It's embarrassing."

"Not for me, it isn't. For you, maybe."

"You are such a dick, you know that?" CJ said. Mrs. Wester slapped her son in the head and he winced.

"Yes, I know. But what are you?" I waited for a response. Getting none, I let myself out the door. "Remember, tomorrow. I expect another rewrite, Mr. Wester." I walked down the front and got into my car just as a beat-up old truck rounded the corner. I assumed that it belonged to Mr. Wester, so making haste I drove off before he had a chance to corner me. I was no coward, but a man who calls his son, 'Christ Jesus' has one of those tempers that make sharks look like the Titanic.

Friday morning arrived with thunder claps as loud as cymbals. There was so much clashing and banging that one had to scream in order to be heard. By the time a person began a sentence, there was more thunder followed by a shattering light, splitting the sky wide open. I didn't mind the rain, but the hellacious foreplay of the storm was about as scary as walking into Dr. Stupid's office with the painted piranha. The mere thought gave me Goosebumps and the tiny hairs on the back of my neck stood on end just like they did when I got married the third time. (For the record, I was not stoned when I said, 'I Do'. But I was when I said, 'I Didn't'. I was caught trying to bang the coffee table. For the life of me, I swore up and down that I couldn't remember how my trousers ended up around my ankles and I was bent over the coffee table when Maggs came into the living room. Little Herman was out shopping and forgot to get dressed and so it looked rather ...... intriguing?? There had been no other woman but, Maggs didn't care. She left and her brother Andrew retrieved her possessions the very next day. It was a very short marriage, lasting all of three weeks. Should-a, would-a, could-a, was out of the picture as soon as that knot was tied. To this very day, I still don't remember what happened.)

I walked into class and there sitting in his seat was CJ Wester. His hair had been cut and washed. A brand new shirt and jeans glistened, and his holey tennis shoes had been replaced with a new pair of black Converse. CJ was grinning from ear to ear at me as he sat in his chair. I'm not sure what happened over night, but CJ was either stoned higher than I ever had been, or, he had a 'Christ Jesus' meeting with his daddy. Either way, CJ was actually a good-looking kid under all that mess he had worn to class. The class was silent as I began my lesson. Something had clicked with those kids. Maybe it was the way I hounded CJ that got everyone's attention. Maybe they were scared I'd pay a visit to their homes if they didn't correctly rewrite their essays. Maybe it was the weight of the school year being lifted off their shoulders as they got closer to eleventh grade. Maybe there had been a fart in the wind and it blew everyone's brain into gear, who knows. Whatever it was those essays were far better than they had been.

I took that stack of essays with me to the coffee shop instead of to my empty house. My red pen barely put a dent in those essays. Then came the essay I had waited for, CJ Wester. It was once again, a one-pager. My anticipation started to ball up in me like a tootsie roll, only without all the sugar.

What I Did Over Summer Break
By
Christofer Jason Wester

After I got out of school in May, or was it June, I took out my stash of weed and began to celebrate.

Before I realized what had happened, I was low on weed and borrowed some from the backyard growth.

Cannabis, a wild weed, grows quite rapidly in the back of the house, and in the lot next to ours. To date, no one has found my precious hidden supply of green wealth, and for the record, I'm not going to share.

Dad has yet to find out how I have no job but always have cash on hand when he needs a beer.

Every day that I have to endure this English class, I want to find a reason not to come. But thanks to Mr. Strickland lurking outside my house, I can no longer hide in my room in the gloom.

Fridays never come fast enough.

Girlfriends I have, guts I have, glory--who needs it, grass I have plenty.

How stoned have I been?

I don't remember much of my summer, only spurts of deranged parents.

Just glimpses of the asshole living here.

Kind of makes me wonder why school is so important when the CJ Sr. never finished school.

Love my mother, loathe my father. Looked that word up at the library.

Marijuana maybe illegal, but it has made me richer than that monster who calls me Christ Jesus.

No one can say I didn't try to make something of my life, not now, old nag.

Perhaps I didn't want to pass, perhaps, I wanted to piss the teachers off and play stupid, perhaps.

Questions tire me out.

Rewriting essays are retarded.

Sleeping in my bed is where I'd rather be instead of stating what sort of summer I had.

Teachers like Mr. Strickland annoy the hell out of me, when I'm trying to make a score.

Understand me now, you asshole?

Virtues my ass; I had to look that one up too, very interesting…virgins?

Weary am I, I'm nearly at the end of this fucking essay.

Xtreme case of who gives a shit what grade I get.

Yelling at me over your glasses and coffee because of this essay, is best done in your house.

Zippity-do-dah-Zippity-eh, my o my, what a wonderful essay!

The End

A brilliant creative development. Everyone fails generally, however, it just keeps leading me near other potential quests. Relish structure to understand. Value wisdom. Xing your zeros.

Congratulations…C, I knew you could do it!

What else could I say……..?

CHAPTER 7

I have decided that once this storm has passed, the one I'm still in and hiding from in the bathroom under the mattress in a bathtub, that I will dig out my "special box" and search for a something that peaks my interest and write a book. This is assuming however, that my ass in still hiding under current mattress in said bathroom, still attached to my house. Each creak I hear, I wonder if the hundred-year-old homestead will survive. Of all things, a tornado this evening. To quote a student I once had the distain of meeting; "I had plans: eat, sleep, and take a dump."

One of my favorite writing gigs is to have my students read the newspaper every day and see if they can make up a story about someone they have read about. That's where my box of articles comes into play. I never know where the next great story or book comes from; it just simply presents itself and like a flyswatter against the counter, I have a most inspiring idea. Too bad the fly didn't get the memo about the flyswatter.

I squirmed and stretched in the bathtub under the safety of Lady Americana. The popsicles were eaten and the empty wrappers laid next to me, making soft noises as I brushed up against them. I found a partial joint in my front pocket and lit it with the butane lighter I always carried with me. It was dangerous business lighting the joint under ma' Lady, but I needed to stay relaxed and go back to napping while I could. Two long huffs on the joint put me back into candy land once again

Farley Cruekshank came into my office one Tuesday afternoon in late September as an 'undeclared' degree seeker. I never noticed him in any of my classes, but I always wondered what the lingering smell was that had settled in the class after all the students had left. It was a cross between dead alligators and swamp moss…musty and downright repulsive. Several of my English students complained of the rancid stench that assaulted them on a daily basis. At first I thought it was the sewer backing up, or even my own gas problem that increased. I couldn't control the gas because it was part of whatever sickness I had. I just had to make sure that when the Pink Panther said, "exit, stage right" I was already on the move to the nearest 'head'. Fortunately, the stench was not coming from me but from an unknown source that stood outside my office like a ripened Greek statute on the bayou.

Farley was about as out of place as they come, and about as dead looking as well. At first I assumed that someone was playing a practical joke on me and planted the statute of Farley in my office doorway to remind me that students were waiting to rip me a new one. As there wasn't a line of students waiting to see me or rip off my head and shit down my throat, I suddenly felt a calm before the storm settle down in front of me. No one stood behind Farley whispering for me to hurry up or dance around as though they had to go to the bathroom. Behind Farley was dead silence and an empty office.

"Mr. Strickland" Farley begins. "I wuz wunderin if youse cud take a look see at me papera." He replied with a drawl so thick that his words came out like molasses.

"You are wondering if I can take a look at your paper." I responded.

"Yea." Farley said. "'Peers that it is all red and I kant make nut'in of it. So I wuz fixing to see if youse cud helps me."

"What is your name, son?" I asked without trying to sound sick. His improper speech made me wonder how in the hell this kid even made it into college, much less graduate from high school!

"Farrrrrley." He stuttered.

"Well, Farley. I will be glad to see what I can do to assist you, okay?
"K."

"No. It's okay. You're in college now, so you need to learn and develop your English, all right?"

"Okay." Farley smiled a near toothless grin. There appeared to be only a few teeth on the top, and while I couldn't see the bottom half of that smile, I was willing to wager that there were only a handful left there as well. Farley walked in sloth mode over to my desk and took a seat. The fear of death suddenly punched me in the stomach. The rotting stench was coming from Farley and it was so massive that I about lost my eggs and bacon! Dressed in a pair of filthy overalls, and the remains of a ripped flannel shirt and flip-flops, Farley looked as though he hadn't seen the inside of a bathtub or shower in well over a decade. His massive head of dark hair was in dire need of a washing and perhaps a debugging as well. Farley leaned over to hand me his paper and I instantly cupped my hand over my mouth. It was not a joke, I was going to lose it. I grabbed a peppermint, unwrapped it and shoved it in my mouth as fast as I could. I offered Farley one of my mints but he refused. His breath was as vile as week old vomit; his mouth would be a dentist's nightmare, and by the looks of the lack of teeth, an expensive trip!

"So, Farley. What do you do when you aren't attending classes here on campus?"

"I sleeps in muh truc, mostly."

"You don't have a place to live in?" I asked.

"Nah, I ain't had no place since I were thirteen or so." Farley looked at his hands and surveyed the caked grease, mud, and whatever else he had been into before speaking. "Ain't no ones like me, I gots moved around a lot times."

"You were in a foster home?" I said trying not to hurl what lay in the depths of my stomach.

"Yea. Muh folks wuz 'rested and me and muh sister wuz took from ours house." Farley wiped his nose on the back of his hand and then on the leg of his overalls. I couldn't even begin to think what sort of biochemical warfare he was carrying on his person. I didn't want to know either. But the stench was making me so nauseous that I had to get up and leave my office for a moment. Oh gothic nightmares, I needed a joint and some fresh air.

"Would you like some water I asked as I left my office?" I turned and watched Farley for a reply. He shook his head yes and I ran to the kitchen to avoid throwing up in the waiting area. I just made it to the trashcan before everything from breakfast flew out my nose and mouth. Good thing I didn't eat lunch or have sex yet, otherwise that would have come up as well. I rinsed out my mouth with a bottle of Scope sitting in the cupboards, wiped off my face, and then grabbed two large cups of water before embarking on the death trip set before me. I handed Farley his cup of water and he engulfed it like it was a new elixir he was being asked to drink. He was shaking so bad that some of the water spilled out of the sides and ran down his face. A clean spot appeared and lurked there like line in the dirt.

"Soury" Farley muttered. "Been needing sum waters and ain't had me no cup to git sum."

"Where did you attend high school, Farley?" I was prepared for the worst as I asked this.

"Oh, I ain't never gots to high school. I kin read and stuff, but I's taught muhself." Farley grinned. Four teeth appeared on the bottom of that smile and two on top. Whatever this kid had been through, it was far worse than anything Alfred Hitchcock could have drummed up.

"You never went to school at all?"

"Nah. Mades it through teachin muhself." Farley took another gulp of water and wiped his face. Another clean spot developed around his mouth. Nightmare or not, I was just handed the challenge envelope and it had "holy demon shit" written all over it.

"Farley, I don't want you to take this wrong way or anything, but, when is the last time you had a shower and slept in a real bed?"

"Mush been since I wuz fourteen maybe." Farley looked at me intently.

"I see. I think before we get started on anything, we should clean you up so that you can at least think and feel better. What do you say?" I was hoping he would say yes so that I wouldn't have to race back to the kitchen and vomit again. Not that I had anything left in my stomach, but there are always remnants left behind, even if it's nothing but dry heaves.

"K. I mean, okay." Farley smiled.

"Groovy!" I got up felt the world do a twisty thing on my mental state. I would need maintenance to spray my office for bugs, vermin and anything else they could find creeping in there after Farley left. My chair would have to be burned, and the carpet would need replacing. Farley reminded me of Pigpen from the Peanuts comic strip. Only it wasn't a cloud of filth following Farley, it was toxic gas and rotting flesh from some nuclear fallout that we had forgotten about. I couldn't leave my office door open, so as soon as Farley left, I took out some room freshener and sprayed the hell out the place. I was pretty sure that it would take several cases to detoxify my office. A good strong fart would set the place on fire so I held one in and waited until we were outside. At least we could smell bad together.

The YMCA was a few blocks from the college and I drove there at warp speed just so that I could get Farley bathed. The guy at the front desk stared at us and then began to shake his head in a manner that said, "Oh hell no!"

"Afternoon" I said looking at the anxious blond-headed kid behind the counter. "This young man needs to freshen up a bit and I would like to buy him a few minutes in the shower. Is that possible?"

"A few minutes? Man, he smells like shit! He will stink up the place and we will have to close down for at least week before anyone can use the place. Take him to the gas station or something!" The kid had backed up against the wall and was waving the air in front of him. All the sudden he threw up and the spray hit the counter and the floor. The kid looked white as he glared up at me. I shrugged my shoulders, took out my wallet and placed a twenty on the counter.

"Farley, here are some towels and the showers are over here." I said pointing to the sign. Farley took the stack of towels I handed him and proceeded to walk around the corner to the shower. I was grateful that no one was back there when Farley entered. The moment Farley had his clothes off and stepped into the water, I found a pair of gloves, grabbed a trash bag and began stuffing his clothes inside it. I was not going to let Farley wear them ever again. I searched the lost and found pile of forgotten garments and located a pair of shorts and a shirt that I thought Farley could wear. "Make sure you use soap too, okay!" I shouted into the shower. I laid the fresh clothes I found on the bench just outside the shower. I found a pair of men's tennis shoes that looked as though they would fit the young man in the process of removing years of filth from his body. I could see under the curtain and the swell of dark water covering his feet.

"Yea." Farley hollered back.

It was sometime before Farley emerged from the showers and walked out to the front counter. The blond kid had been replaced by a bulky older gentleman wearing a life guard uniform and carrying a whistle around his neck. He was standing guard like a jailer when Farley came out. He surveyed the kid who now looked like he was six feet tall and not five-feet-something when he first walked in.

"Feel better?" I asked.

"Yea." Farley said. "I ain't had me no clean clothes since foster care, Mr. Strickland." I shook my head at Farley and motioned him to follow me back to my car. I had doused Old Spice on the seats of my Rambler and left the windows open so that the stench wouldn't cause me to pass out and hit a tree or an alien. Had I hit an alien, I'm quite certain they would have sent a decontamination squad to Earth to rid it of things that smelled like death and went bump in a nightmare. I did not want to be mistaken for roadkill and eaten. This was a thought I was not entertaining would happen but if such an occurrence presented itself, I was preparing myself for retirement.

I found a 'hole-in-the-wall' diner. Immediate seating next to a window. No waiting. Had I done this in reverse, we would have been escorted out of the place and our food tossed at us like wild dogs. Farley surveyed the menu; there wasn't a doubt in my mind that he had never been to a diner. I was pretty certain that the pickings had been grim at his 'real' home and probably not much better in foster care.

A fair-haired waitress ambled up to our table, smacking gum like she was chewing her cud like a cow.

"What 'cha fellas want?" She queried. I felt as if I had left the peace of solitude and had embarked in a land full of ignorant, and illiterate working-class people. She adjusted her apron and messed with the buttons on the front of her uniform while I waited for Farley.

"Farley, I'll order for both us if that's all right with you." I smiled at him. Farley nodded and looked relieved.

"Well hurry up then, professor, I ain't got all day." She said smacking her gum. I looked around the diner and it was as empty as a trashcan after trash day. I opened the menu back up and took a quick glance.

"We'll take two cheeseburgers with fries, two strawberry shakes and a couple pieces of your apple pie, Miss." I handed her the menu and she grabbed it from me like it was a roll of cash. The waitress returned to her fortress behind the counter and yelled out our order to an unknown cook. A tall white hat popped up from out of nowhere, grabbed the ticket off the wheel and proceeded to complete the assigned task. I looked over at Farley, "she wasn't very nice, was she." I stated. Farley shook his head back and forth and stared out the window. The silence was awkward while we waited. I spied a jukebox in the corner of the dinner and left my seat to see what was playing. I chose a Frank Sinatra song, old blue eyes always made me smile when I was going through the shit. I got back to my seat and was butted into by our waitress. She slid both the plates of food across the table like flying saucers and then put our shakes next to silverware.

"You want anything else?"

"Our pie." I replied.

"Yea, I know. Coming right up." She said walking away. I could hear her muttering under breath about rich folks and her crappy job. I felt her pain. I really did. Based on our service thus far, her tip was going to be rather minimal. She would have to kick it up a notch if she expected anything from me.

Farley gummed his food while I chewed. Old Blue Eyes serenaded us through our main course. I had never in my life, ever seen a kid blow through a cheeseburger and fries in less than five minutes. He drank the strawberry shake, wincing a few times at what must have been a brain freeze sitting at the forefront of his head. He polished off the apple pie in two bites and then sat silent, watching me eat. I lost my appetite and slid the remainder of my pie over to Farley.

"Hungry?" I asked. Farley nodded. "Feel better?" Farley nodded again. "So how did you manage to get into college?"

"I jus walk in da main dur aun e'ryone pointed muh to dis hir room. I axes if I cud talks to someone 'bout school and den the next thing I nos, I wuz enrolled in this hir school." Farley was very nonchalant about the whole thing.

"So what did you do before you came here to Metro State?"

"I'd ben gater huntin in Texs, and Floda, and Orlens."

"Texas, Florida, and New Orleans?" I repeated.

"Yea." Farley bowed his head.

"Alligator hunting is important work, right? People have been alligator hunting for several hundred years. It keeps them working so they can buy things and have food, and a roof over their head. Nothing to be ashamed of son."

"I don git mus do. Reckon its cuz I werk on a crew and they don't pay me but a foo dollar." Farley picked up his plate and licked the pie crust crumbs. The waitress appeared out of nowhere and retrieved the plate as though it were the last one in the set."

"You best take your dog back outside were it belong." She said, glaring at Farley. "Ain't you got no manners?"

"You would do well to bite your tongue, Miss. Your tip is dwindling away faster than toilet water." I stared at her. She huffed at me and tossed the check in my lap. "We're going to stay a while and chat. Maybe annoy her some more before we leave. What do you say?" I snickered at Farley.

"Yea. Dat be fine by me." He said giggling. "Do you know what youse call a gater in a vest?"

"No, what?" I was surprised by the humor that suddenly leaped out of Farley.

"A vestigator." He said smiling as wide as the Mississippi River.

"Investigator." I said laughing. Farley slapped the table and laughed like a pig in heat. The harder he squealed, the harder I laughed. I snickered as Farley took a long drink from his glass. "What are your plans after college, Farley?" I saw a gleam in those eyes that reminded of my first train set I got for my birthday. My uncle Ned brought it over as a surprise and my parents weren't too thrilled about the idea. We spent several hours setting up train on the tracks before supper. Ned was my father's youngest brother. There was a fifteen year difference between them and I guess that made Uncle Ned my playmate on more than one occasion. As I stared at Farley, I was reminded that my Uncle Ned would be a few years older than me. Now that my parents had passed on, maybe it was time to look Ned up and see what he was up too.

A sudden noise woke me up from my slumber under Lady. I heard a crash and was mentally trying to locate the damage, but I was too groggy to care and fell back asleep on top of the towels I had grabbed off the towel bar in my sleep. I was safe and secure. Lady would protect me.

"Sweet baby Jesus" I said under my breath. "What did you say?"
"Wanna be a vumpre kilr." Farley repeated.
"Let me get this straight to make sure I'm not misunderstanding you. You want to be a vampire killer?"
"Yea."
"You mean with stakes, and garlic, holy water, and silver bullets and stuff?" I was trying hard not to choke on my water. I was trying not to laugh and I was trying to hold on to my bladder. I excused myself and hurried to the head. I unzipped my trousers and let out a heavy sigh. "Sweet baby Jesus! Vampire killer? Fuck!" I finished my business and washed my hands. I was staring at myself in the mirror when a crazy thought lodged itself in the vortex of boxed up thoughts. "I wonder if they smelled him and left town because he smelled worse than they did! I bet they smelled him the minute he crossed the county line and fled faster than a flock of sea gulls out of there!" I was laughing so hard that tears were running down my face. I was leaning up against the wall laughing when Farley came into see what all the ruckus was.
"Youse okay, Mr. Strickland?"
"Son, I am just fine. I let out a fart that sounded like a lighthouse bellow. Made me laugh. Never had gas quite that bad, ever." I was still laughing and I was trying to control it but then Farley joined in that made it worse. He had all of six teeth showing and he laughed like a donkey. The notion of Farley killing vampires, slayed me. Every time I would think of Farley in the state he was when he first entered my office and the awful stench that enveloped him like a disease, I would burst out with a fresh wave of laughter. My sides hurt something fierce and when I bent over to settle myself down, I damn-near blew out the crotch of my trousers. Farley gave me a look that said it all and then we both started laughing even harder. Hey had to leave the head because the smell was just down right rancid. I had been accustomed to it but this time it was worse than ever.

We blew off sitting in the booth next to the window. I took out a rumpled Jefferson and let it fly from my hand to the table where it landed next to our ticket. There would a minimal tip; five whole cents for our less than merry waitress to spend on whatever she chose. I suspected that it was not enough to send her to charm school, so I didn't worry about her hateful gaze she gave us as we left the diner. I caught her flipping us off when she saw her tip. It was as if she wanted more but did less to earn it. I didn't feel sorry for her, but I felt sorry for the poor soul that walked into the head after me; it would be a righteous awakening.

I brought Farley home with me and put him up in the guest bedroom. He instantly fell asleep. I noticed for the first time how tan the young man was. His snores threatened to rip the sheets right off the bed. He had used soap and water at the Y but one cannot wash off a tan that dark. His hands belonged to a man that was no stranger to hard labor; calloused and scarred from pulling on the toggle lines loaded with alligators. Through his short-sleeved shirt, muscles emerged as if he was in weight training for a school wrestling or football team. His build belonged to someone twice his age, not to a young man all of nineteen and still learning about the world around him. From the way Farley fell asleep, it was quite evident that it had been a very long time since he had slept.

When Farley walked into the kitchen the next morning he found a note sitting on the counter.

HELP YOURSELF, PLENTY OF FOOD IN REFRIGERATOR. THERE IS A BAG OF TOILIETRIES IN THE BATHROOM THAT ARE YOURS TO KEEP. I WILL BE BACK AFTER MY 10:00 CLASS.

--HERMAN STRICKLAND

I got back home to find Farley sitting on my couch, eating the biggest bowl of cereal I had ever seen. So much for my Cocoa Puffs. Farley had by-passed the cereal bowls in the cupboard and opted for my mixing bowl, or the meatloaf bowl as I sometimes refer to it. The entire gallon of milk was gone along with the box of cereal, bottle of orange juice, and a partial box of doughnuts had been devoured. Farley hadn't been hungry, he had been ravenous!

"I see you found everything." I smiled as I walked over and sat down on the coffee table.

"Yup." Farley had found a National Geographic and was looking at the pictures and balancing the bowl of cereal on his knee.

"Anything interesting?" I asked.

"Ded youse no dat these hir monkeys eit theys shit?"

"Gorillas" I said correcting him.

"Okay." Farley looked up at me and then pointed to the picture. "Goreyas."

"Gor-ill-as" I said, sounding out each syllable. Farley took another large spoonful of cereal. He was using a serving spoon to eat with. I shook my head and chuckled.

"Wat funy?" Farley frowned at me.

"You. That's a serving spoon you are using. I've never seen anyone use it to eat with."

"Why?"

"Serving spoons are meant to serve food with. Like mashed potatoes or something."

"Like gater innerds?"

"Sure. Absolutely." I said swallowing hard. "Do you eat alligator intestines?"

"Yup. 'Specially, if nuthing else around." Farley said matter of factly.

"I bet that's, ah, interesting?"

"Nah, I's yoused to it."

"I see." I watched Farley take the last spoonful of cereal. He placed the spoon in his lap and picked up the bowl and drank the rest of the milk. Milk dribbled down the sides of his mouth but this didn't bother my houseguest, no more than it bothered him to eat alligator intestines, or that he was grossing me out. Nothing bothered Farley, at least not that I could tell. Farley was so intent on the article about gorillas that he forgot about me as he mouthed each word, trying to read, but with some difficulty. I reached over and took the bowl and placed it on the table and slid next to Farley on the couch. I had a good idea that while Farley could read, it wasn't good enough to get him where he needed to be. From that particular moment on, Farley became more than just a project for me, he became someone I could mold into a man.

CHAPTER 8

The days flew into weeks, into months, and before we knew it the end of the semester had arrived. Farley had grown. He had become a sponge, matured, and dressed better.

"Mr. Strickland" Farley began one Wednesday afternoon. "When there is no school, what do I did?"

"When there isn't school, what do you do?" I said correcting him.

"Yes, sir."

"Most students have jobs, or they go home for the holiday break."

"I ain't got no home but this here one."

"You don't have a home but this one. I know that Farley." I said. I had grown annoyed with Farley as of late because he was not using proper English and my own annoyance was crystal clear. I gave him credit for trying, but it was as though he was giving up. I needed to find out what the hang up was or I would end up strangling him while he snored a forest down in my guest bedroom. "Is there something bothering you, Farley?" I asked after the beginning of the summer break.

"Nah. Jus that youse keep riding my ass about muh language, is all!"

"Proper English is important in order to communicate effectively with others."

"I don 'spect to be going no wheres with muh proper English. Is fine, the way it is." Farley annunciated the 'fine.' Dressed in a fresh pair of overalls and tank top he sat down hard on the couch. The couch creaked under his weight and then adjusted to the gesture sitting in its lap.

Farley had started out as my very own abecedarian, enamored with ideals of slaying vampires, and chasing things that were mere fantasies and not truths. Eventually, Farley grew tired of pursuing his desires of slaying the ever immortal vampire and resolved to just tag, bag, and gag a few hundred alligators as his chosen profession of survival.

"Mr. Strickland" He began as he started polishing off a bag of popcorn sitting in his lap. "It purd 'near time for me to head out. I appreciate all youse don fur me n'all but, gater season is fixing to start and I needs to get on da road."

"You mean are getting ready to leave to hunt alligators?"

"Yah, that's what I say. Gator season in the east zone of Louisiana fixing to start in a couple weeks."

"But you'll miss the fall semester of college!" I started to argue.

"Yah, but this year is goin to be muh year, I kin feel it. So I'm fixin to leave tomorra."

"You're getting ready to leave, not fixing to leave. Fixing implies that you are repairing something that is not working properly. Therefore, you are getting ready to leave, okay."

"Sure. Whatever you say." Farley almost snarled at me. The tension between us had begun to mount over recent weeks. At times I felt like Farley was the alligator and I was the prey; I most certainly did not want to be ensnared in his wrath. I had already witnessed the streak Farley kept hidden deep within that exterior frame of his. It was as if a prehistoric monster found its enemy lurking and he was waiting for the right moment to snap the jaws of death down on whatever or whomever set it off. I decided that having this young man ripping out my throat was not in my best interest and I would let him go.

"So alligator season begins in a few weeks. What then?"

"I goes to the next location and hunt fuh more." Farley wiped his hands on the front of his overalls and looked at me. "See gator season starts in late August for thirty days, and then when it's over, I kin go to the west part of Louisiana and see if I kin get some tags there, but that there season will be nearly plum over by the time I gets there. See the west part where all dem other parishes are, fixes to open the first week of September which means I gots to git what I kin in the east part of Louisiana so's I don have to go to the west end. Lafayette has the best gator hunting and so do Morehouse. But New Orleans and Livingston have even better spots on the east end. So's I gots to figure what I gots to do. Georgia has sum gators too but thems a lot more worse. Gots to git landowner permissions and crap. Texas gator season runs from September tenth to the end of the month. Other counties runs in April first to da ends of June. The Florida gator season allows you to hunt a few gators, mostly trophy ones if'n you kin find 'em. See, each state be different but it's a living." Farley looked at me the way he did when we first met. I saw a spark in his eyes that had not been there before. Farley was an alligator hunter, not someone who chased after animals that hunted humans and sucked them dry.

"So alligator is good money then, is that right?"

"Yup."

"Are you going to join someone in this adventure or are you going to go out on your own?"

"I recollect I got's enough to start on muh own."

"And how do you figure that? You don't have a job, and you don't have any money that I know of."

"Oh, I got's, money, Mr. Strickland. I ped cash for an s'mester of schooling. I got's to learn things I ain't never learnt before. I saved what I's got from da last season. It weren't much, but I saved it. Anyway, I never let no one no's that I got's money because everyone's always trying to steal it from me." Farley was watching me as I listened to him. "Fact is Mr. Strickland, no one's never done nothing for me likes youse has. Youse the firstest purson to ever help me and not s'pect nothing in return. Youse teaches me lots." Farley grinned his toothless grin. He wasn't wearing his dentures that I managed to get him a few weeks back. A dentist friend of mine helped Farley get some teeth so that he wouldn't have to eat everything pureed.

"So you have money! You've been running a scam on everyone?" I said accusing.

"Nah, it ain't nothing like that." Farley said calmly. "I was fixing ta tell y'all that I had sum but I jus never got 'rund to say nothing."

"Fixing is being used in the wrong context; and I will continue to ride your ass about this until you learn. Y'all is a lazy word which is a contraction of you and all and is prominently used in the South. I loathe that word more than anything and I wish for the remainder of the time you are in my presence, that you refrain from using it. And for the love of

Hercules, please annunciate your words as it is making it rather difficult as of late to understand anything coming out of your mouth despite the new set of teeth." I was pissed, torqued, and beside myself with disdain. If I had been a prehistoric anything, a Carnotaurus perhaps, I would have ripped off Farley's head and shit down his throat for pulling the stunt he had. I might as well have thrown caution into the wind, and yet, I wondered for a brief moment why Farley played such a game.

"Mr. Strickland, it ain't no lie, I tricked muhself into believing I could be like everyone else. Hell, I even talks better than youse too. It weren't no game. I jus be carful."

"Not by much" I said patronizing him.

"I does deserve that, I surely does. But fact is, I dunno if keeping it a secret was a bad idear." He said bowing his head. His long locks fell around his face before he brushed his hair aside and looked up at me. Clearing his throat, he began annunciating every single word with care. "Did I ever tells you about Flower?" I shook my head. I waited in anticipation for something I thought I would never hear from Farley, my backwards houseguest. "We was close. We ate together, slept together, took walks together, and even took baths together. One day we was bathing together and we was sitting there playing in the water. I shows Flower mine thing and Flower comes over and licks it. Flower keeps licking until my thing grows almost double in size. I didn't understand why but Flower did, 'cuz Flower kept licking until this stuff came out like muh pee-pee, only it wuz white, spilling out from me. I suddenly felt all gooey inside and I wus smiling real big like. I hugs Flower and Flower hugs me back. Flower and I wuz closer, a lot closer after that. Every time we got to take baths together, we played just like that. One day I found Flower lying dead in the drive when I came home from school. Her head had been bashed in and her ribs were all poking from her sides. I saw the baseball bat next to Flower and knews that someone's had kilt my Flower. I ran to Flower and cried and cried until there was nothing left to cry. I found a shovel in the shed and dug a hole out in the field, where I buried Flower. Flower weren't no bigger than I wuz so, I did my best to carry her into the field. I don't recollect much after that cuz I fells asleep after I buried Flower. Muh mother found me in the field and took in me in the house and put me in bed. I had a dream that night that Flower was curled up next to me, sleeping on my chest, snoring away. But Flower was gone, gone for good." Tears flowed down his tanned face; he used the back of his forearm to wipe his nose.

"I'm so sorry, Farley." I murmured. "You must have loved Flower very much." I waited a few minutes before I finished. "So Flower was your dog?" I watched Farley and he got up off the couch and walked out the front door. I didn't see him for the rest of the evening. I knew the loss of losing someone you had cared for, knew it as well as the next guy.

The next morning clouds hid the sun from view. Fresh dew lined the streets and sidewalks, blanketed the leaves of the plants around my yard and covered the grass with moisture. It was weird weather for an August morning, but, this was Colorado weather after all so anything is possible.

I poured my first cup of coffee of the morning when I saw a note lying on the counter. I recognized the scrawl right away.

> Mr. Strickland, I Farley, I gone for a spell. Be back soon as I get enough gators to pay you back fur all youse has dun for me. Goin ta make sumthing of muhself. I be fine, so don you worry none 'bout me.
>
> Farley--

Truth is, I did worry about Farley. I missed the company, the empty boxes of cereal sitting on the kitchen counter, empty gallons of milk left in the refrigerator and on the coffee table. I missed the pile of clothes tossed in a corner or hanging on a hook somewhere. Missed the conversation and correcting his language. I missed finding books sitting on the couch and not on the shelf. I missed all the peculiar things of my young mentee in my neat and tidy world that I guarded and dared to keep in an orderly fashion with a meticulous eye.

The fall semester started off with the same vigor as always; new class of students, new ideas and a cluster of English faux pas and fubars. A friend of mine from graduate school used to say some of the weirdest phrases on a daily basis. I used one of his phrases one morning after I walked into my class of college seniors all acting like a bunch of preschoolers.

"You are excrement, you can change yourself into gold." I stated. The class of over-zealous students quieted down and looked at me. Each student looked as though I said something so deep and profound that they clung to that phrase like parasites. "How is it that each of you managed to get this far in your educational process without maturing. Buttermilk performs better under worse circumstances than you do. You are about as useful as a washing machine left on Mars."

"Professor Strickland, we haven't thought of going to Mars yet." One innocent voice said shattering the silence.

"Does the word sarcasm mean anything to you students? Or do I just preach up here and give you ways to improve yourself for the pure agony?" The class was silent. "That's what I thought. Act your age, not the number of popsicles you consumed over the course of a day." Several students snickered, but I was not in the amusing mood. I missed Farley.

The day wore on into the next, and the day after that and so on until Friday afternoon peeped its head into my office and chimed four o'clock. I surveyed the waiting area, saw no one waiting and closed and locked my office door and was about out of the entire area before confronted by Dean Honeywell. Our fatal collision happened several times a year. More often than not, Bert Honeywell and his bald head, swanky dark blue pin-stripe suit, colored shirts, and paisley ties always tried to turn me into a religious man without much success.

"Drinks, old man?" Honeywell said to me.

"Think I'll skip this round, Bert. Can I take a rain check?" I said as I hurried past the tall, stick man holding a brief case. The cold green eyes bore a hole into my back and I felt a burning sensation as I headed out into the main hallway. The stick man yelled after me, but I was already too far down the hallway to hear what Bert had to say. Bert Honeywell wanted more than drinks. He was trying to change my religious beliefs to match his and it wasn't working. Before the end of spring, Bert and I had conversed about a great many things, some topics should have been left alone while others were safe. Bert was the type of individual that kept his finger on the annoy button until you gave in. His favorite topics were religion and sports.

"So Herman, what do you think of Genesis?" Bert had started off one day. It was like asking me how I liked having sex in the conference room during planning period.

"What about it?" I said sipping my Budweiser from the glass at the bar.

"It's the first book in the bible."

"A fact I am quite aware of." I answered Bert in a minor mocking chortle.

"Followed by Exodus….." Bert had started to ramble. At the mention of Exodus, I made my escape and never looked back. The following day Bert was at it again. "Herman, you really should think about what happens when you die. You could end up going to hell, you know." Bert started to preach.

"Well, it will be a hell of a journey then, Bert. I look forward to warmer weather in the afterlife."

"That's not funny, Herman."

"Frankly Bert, I don't care if I can make s'mores and tip back a cold brew in hell, this discussion is over."

"Herman, you are going to burn and I feel sorry for you. Just like I feel sorry for the Broncos when they lose. I will pray for you both."

"Bert," I said. "Sports and religion is like a penis; it is a fine thing to have and to be proud of, but, when you start waving it in front of my face, then we are going to have a problem. Understand?" I said looking at Bert in one of my annoyed and callous looks.

"You are a cold-hearted bastard, Herman. I feel sorry for you. I am going to pray for you to change your beliefs." Bert started to bow his head and pray but not before I stopped him.

"Bert, of all the people I know it boggles the mind that you, a self-righteous, self-indulgent bastard, can fuck a graduate student and become dean of the department and then have the inflated balloons to tell me I'm going to hell, because I don't believe what you do. If it had been me caught with my pants around my ankles screwing the graduate in my office behind my desk, I would have been fired, not promoted. Keep your discussions away from me and let me rot in hell if that's what I have to do. But it's a damn sight better than where you're headed, I guarantee that!" I stormed off. I felt as though my intelligence had been molested by the biggest hypocrite on campus. For a while, the conversations ceased and I was free. But the moment fall semester began, Bert was hot on my trail like one of those door-to-door sales guys. They know you are home because they see the curtains move so that becomes an open invitation to keep pounding on the door, until you answer. Once you answer that door, you are sucked into their vacuum faster than you can say, 'Hoover'.

I sat in front of my Motorola with a TV dinner watching "I Love Lucy" when the doorbell rang. I must have jumped ten feet off that couch, knocking over my freeze-dried TV dinner in the process. It was late October. The snow beginning to dance a waltz and end casually on every surface it could to make things slippery as hell. I recovered myself and got up from the couch.

"Who is it?" I called out.

"UPS!" The voice on the other side of door sang out. I opened the door and saw a middle-aged fellow wearing a chocolate brown uniform carrying a box that appeared to weigh more than my coffee tray. "Sign here, please" the guy pointed to the sheet of paper clipped to a board. I scribbled my name and he handed me the box.

"Thank you" I replied. The guy nodded and ran off to his truck, climbed in and drove down the street and around the corner. "Wow, in a hurry?" I carried the box inside. The contents seemed to shift a bit as I set it on the coffee table in the front room. No return address except Louisiana. I took out my pocket knife and sliced down the taped section of the box. I suddenly felt a twinge of anticipation as I peeled back each section of the lid. By the time I had all four panels open, I got the most uneasy feeling in the pit of my stomach; a feeling that made its way up my spine and took my heart in its hands and was ready to squeeze. I took out all the paper stuffing and saw a white envelope sitting on top of something dark. I turned the envelope over and reading the typed font. Running my index finger along the print I felt each raised letter graze the spirals of my fingerprint. I gingerly opened the envelope and took out the sheet of paper that had been folded into thirds. This to, had been typed by someone who used an old typewriter. Each letter carried a shadow with it, marking the space to the next.

Dear Mr. Herman Strickland,

This is me, Farley. I am sorry fur not saying good-bye the way I should've. I gots me some money from gater hunting this season. Every night I practiced my writing so's you would be proud of me. I dunno that I should have left the way I did, but I dun remembers everything you teach me. So's enclosed in this here box is a gift from one of them gators I hunted. I hopes you like what I had done with the skin. Also sent you something else, knowing that you will put it to good use when the time comes. Thank you for beings the best teacher I ever had. I hopes this finds you well and helping others the ways you helped me.

Sincerely,
Farley Cruekshank
P.S. Flower was my dog. My sister, Anabelle, I can't find no wheres, but I still keeps looking for her.

I let the letter drop to the floor and removed the rest of the packing in the box. Wrapped in plastic was a pair of alligator boots. I couldn't bear to remove the plastic for fear that the toes of the boots would bite off my hand. Another envelope laid underneath the boots. This one was so thick it scared me. As I opened it, I expected the claws of the alligator to climb out and rip out my intestines. Instead of claws, it held fresh hundred dollar bills. Attached to this envelope was a baggie with a dozen of the biggest joints I had ever seen. They were quarter-sized joints and as long as my middle finger. I had to laugh. Farley managed to smuggle contraband to me and no one would ever know how good the joints are because I won't smoke them until later.

Journal entry: Dr. Stupid calls, says it's urgent I contact him regarding my condition. I delete the message. Dr. Stupid is no longer my physician of choice. My right hand cramps up and I mutter a few choice words into the silence. *Wish the frigging asshole would leave me the fuck alone! And what's with this feeling of bugs constantly crawling up and down my legs? Do I have ants inside me? Roaches? Like that scene from Creep Show…. wouldn't that be swell…roaches crawling about in the House of Herman!*

A month or so after Farley's box of alligator boots, historical and cosmic rushes, I received another envelope. This one looked as though it had been dragged through the swamp and then left out in the rain for a few days before it had been mailed out. The putrid smell of decay drifted out from the edge of the envelope as I pried the letter out. I looked inside the envelope for a dead animal. Finding none I pitched it immediately into the garbage. I unfolded the sheet of dirty paper and found the familiar Farley language.

> Dear Mr. Strickland,
>   I write this to tell you that me Farley, found my sister. She is in Kentucky living with some peoples that came to take her away from the foster home she was put into. Now she lives wit them. My sister and I is getting married and wanted to let you no that. We be living hir in Kentucky for while 'til we gets are selves situated.
>   Good bye for now. Farley Cruekshank

I walked over and took down Gulliver's Travels, removed a huge joint and took one hit. That's all I did…..because that's all it took to erase the image of Farley and his sister and the dog from my mind….. for good.

CHAPTER 9

Rene Carter was the sort of woman that most people steer clear of in any situation. In the spring of 1998, Rene Carter walked into my English class and demonstrated that she was a loud mouth, arrogant, uncouth and foul-mouthed bitch the lord of darkness had ever had the right mind to create. While the rest of my class was busy trying to wrap their heads around Rene Carter, she wanted to know why the world had so many mistakes and why everyone hated her. I had a few opinions of my own as to why the latter had happened but I chose not to say anything right away. I saved my remarks for later in the semester when it would matter more and she would matter less.

As fate would have it, my less than charming comments made it to the head of the class several weeks into the semester.

"Why is it when I have something to say, that y'all ignore me and y'all act as though I ain't hir. I just want to know why y'all behave this way. Y'all are just a bunch of fucking morons without no sense at all." Rene spat out, interrupting a conversation taking place between myself and another student.

"Miss Carter, what on earth seems to be your malfunction?" I asked her.

"My what?"

"Your malfunction. Your problem. What is it?"

"Y'all are fucking bunch of losers." Rene squawks as she stands up.

"And what does one know about losers, Miss Carter." I question her. I wanted to reach out and yank Rene by the nap of the neck and toss her on her ass into the hallway; I refrained, but only just barely. "You have demonstrated that you are rude, crude, and socially unacceptable numerous times. You willingly put yourself out in front of others to be ridiculed and made fun of. You speak like someone who has never had any formal education other than that found on the back of Cheetos bag, and you fail at turning in assignments and wonder why you are failing my class. Need I point out the obvious or do I need to write it in Twizzlers style for you to understand?" I stood my ground while Rene put her hands on her hips and acted like she was going to do a dance. Her too-tight top exposed the bounty held firmly in place. I could tell that Rene had about as much fashion sense as a walrus. One might as well paint a target on her because that was how she presented herself to the world. "Once again, what is your malfunction or in your case, dysfunction?" I stared Rene down and she took a step backward and sat in her chair. The all-too-obese Rene oozed over the chair like dough, the sight churned in my stomach and I was repulsed by the woman that had interrupted my class. As I turned to walk back to the student that needed help, Rene started running her mouth again. This time I wasn't playing nice with her. This time I was down-right hateful with her and I was sure that this confrontation would get me fired from Metro State College.

"Like I jus got done sayin, y'all a bunch of losers!" Rene shouts even louder.

"Ms. Carter, pick a verb and leave my class."

"What you mean, verb?"

"Are you kidding me right now? You don't know what a verb is?" A look of shock broke out on my face. This was not going to end well.

"No."

"Where did you attend school?" I asked as I stood at the front of the classroom.

"Oklahoma."

"Where in Oklahoma?"

"All over. Mostly on the north side of Oklahoma City. We has gangs and shootings there all the time."

"So what brought you to Colorado?" I was quite sure I didn't want to hear the answer. I wanted to block it out but I kept plugging away. It was like picking at a scab on my arm; peel off the scab, lick the blood, wait for it to heal. Pick the scab off. Lick the blood. Heal. Pick. Lick.

Heal. A vicious circle of never-ending picking and licking until a scar appeared marking the place where I plugged away.

"My auntie lives hir." Rene indicated.

"It's pronounced 'here'." I wrote on the chalk board the way I heard Rene speak. I watched Rene's reaction when I wrote the way she said it. "This is what you are saying, Rene, 'hir' not 'here.' You need to learn proper English because that is what this class is about. Everyone here speaks well."

"I don't care. Y'all are stupid." Rene motioned with her middle finger circling the class.

"It would behoove you to read a book wherein you pick up a few new words and use them property within a sentence. As we have been horrified by your lack of bel-esprit, I, for one, would admonish your teachers for not educating you in more appropriate terms. You are by far, one of the reasons why current education levels in your state are far below par. You are lazy in the way you speak, and apparently have no self-esteem or confidence in the way you have presented yourself to this class. You act as though we owe you a favor when in fact, no one owes anyone, anything in this class. Everyone is doing their part to improve. I have thus far not seen that from you. So, if you please, pick a verb. Any number of them for that matter, utilize them posthaste to take your leave of my class."

"Is you kicking me out of your class?" Rene said scrambling to her feet. Her dreadlocks catching in the chair as she got up. Several of them dangled like streamers on a tree. Rene didn't seem to notice.

"To quote a dear friend of mine, 'I believe I am.'"

"You kant do that. I done paid for this here class." Rene spouted as she further annihilated the English language.

"I assure you Miss Carter, I can and have. You have already taken up too much time arguing and being disruptive in a class of students that are clamoring for assistance. Good day." I loathed confrontations, but there were days when some students just needed a good swift kick of reality.

"Well, I never!" Rene huffed, yanking up her bag and left the class. There was a huge sigh of relief from every single student, myself included. If there was ever a time when a student crossed the path of ill-repute, it had just happened.

* * * * * *

No one could have foreseen the dynamite that exploded in the president's office later that day. There was so little warning that the fallout was enormous. Rene Carter walked into the college president's office and went off like a blown fuse. She was the force no one expected to deal with. All I heard was that some student went to the president and started swearing up a storm and vowed to bring suit against the college for not allowing her on its campus. No one ever could understand why Miss Rene Carter felt that she needed to create the drama she did in order to get what she wanted. It wasn't the education she wanted, it was the notoriety of her hateful attitude that caused her to behave like a social ingrate.

The morning paper identified Miss Rene Carter as a rejected student of color, upset over her dismissal from my English class. As the Chinese would have said, 'she bad fortune, cookie.' Several days after my run in with Rene Carter, Daryl Frey cornered me near the Sigma Tau Delta sign posted outside the faculty lounge.

"I see you have yet another satisfied student, Herm" Daryl grinned. I looked at Daryl over the rim of my glasses and swore up and down that his toupee was on backwards. The small indent on the top looked to be in the front this morning instead of near the back. I motioned to Daryl's toupee and without so much as a gasp, he adjusted the wig without thinking of it. I gave up trying to figure out Daryl long ago. Like many of his kind, Daryl came from a mixed culture of British and Asian. His accent was not pronounced and not terribly attractive. Every time Daryl would talk about whatever was on his mind, he would dance around like he was playing Twister or spin the bottle; you never knew what answer or excuse lulled him into his current predicament. Aside from his drab clothing choices of pea green slacks, washed-out green polo shirt and dulled brown shoes, Daryl was an unremarkable character. He reminded me of a garden gnome gone camo. He didn't have definition or hardcore values; he was the sort that just came along for the ride and if you happen to stop for a quick bite, he was right by

77

your side. That's how Daryl landed the job at Metro State a year ago; his brother invited him to a faculty dinner. He lathered on a tale about all the stuff he had done, and then got some big wig to hand him a job that he had no clue about. As it turned out he was an average teacher, but that's all one could say. His reviews from students were satisfactory. Nothing ever stood out as being exceptional. Daryl was a hitch hiker with an agenda donned in camo green.

"As always." I coughed. "I see you donned the green again."

"Green is a safer color than anything."

"Sure. It's also the color of currency too, but that doesn't mean I'm going to wear it as a shirt." I said with my usual sarcastic flair.

"Feeling bold this morning, are we?" Daryl commented.

"Cut the crap Daryl. Not nearly as bold as you; wearing pants that high makes me think that 1) there is a backed-up john somewhere, 2) your ass has grown and its sucking up the excess pant space and 3) you don't own longer pants and have therefore opted for thrift stores rejects and last but not least, 4) K-mart had a special and you bought five pairs of everything. That means you are butt-ass naked for two days and can't pass as a camouflaged idiot stuck on Normandy Beach."

"That's out of line! You're a fool and you deserve everything you get! Your attitude sucks!"

"You're toupee sucks. If you don't like my attitude, quit talking to me. Let me take another crack….Ho Chi Minh Trail. They wore all green and blended into the jungle like one of your green health shakes."

"What's wrong with my health shakes?"

"Nothing, except its gives you the shits all day which is why is you are gone from your class three-quarters of the time. Do your students even know about the Truong Son Trail? Or that it was known for being a series of trails used by Vietnamese troops of the north to gain access to South Vietnam?"

"Meaning what, exactly?"

"Let me refer you to a certain faculty dinner; you said that history was your forte and that you were 'aces' in that area. So I ask myself, what the hell are you doing selling everyone the bullshit that this particular trail was used to traffic prostitutes and human slaves to rich Chinese and Russian businessmen?"

"It was!" Daryl argued.

"Really? And all this time, the one person standing here next to me, who is supposed to be prolific in History has absolutely no idea, let alone remote, as to why his students only take the class to pass the time away to earn an easy A. Don't you think management has figured out that you are a fraud? For all intents and purposes, they made your brother a deal that they would bring you on staff, as a temporary. You are going to be replaced." Daryl is the last cookie in the jar, the one no one wants because it's all crumbling and soggy. That's the cookie that gets taken out and dumped. So long Daryl. I walked over to my mail box: assorted junk, messages, student papers, and fliers. I took the stack of non-important things and tossed them in the trash. I watched Daryl for a moment before I headed back to my office.

"How is it that you know all this" Daryl asked all puzzled.

"How else does one learn about things, Daryl? I don't read Enquire or Playboy just for the hell of it!"

"Then what do you read?"

"I read stuff that would make you squirm like a worm on a hook above the gapping jaws of a Megaloden, or a Carcharias adneti. I don't have to lie about my knowledge the way you do. I earned every letter that sits after my name. When it comes to you, the only letters I see are BS. That's what you teach, BS. When the final bell rings, you will still be teaching BS and retired to a home where everyone wonders how the hell you managed to cross the BS desert unscathed. I tell you Daryl, there are more and more of you each and every day, telling everyone how great they are when in fact they are just another turd in the toilet waiting to get flushed with all the other shit. In the end, your future is still as grim as ever because no matter how you slice and prepare it, bullshit still walks with its hands stuffed in pockets." Daryl hung his head like a dog and walked out of the lounge. He already had a sign draped around his neck that said 'Fraud'. He didn't need reminding that some people around him had already caught on to what he was up to and that was enough knowledge and power to send a guy to Mercury and beyond.

I felt a sudden pain of repulsion dance a jig in my lower intestines as I walked into my first class. My sickness wasn't the only thing giving me grief. I had refused to see a Doctor Stupid and had missed more than my share of sick days. Back spasms caused me to hunch over and moan in pain. Invisible bugs climbing up and down my legs and I can't sleep for shit unless I have a joint. The tapioca diarrhea was worse and my ass hurt every minute I was awake.

Rene Carter was seated near the back wall, waiting for my arrival. I saw her and I wanted to run like Babe Ruth did around the baseball diamond, knowing full well she would never catch me. I froze in my shoes and almost let my bladder and rectum go in the process.

"Heller, Professor Strickland." Rene sneered at me. Her heavy bosom heaved back and forth like boxers in a title match under a shirt that was entirely too small for her. She waddled up to the front of the class, the swish-swish of her jeans barely muffled the snickering behind her.

"Miss Carter. What an un-delightful surprise. Are we going to behave?" There was a reasonable air of disdain in my voice.

"Too bad for you then, ain't it. B'cuz I done got this hir piece of papa that says I am in this hir class."

"Not without much pomp and circumstance either." I replied. My tone was flat as I surveyed the paper.

"Says hir that you have ta let me in or else."

"Or else?" I queried. Prior to Rene's story making the paper, I had been summoned by the president of the college. Our conversation was simple: Yes she was violent in class. Yes she was menacing and took up valuable class time with her pointless ravings. Yes I told her to leave my class. No I did not swear at her but asked her to pick a verb and use it to leave my class. Based on the ranting and raving, and the introduction of her "attorney" (might have been her aunt because there was a HUGE resemblance between the two), I had to allow Miss Rene Chantel Carter back in my class. I was still reliving the conversation with the mighty 'tons' when Rene tossed her paper at me.

"Or else, this goes to all the television stations." Rene turned around and waddled back to her seat. Her waddle reminded me of two guys duking it out; dancing around, bouncing back and forth against the ropes until someone got a lucky punch and jab for the knock out. I picked up the paper and noticed a smudge on the corner. It was sticky and smelled like grape jelly. I looked up and there was Rene stuffing her pudgy face with a jelly filled doughnut.

"Sweet baby Jesus," I breathed silently. I turned back to the paper and saw that our glorious president authorized Miss Carter back into class and was to be allowed to finish out the remaining term without incident. *Shit.* I rifled through the stack of notes that I found in my mailbox in the faculty lounge and uncovered the note from the president. It had been attached to the same paper Rene had tossed at me.

Herman: If at any time you feel that you or the students are in danger, please do not hesitate calling security and having her African roots escorted out of your class.

Bob Ware, President
Metro State College

To avoid any outbursts, I turned around and wrote on the chalk board:
No talking in class, just write in your journals. The only noises are those of your journal pages, the stroke of your pen across the page, and the air coming from your mouth/noise. Anyone violating this, will be escorted out of class and asked not to return. Please, no questions. Today you write about why you feel you must have a college education from this particular school. I expect your journal entries to be on my desk at the end of class.

By and large that was the longest eighty-minute class I had ever had. It dragged as tough I had taken ten hits from Farley's swamp joint. It was very painful and yet rather interesting to see the reactions of the class as they began the task of writing. They were puzzled and I could see the questions written all over their faces like track marks of a junkie. One could practically connect all the dots of those questions and it spelled Rene Carter as big as a whale. I shook my head and began reading my mail. The worst part of being an English professor are students who make a job harder than it needs to be. The constant essay submissions were far easier. My red pen uncapped as I began to riddle each line with blood.....

CHAPTER 10

Somewhere I heard a crash and I woke up from my slumber under Lady Americana. The winds were still howling. A banging a gutter had been knocked loose in the storm and was hitting the side of the house. Hail was crashing against the window in the bathroom and my ass was numb and cold in the bathtub. Bugs were busy climbing up my legs again and I swatted them, knowing full well they were invisible. I was stiff from the weight of the mattress and I ached way worse than usual. A quick look at my watch indicated that I had been asleep for less than an hour. I could no longer hear the storm report on the radio as blaring static filled the air. I shoved the mattress up against the wall and poked my head out from behind the ripped shower curtain. I couldn't tell if there was still a tornado going on or not. I was about to pull myself out of the tub when the tornado sirens blared to life.

"Fuck, again?" I ducked back in the tub and pulled Lady back over me. This time I readjusted myself so that I wouldn't be so stiff. I fell asleep as soon as I hit the rumpled up shower curtain in the tub.

The last student dropped their journal on my desk on the way out the door. The classroom was empty save for the remnants of candy wrappers and cookie crumbs where Rene Carter had sat. I did not relish the idea of reading her journal, nor did I want my intellect afflicted with her writings. What I wanted to do was burn the sum-bitch and let her watch. However, I resurrected the idea that perhaps she could write better than she spoke. I was wrong, so very, very wrong.

I pulled the flowered journal off the stack of journals and opened the cover. The inside page had a drawing of a rather enlarged penis being sucked by a rather large mouth. I got the gist of the drawing right away.

"Cute, Miss Carter. But I am not the one to suck a dick." I turned the next page and found powdered sugar all over the page and droplets of jelly filling smeared everywhere. "Shit. Who the hell is she kidding here? Bitch is making a mockery out of this whole process. The president is going to hit the ceiling when he gets a hold of this." Sweat started to form on my upper lip and brow. I could already feel the heat breathing down my back. I turned the page, my red penned poised and loaded......I was aiming to fill up a journal with so much blood that a vampire wouldn't need to feed for months. However, what I found was beyond appalling.

> To Whom IT May Concern:
>
> I ain't going to tell you shit about why I came to Metro State to get some schooling cuz it ain't none of your bizness.
>
> I ain't sum freaking wannabe haf-ta-be educated ho that needs to be herd. Fact is, I came hir because I knew ya'll wouldn't refuse me what I did deserve. What I learnt was that no matter what part of the states I comes from, ya'll treats us niggers the same way, like we is animals. My auntie said that you white crackers don't teach, you just toss us stuff 'n to do, and s'pect us to understand what ya'll want. Like back in dem slave dayz. My auntie nose about dem cuz dats my line of blood. There ain't nothing ya'll teach me cuz I already nose everthing there is ta know. Knot that I need an educations, but to sit in a class and be among ya'll was enough for me to say that I done did go to college.
>
> All ya'll need from me is my attorney knocking down yer door, threading you with a law soot, so's I can continues to be fat and happy. I already don screwed another college professa so you ain't going to be the last on my lest.
>
> I would however appreciate you sucking my dick and giving me sex so's I kin gets ya for sex abuse. See I figure that you kin lose yer job and I'd be set fur life

cuz no one would ever belief you over me. I nose how the system werks so I nose what to do and when to do it. Ain't nothing you kin do to me, cuz I already started holding yer job in jeopardi.

So if you think fur one mint that I kant do nothing to ya, guess agin, cuz I CAN AND WILL! Make my auntie happy to seeing you twitch in the president's office. See I didn't come to see how fare I cans git, I cames hir to shew ya'll that this nigger ain't playing 'round. And I can call myself a nigger but you kant. The reason being is that we can do that as a sigh of respect, cuz that's what we is owed. Respect, you cocky bastard, is sumthing ya'll take cuz ain't no one ever gives ya respect, not wit out no fight.

In con....whatever that werd is, I be back for my papar and I best see an "A+" on it sum wheres or else I be telling them news people what ya'll did to me hir. Now, you can sux my dick, Mr. Strickland cuz that's all you is gout fur.

Cincerly, Miss Rene Chantel Carter, from Okliehoma, US of A.

My mouth dropped as I read the page for the first time. I went back and reread it to make sure that I understood the threat that lay in the shortened depths of that entry before I wrote my comments at the bottom. Uncapping the bottle of 7-UP next to me I took a long drink, belched, and began to fire away. Ah, the power of RED……..

Miss Carter,

While I admire your enthusiasm and passion for displaying your hokum, you have a very limited grasp of the English language. The assignment was to address why you chose to come to Metro State for an education, not a summation about threatening a well-liked, well-versed English Professor. While you seem to need a daily dose of drama to satisfy your craving, might I suggest watching drama television like "General Hospital or All My Children," for starters. They seem to have enough drama that it's hard to keep track of who is screwing whom. I might also recommend that you inquire about getting a tutor to help you to write a proper threat letter. In addition, I recommend that you visit the Tattered Cover in the Cherry Creek Mall and sequester a recent copy of Webster's Dictionary to broaden both your vocabulary and spelling, which is not to say are both horrendous and atrocious. It is not necessary to draw pictures to prove a point, but you must show the reader what your intentions are...this is not a 'show and tell' segment that you participated in while attending preschool or kindergarten. I dare say Miss Carter, you have failed to address the intended reason for your attendance at this college or in my classroom. While I am quite certain from the reading you intend to earn a sizable income from us, I assure you that nothing of this nature will occur. You might inquire at an employment agency about acquiring future employment. Based on your lack of interpersonal skills, I would speculate that you are not the sort of individual a retail store would put on their staff. I say this not to tarnish your image of how you dress, but how you behave in the presence of others. Since you feel the need to cherry-pick your way through the English language, perhaps you would be best suited as a grease monkey at one of the more popular Lube shops. In conclusion, (I believe that is the word that you were seeking previously in your attempted scribbling), your indelible remarks cannot be so, easily removed as you can. In light of this, I would suggest that you and your beloved, look-alike, obese aunt find yourselves a damn good attorney, because as soon as the president of the college sees this, 'your ass is grass and we are going to be the lawnmower.'

Sincerely,
Herman G. Strickland, PhD
Professor of English
Metro State College

I capped my pen and slammed it down a little too hard on my desk. There was no reason under the moon why anyone needed to be subjected to that crap, which had been spilled forth by someone who was as obtuse as they come. I retrieved the journal from my desk and tucked it under my arm as I left the classroom. A pink slip with my name typed across the top of it was going to be in my near future but not before I had addressed this unfortunate problem. The distance between my building and that of the president was about three blocks. The trek across campus was a quick and unfettered, empty of students and faculty, only the grounds-keepers were out and about.

Climbing the four flights of stairs to the president's office was probably the hardest climb I had ever had. Every joint in my body screamed and my knees threatened mutiny. The office lights were still shining through the frosted glass in the door; I had almost wished that Rene Carter and her auntie were present for this meeting. I knocked on the door to Mr. Ware's office and waited for a response.

"Come." Said the deep voice behind the door. I opened the door and saw Bob devouring the remains of his lunch.

"I've interrupted your lunch." I said. "I can come back." I turned to leave.

"Herm, I've know you a long time. The only time you ever see me is at the faculty dinner or luncheons, holiday parties, or graduation. When I see you the way I do right now, it concerns me, because I know that whatever brought you here is mighty important and cannot wait until I'm finished with my salad. So, let me have it." Bob sat up in his chair while I approached his desk.

"Rene Carter." I began. "She has written something that I believe you should see. My comments are of course are in my usual shade of rip-them-a new-one-red at the end of her, how shall I, put it, essay."

"Give it here. I hope she writes better than she speaks. The way she talks is like listening to a symphony playing all the wrong notes. Who the hell let her in our college in the first place?" Bob said looking at me. He squinted in the glare of the afternoon sun as it beamed through the row of windows in the office. I forked over the journal and took a seat in the chair facing Bob's desk. I waited for the grenade to go off. Bob opened the front cover of the journal and sucked in his breath. He looked at me over his reading glasses and I motioned for him to continue. Bob was right, the only time we saw each other were at events that were important. We didn't see each other outside of our equally important environments until those events arose.

I had only been a professor for a short time at Metro State before I met Bob. I liked him immediately; down -to-earth guy, low key, straight forward, no obvious character flaws that I could find, and he dressed the way college presidents should dress. Impressive and impeccable but not over the top. Today, he wore a light blue dress shirt, yellow stripped tie and a black JoS. A. Bank suit. Top of the line suit but reasonable, a bit pricey and befitting of a man that presided over a college. His reaction to the essay did not surprise me in the least. Bob remained calm as he spoke.

"It would appear that Miss Carter is threatening to sue us, is that your take on this?" He reread the entry.

"Yes."

"It would also seem that Miss Carter feels that we owe her an education and that if we don't give her one, she will file sexual harassment charges against you as well. Is that your understanding, Herm?"

"Yes." I had been mildly annoyed with the way Bob first addressed serious issues that surfaced, but I realized that it took a cool head and sharp focus to maintain that manner so that no one would ever presume college presidents allow their emotions to take over. I scooted up a bit in the chair and waited.

"You know what I really like about Miss Carter's essay?"

"Surprise me, Bob."

"Not a mother-fucking thing." So the master of the college swears like a sailor after all. That was a surprise that I would treasure for the rest of my tenure. Wild boars wouldn't be able to drag that secret from my lips, even if they ate my lips first. "I especially love your comments at the end of her essay, if that's what you call it." Bob smiled. All of his teeth perfectly aligned and sparkling white like stars in the evening sky. "Is this powdered sugar in the crease?"

"I believe it is. Those smears are jelly filling. She was devouring a filled doughnut while doing the assignment and I don't think she took the time to care about her presentation either. She was just so nasty and foul. I've had students complain about her."

"Did she disrupt the class in any way?" Bob asked as he sniffed the smudges on the sheet.

"No. But she did leave quite a mess where she sat; candy wrappers and other miscellaneous food wrappers."

"Did she talk in class?"

"Not a word. Actually, I advised the class to refrain from any sort of communication and that they were to just write for the entire class period."

"I see. And this is what she wrote today?"

"Yes." I cleared my throat.

"Wow." Bob looked up at me. He wasn't a tall man but he was tall enough to sit in the chair and his feet touched the plush carpet. Reaching over his desk, Bob took the phone and dialed a number that he found on a card stuck on his desk. "Reggie Adams, please." There was a few moments of silence before the other end was answered. "Reggie, Bob Ware here. We spoke the other day regarding the Carter case?" It sounded more like a question rather than a statement. "Listen, we have a threatening document here and Professor Strickland has also been named. We need to hop on this bunny before she drops more eggs in our basket." Bob read aloud the document he held in his hand. I saw him wince and writhe in pain as he read the writing that had showed Rene Carter's ignorance. I wouldn't need to worry about getting in trouble, I was safe. The preverbal pink slip was now non-existent.

* * * * * *

The next few days were gawd-awful. Rene Carter never did show up for class. Those students that had been present for her appearance, were relieved that they did not have to endure another moment with her. I seconded it.

Thursday afternoon sneaked up on me as I was entering grades. My phone rang and I about tossed my desk over as it rang.

"Hello?" I answered.

"Herm, Bob Ware. You busy?" I stopped what I was doing and paid attention.

"You have my undivided attention. What's up?"

"Just thought I would bring you up to speed regarding the Carter issue."

"Okay." I waited for the grenade to blast my day apart. I waited for the ball to drop in my lap, and for my career to be a flashing light at the end of the hall. I could hardly wait to get the horrific image of Rene Chantel Carter out of my mind. I shivered.

"You can relax, Herm. The walrus has been reeled in and placed in a zoo with all the other animals."

"Arrested? When?" I felt a rock drop in the center of my stomach. Butterflies leapt with glee and sweat glistened on my brow.

"Late this morning. Both her and her auntie were caught trying to pull the same scam on another college campus, only they had been warned in advance of her arrival." I tuned Bob out briefly while I gathered my thoughts and let the events of the last few days replay themselves in the corpuscles of my brain. There was nothing left to Miss Carter or her auntie, Adella. They were not just numbers, they were menacing vermin that had been directed to their very own shit storm. Their expectations of wealth, dashed. Expectations of living in freedom, erased. And the expectation of finding a way into the funny papers, turned out to be court papers instead.

The House of Herman had survived another shit storm; it had passed over, through and around me without so much as a "may I kiss you first." I survived another term.

Dr. Stupid's office called for the um-teeth time to remind me that I need to have my blood drawn and checked. There was no way on the face of whatever planet I would die on, that I would ever go back to see the painted piranha or her boss, Dr. Stupid.

Dr. Stupid called. No I cannot have a refill on the pain medication unless I schedule another visit. Reminder: we do not accept credit cards for copays. Cash only. No checks. *What kind of a fucking doctor am I seeing in the first place? A bookie?*

CHAPTER 11

Sometimes life throws you a curve ball and it's up to you, the hitter to whack the hell out of it. There are other times however, when life hits you like a bus and you have no idea what body parts are usable or not until you move and find out that everything in your body is either buzzing or non-feeling. As of late, that's how I felt ever since the Rene Carter incident. A part of me no longer felt like teaching people who cared so little about anything in general, and the other part of me buzzed like a swarm of mad wasps in search of a good ass chewing. The other buzz was also due in part from the Farley joint that I took every so often just to defrag from the idiots that trashed my day. It was by far the best buzz ever until a slender young woman of twenty-oneish strolled into my Tuesday afternoon creative writing class and crossed her long legs so that the hem of her skirt rode up her thighs. My eyes wandered up until I saw the hazel glints in her eye and her soft brown hair spiraling down her face and falling around her shoulders. Her smile lit a fire in my stomach and I felt like a puddle of chocolate ice cream in her presence. My breath caught in my throat. I was frozen in time and I couldn't see anyone or anything but her. She was the most beautiful angel I had ever laid eyes on. I gathered my wits and turned my attention to the task at hand. It was against protocol to date students, but damn almighty, I wanted to dive into her swimming pool, do a few laps and sleep next her until I could no longer feel my body.

I went numb under Lady. During the wonderful hitching and pitching storm, Lady had shifted her weight and began to bare down on me like an anvil. I pushed the mattress up and heard the muffled blare of the tornado sirens.

"Fucking storms!" I yelled into the empty bathroom. "You have ruined a perfectly wonderful evening. Fuck you very much!" The mattress shifted and hit me off guard and I fell back against the wall of the bathtub, hitting my head on the edge. Birds, stars, and legs pranced around in my vision as I passed out.

Since the Rene Carter incident, I pretty much stayed from people that gave me grief and added drama. This included the green garden gnome in the faculty lounge. Negative energy messed with my mojo and caused whatever the hell was wrong with me to go full throttle bat shit crazy.

Duke Greywolf found me one afternoon sitting in the middle of the campus gardens. He sought me out as he needed an advisor to guide him through the maze of requirements for graduate school. Duke towered over my five-eleven frame. Several times he would lay his arm over my head, not in a disrespectful way, but in a playful way to emphasize the fact that he was a tower and I was not. Had it not been for his waist length hair tied at the back of his head, I believe he would have been just like every other average college student, higher than most and doing rap in his off time. He was bright, articulate and had a vile disdain for people interrupting him while he spoke about his educational accomplishments and his dreams for the future. He was in my opinion, one of those dangerous little bugs that longed to be something more than just a dangerous little bug.

Quartisha Mohahn was a student that came to me after the Rene Carter problem. She was like one of those huge flashing monikers on the side of a building: Buy me! Although I don't know what she was selling other than her shapely five-foot-eight-body, extended posterior, ample boob-age, kinky hair, and dark skin, I was suddenly aware that she could have been one of those June bugs that dance a jig on my front porch every spring and then dies when fall has leaped into the air. The universe has a very curious sense of humor; just when you think everything will be as right as peach cobbler, some biscuit finds a way to be all doughy inside and ruin the expectation. And so it was with

Quartisha, she was the doughy biscuit inside the peach cobbler that you cannot over look. Looks are deceiving.

Then we have Jade Wimberly, the swerve damsel who takes my breath away every time I see her enter my class room and slip into her seat like she's modeling swimwear for Playboy. She's easy on the eyes but holy sneakers, she was one naughty girl, always dressing like a slut and putting on airs like she was starring in "Gone with the Wind." I shutter, to think what Clark Gable would have done had he gotten Jade in his arms. Fortunately for me, Jade was not the sort of girl that guys or girls shied away from; she was a finely-tuned engine and when she stepped on the gas, everyone purred and I do mean everyone. I was no exception. I left that bait alone because there was something oddly familiar about her, and yet, I wasn't able to put anyone finger on what it was exactly about her that made me cautious as hell. She's the thistle and not a delicate flower I thought her to be; a most outspoken and stubborn individual I had ever met, other than Rene Carter.

"So, Professor Strickland" a familiar voice sounded out behind me as I walked to my office. "I have something I need to discuss with you, if you don't mind." I turned around to see Jade. Her pigtails dangling and riding on top of her cleavage, the red in her cheeks suggested that she had been running to catch me. Her heavy breathing confirmed the latter observation. Today she was wearing a pair of torn red shorts which showed off her shapely legs, and a button up shirt tied in a knot at the waist; very Beverly Hillbilly style, but damn sexy too.

"Jade, what can I do for you?" I inquired, backing away from her. I felt myself growing in an area that needed to be quiet.

"I have something of great importance to discuss." She continued. "It concerns you and me." Jade smiled. Two dimples appeared on either side of her mouth. The hazel glint in her eyes was beckoning me and I suddenly felt as lost as a lamb on the way to a slaughter house.

"That what be what?" My breath caught as Jade laid her hand on my arm.

"We just need to talk in your office, okay."

"My office? We can talk here in the open, in front of everyone, with no problem." I was feeling uneasy.

"You don't trust me much, do you, Professor Strickland?"

"Ah, well, trust isn't the problem."

"Are you attracted to me?"

"Certainly not. You are my student!"

"I think I am more than just a student, Professor Strickland."

"A lynx would be a good classification, or at least a start to a good classification." My head was spinning.

"You're so funny, no wonder everyone likes you. You are after all a kickass professor don't you know." Jade said casually.

"Well, I try. What is it that you want Ms. Wimberly?"

"You."

"Me?" Sweat had started developing under my arms, around my groin, spilling down my legs, around my neck, and every other place covered by clothing. *Sweet bloody fucking Jesus.* At first I credited everything to the sickness eating me up. But Jade was as hot as ever and she had turned me into a rainbow Jell-O shot.

"Can we talk alone, in your office?"

"My office is under attack by roaches. Exterminator is coming." I lied.

"Roaches, huh. Too bad. I could have shown you something that would have made your growth sag clear into your socks and tickle your toes." Jade said stepping closer to me. She placed her hand on my chest as though she was testing the beating of my already fast pumping heart. "Perhaps, when you are not so busy, cleaning up bugs, or grading papers, or whatever else you professors do in your office, I can come visit you and then you and I can get to know each other better." She licked her lips and placed her fingers on my lips, feeling the dryness that made camp in my mouth.

"I don't think that would be such a good idea, after all you are so very young and I am older and I don't need the hassle." I faltered. In the back of my mind I could see myself banging the living hell out of this girl and I could also see myself losing my tenure, career, and friends as well. It wasn't worth the headache; I already had three ex-wives, didn't need a scandal to add to the mix.

"Okay, it's your loss." Jade smiled as she left my presence. I felt a huge relief fall over me and the numbness that I had felt earlier was replaced with a dire need for a joint......so help me Hades, I needed a hit like a junkie needed a fix. Jade was a lynx and I was damn near twice her age and she had about entrapped me like one of her playthings. A rabbit I was not. I sure has hell felt the life being sucked out of me by the most beautiful pussycat on campus. Meow!

I was still watching the gentle swish of Jade Wimberly's ass in her torn shorts when my office phone sprang to life, scaring the living piss out of me.

"Professor Strickland." I answered shaking.

"Herman Strickland?" The voice asked.

"Yes. May I ask who is calling?"

"It's Uncle Ned." The accent gave him away.

"Wow! This is a surprise. How on earth did you find me?" I asked.

"Your mother told me that you had pursued a teaching career and then I lost track of her and everyone after I moved away. I came across an old clipping that mentioned you, it was something your mother sent me years ago in a letter. I took a chance that you were still at Metro State." I hadn't seen Ned since I was a kid. After the passing of my dad, things were strange in the family. I turned to rock and roll and Mary Jane, and mom took to the bottle and pills. I fared much better than mom had after dad died. Then mom died, and I became orphaned.

"Yes, I've been here a few years." I said

"Bloody great! I have a favor to ask of you."

"Okay, I'm listening."

"It's about my daughter."

"Your daughter? I didn't know you had any family. When did you get married?"

"I didn't. I was young and foolish, did the whole Woodstock thing, met a girl, we hung out for a while and then I left. Well, she's been living with me for the last five years here in Paris, and now she's gone state side to attend college." Ned explained.

"I see. And this concerns me how?"

"She's a bit wild and precocious, outspoken, attractive, smart as a whip, and she can twist you into a knot without even realizing it. I sent her to see you." Ned continued to point out his daughter's attributes. I had the queerest feeling come over me; the girl in question sounded a lot like Jade Wimberly. I felt like puking right about then but held the feeling in check.

"So when is she due to arrive?" I asked.

"Oh, she's already there. She phoned me as soon as she landed in Denver."

"She's here? When?"

"About a week now, I should think. Yes, that sounds about right. She enrolled at your college not too long ago. You may have already met her or if not, you soon will. But be careful because she is more than a handful. She's got a bagful of tricks I have yet to see the bottom of."

"So what is the favor?" I asked. My mouth suddenly felt as though I had eaten part of the Mohave Desert and the sand had caked in my throat making it virtually impossible to speak.

"I want you to look after her. Make sure she stays out of trouble. She's a good kid, but very misdirected and wild. Her mother dumped her off at my place shortly before she died of cancer. I don't think Jade ever got over the loss of her mother."

"Jade?" I whispered into the phone. "Jade Wimberly?" I nearly passed out from dehydration.

"Ah, you have met her after all. Good!"

"Good?" I yelled.

"She's my…..bloody crapshoot. You're telling me that the young hot girl wearing pigtails with ripped shorts, legs to her neck, hazel eyes, and button-up shirt tied at the waist is my….." I couldn't even finish the sentence. I went into deep, deep, deep shock and hung up the phone.

While my brain was still trying to wrap itself around the news of Jade, my body had found its way to my 1967 Porsche. I slid my molecules in behind the steering column and placed my hand on the gear shift. I couldn't recall walking through the xyst of shrubs, trees, and assorted petunias before reaching the parking lot. Certainly the sort of hokum that Ned hit me with couldn't possibly be factual. A scene from Dragnet clicked into play and I could almost hear Detective Joe Friday in the outer reaches of my mind.

"Just the facts, Herman. We'll take it from here." He would say in his most professional Sergeant demeanor.

"But she's my and I almost.......!" I screamed into the steering wheel. "What the hell! Shit. She's related to me and that makes me her......" I closed my eyes and bowed my head. "It's just a joke. Ned used to do this when I was a kid." I tried to convince myself of the improbable but there was a great deal of doubt sitting in the sit next to me, sharing the moment as though it were an old college roommate visiting from Berkley.

"We'll take it from here, sir." Joe Friday spoke up again. I could see him nod at me and then walk away off into the Twilight Zone. This wasn't a season premiere of Rod Sterling's nightmare, it was MY nightmare and its host was one of the hottest college women I'd ever laid eyes on in quite a long while; Jade Wimberly.

I don't remember driving home, or parking the Porsche in the driveway, or retrieving the mail from the box, unlocking the front door and latching it from the inside. Everything had become Jell-O and I was moving at a pace I couldn't comprehend. I sat down hard on the couch with the mail still in my hand when the phone jarred me back to reality.

"Yes?" I answered.

"Herman, its Ned.

"Yes, I know."

"I know it's a shock, and I will have to admit that Jade is a fairly attractive young woman but….." Ned's voice trailed off leaving me on another plain of anxiety.

"Yes." I said feeling more like a robot.

"Still in shock aren't you, Herman?" Ned inquired.

"No shit. What gave that away?"

"Your reaction, mostly."

"Not transparent, am I?" I said a little too flat. My tone sounded far worse in my own ears. The shock was as obvious as a black flag on a can of Raid. There appeared to be a giant sized bug that had found its way into my universe and I was stuck with it, for lack of a better term.

"I've sent you a letter, explaining what happened. When I hadn't heard from you, I called." Ned said in a parental way. I was about to put the mail on the coffee table when a letter fell out from all of the junk. It was an Airmail letter from Paris.

"Well, it appears that it came today because it's sitting in front of me."

"Read it Herman. It will explain everything, I promise. I just need you to keep watch over her and make sure she doesn't do anything that gets her into trouble."

"Oh hell no! Don't you dare make me responsible for that little minx! She spells danger in my day timer. My social event calendar is booked for three years and……"

"Herman, I need you. Please." Ned was pleading.

"Do I even have a choice here?"

"No, not really. You are the only family that's left." You are all she has."

"But she's…."

"Please Herman, do it for your uncle Ned, okay?"

"Alright, but please know that your daughter is not going to stay under my roof, now or ever."

"That's fine. Thank you Herman." Ned hung up. I heard the click on the other end and knew that whatever lay in store for me was going to be a test, a challenge, and probably one of my nightmares. I laid the phone down and took the Farley joint out of its favorite spot. One hit is all I needed, just one long, large, elevated high to calm me down so that I could focus. Focus and clear my head of all the shit that had been swept my way-- as if someone just cleaned their house and sent all the dirt flying through my open window. Damn bastards. Always flinging shit my way. Always. Never any relief. I could never remember half my students' names without writing them down in a journal along with their story. I could barely fathom most of my days unless of course you count the number of blowup dolls stashed in one professor's closet…I could remember that shit. I don't suffer from the almighty old-aged brain fart that many have; my brain completely shits its pants from time to time, but that's about the size of it. But this new development caught me way off guard.

I took one extended healthy hit from the joint and let it fill my lungs, unplug my nerve endings and send me over to the other side where I could pilot mushrooms and dodge shit storms. My brain let go of the numerous thoughts and set me sailing on a river of rainbow candies to where I didn't care. My lids slipped silently over my eyes and I was down for the count.

Last thought........she's my fucking cousin.

CHAPTER 12

"I exist as I am, that is enough,
If no other in the world be aware I sit content
And if each and all be aware I sit content"
---Walt Whitman---

I woke up several hours later as the evening tip-toed on my porch and set up camp. I didn't dare turn on lights or turn on the radio or television. I just sat there enjoying the peace and quiet; I was content and I had seen a solution to my Jade problem. Finding my way to the kitchen, I opened a cabinet and pulled out a box of cereal, the flavor didn't concern me at this point, because I was starving. I pulled out the mixing bowl, the same one Farley used to eat from during the brief time he stayed with me and poured the remains of the cereal into the bowl. Sitting in the icebox was a half-gallon of milk, close to expiring. I poured enough to cover my cereal. I hopped up on the kitchen counter and planted that bowl on my lap and feasted as though it was the first and last meal of my life. Finishing the last of the cereal, I got down off the counter and walked back into the front room, sat down on the couch and pulled a blanket over me and crashed. I slept so sound I never heard the crickets or my neighbors yelling. It was the sort of sleep one has when they have been up for forty-eight hours straight and when they finally close their eyes, it's as though they have not slept since they were a child. I was content. I was at peace.

The following afternoon Duke Greywolf greeted me in his usual Native American "How". I smiled at him and motioned him into my office.

"What's up?" I asked.

"You got high, that's what's up." Duke's smiling eyes said it all, knew it and felt it. Duke watched me for a minute before saying anything. "So you have a new problem to deal with, Professor Strickland. Find a solution in that high you had?"

"How do you know I got high?" I asked."

"Professor, I look the same way after ingesting peyote during my vision quest. It's the way your entire being looks. There is a sense of contentment that only comes after the vision. You know what has to be done, the answers are there and all you have to do is have the courage to follow it. It's like a meditation, similar to what Buddha did, only without the peyote or weed. Of course he went without food for a while, which made his visions more profound, but it's still the same theory."

"I know. On the shelf behind you are a few books about Buddha. You are not the only one that's smart, you know." I pointed to the line of books just behind Duke. Turning around, Duke found the books to which I referred. I watched him skim the titles until he picked one out and starting thumbing through it. "And no you may not borrow it."

"That's cool. I don't blame you. I don't share my library either. Took me too long to acquire all the books."

"So, what's on your mind, Duke?"

"I heard from a bird that Jade is a ….." Duke saw me holding up a finger.

"She is a relative, yes. So let's leave it at that and don't mention anything outside of that relative aspect." I instructed.

"Got it" Duke saluted. "So, your relative is pretty hot. She's also a mess from what I can tell. Can't be too careful around her. She's like one of those nasty scorpions; hateful monsters full of venom."

"No shit. How can you tell?"

"I am not the only one that has been bitten by her. She entraps just about everyone, few escape, but others have; you for instance did but just barely from what I was able to tell. The universe has a rad sense of humor which, if you pay attention, always has a message to share. The universe is full of messages if you are open to them."

"Duke, what is your area of study? Because creative writing doesn't seem to fit your curious nature."

"I take creative writing as an extension where I journey into my thoughts. I'm a philosophy major. Why?" Duke sat down in the chair next to my desk, still holding the book from my shelf in hand.

"Because you are the first student I have ever met, Native American heritage aside, with that much insight and strength for someone as young as you are. I would think that you could be using your talents elsewhere, perhaps as a professor yourself."

"That's funny you should mention that. Quartisha said the very same thing. Said I was a whole lot wiser than many of the professors on campus, except for you."

"Of course." I nodded my head. I was waiting for the bomb, the grenade, C-4, a hand-held detonator to set off an explosion that would send me flying to the outer limits of the universe. Duke only starred at me. I was beginning to question his motive for his visit into my office when the fuse on the dynamite started to twitch into the 'GO' position. A knot in my stomach started to form, something bad was on the horizon.

"So you are wondering why I came to see you, when I never talk to you or see you during office hours. I never participate in class, but I'm always there and my writings are always turned in."

"The thought had crossed my mind." I acknowledged.

"Well, during my vision quest, I had a visitor come see me and tell me that a certain professor I admired is seriously ill. I never ask why, they just come. I listen and remain open. The reference was made to a certain book I would find on a book shelf in the office. Should I find it, I would give it to you with the message. I found this book on Karl Marx's writings which was the same book I saw in my vision last night. You are the only professor I know that is the most sarcastic, insightful, intelligent, and witty as hell. I admire you because you don't hide shit from anyone, you don't take shit from anyone either. So here is your book." Duke laid the book on my desk.

"Okay. So what is the message, Chief?"

"You need to get to a doctor before the end of the week. Something is wrong with your insides. Like a super bad disease that no one has been able to identify. It's bad and it can kill you if you don't get to the doctor pretty soon." Duke frowned. It was a deep frown, the kind that leaves lines after you hit forty.

"Probably because I smoke weed more than I need to. However, I find that it helps me stay relaxed and not feeling like a dump truck has been parked on my body."

"It's not the weed, Professor Strickland. Of course it helps you keep calm, but its way worse than weed." The serious look on Duke's face said it all. He wasn't playing around or trying to scare me. He was warning me of impending danger. I had noticed that when I felt overwhelming pressure. I lost focus and I smoked the Farley joint to relax. It helped take the edge off things, especially when I found I that I couldn't get to the john fast enough and shit all over myself. Embarrassing part of getting older, I suppose.

"Okay, but if it's nothing serious, then you owe me some of that peyote, okay?

"Can't give you the peyote, but I will invite you to a vision quest and you can have your own vision." Duke said matter of factly. "Besides, peyote is only used by Native Americans, and by the looks of it, you aren't anywhere close to that territory" Duke smiled.

"Very funny, but you are right. Herman is about as far from the plains as Karl Marx" I picked up the book, grinning. "I promise I will check into it all right?"

"You better, or shit will hit the fan before you know it." Duke got up and left my office. I wasn't sure what the last referred to but I shook my head and shelved the book.

I made an appointment with Dr. Redblum for the next morning. The offices of Dr. Redblum housed dark gothic furniture in a waiting room of yellowed and brown wall paper. The plants were rubber and sitting in the corners like forgotten statues. I wiped my finger across one of the plants and dust about an inch thick came off in my hand.

"Cleaning crew needs to be fired, that's for sure." I said to myself rather than to anyone in general. I walked to the reception desk and saw a familiar face smiling me.

"Professor Strickland!"

"Quartisha." I grinned. "So this is where you rush off to in a flurry of excuses after class. You need to tell whomever cleans this office that they missed the plants during the dusting phase."

"I know. I always forget them. I'm the one that is supposed to do it before I lock up but I always forget. Always in a rush to get home, you know." She smiled a large white grin. Her afro had been pulled back and she was wearing a headband, exposing her dark African features and brown eyes.

"Yeah, I understand that. So, I have an appointment with the doc this morning."

"I see that. The nurse will call you in a moment, so just make yourself comfortable."

I sat in one of the high-cushioned-backed-chairs with the all too rigid seat. I was trying to situate my frame against the stiff back but my ass hurt and I was getting cramps in my feet when the nurse came out to get me. Wanda was dressed in white from head to toe. She could have been an ice floe in the middle of a desert for all I cared except, her blue-grey hair sat twisted atop her head like a champagne cork. One little twist would be all it would take to extinguish the enemy. I followed her to the back where she preceded to take my vitals and weigh me. I hadn't noticed the weight loss, because I always wore Hawaiian shirts and khakis to class. Although not the professional attire my colleagues enjoyed, I preferred to be comfortable not in pain. The grey-haired nurse handed me a gown and told me to disrobe all the way to my skivvies. There I sat with my clothes neatly laid on a chair next to me and I, in the largest gown in the world, wondering what the hell was going on. The last time I had been in an office like this, the gown was a lot smaller on me than it was now. Dr. Stupid's office. Maybe it was just me, but I swear that nurse was looking at me all funny like I had a bug or something.

Dr. Redblum came in and did his usual doctor thing: check heart, yak about his wife, check mouth, yak about business, check my ears, yak about how great Quartisha was and how he loved hearing her brag about me, checked my groin, yakked about his trip to Japan, check my reflexes, yak about the golf game he had, and then he pulled up a stool, wrote down some notes before looking at me the way a doctor looks at a patient. The receding hairline Dr. Redblum was sporting was similar to a spaceship landing in a corn field, a huge white spot surrounded by sprigs of grey-red hair popping out. Cool green eyes stared at me as though I was the center of a bug trapped under a microscope. His glasses dropped down over the bridge of his bulbous nose, making him look like a Ferengi during a business transaction. He took off his glasses and stuck them in his pocket before addressing me. I wondered briefly which rule of acquisition I fell under in this proceeding.

"Herman" he began. "You on a diet or something?"

"No. Why?"

"Records from Dr. Haggel suggests you are about hundred pounds off."

"Well, I had this dress I was trying to get into, but my damn hips were a bit too big for it." I grinned. *I hope it was a moo-moo.*

"Uh huh." He was not amused. "Do you have problems going to the bathroom? Blood in the stool?"

"No. I go more than I used to. Have the shits all the time, but nothing outside of that. Sometimes I don't get to the head fast enough, especially if I'm grocery shopping. People blocking my way, won't let me pass, no matter what I yell and sort of stuff. I get bad stomach cramps, my stomach yells out at ugly kids and bag ladies. Some days the sight and smell of food makes me toss my cookies and I have to get out of "dodge" fairly quickly. Why?"

"Anything else?"

"I get the most awful heartburn in history. Makes Pandora's Box look like a cookie from the Keebler Elf factory. Probably gone through a case of Tums and Rolaids, followed by two cases of peppermints to keep things from pounding down the door to my throat. I even have these invisible bugs climbing up on my shins. Annoying things."

"Okay." Dr. Redblum looked at me for a moment. He pierced his lips for a moment and then a quizzical look sprouted on his brow.

"And another thing......I get mouth sores. It hurts to brush my teeth. It goes away for a few days, then it comes right back." I sat there with my hands in my lap waiting for the time lord to drop in and take me away from this sterile white hell. The doctor noticed the rash on my lower leg, a matching one had bloomed on my right wrist, side of face, and eyelids overnight. They itched like hell. No over the counter drugs were able to curb it. I discovered that scalding myself in the shower gave me temporary relief. "Nearly forgot the last of my alien symptoms. My ass hurts all the time. Hurts to sit. Like maybe I have hemorrhoids or something. Told Doctor Morgan about it, but I never had the surgery done because of blood transfusion." I cleared my throat and waited.

"Anything else you want to add?"

"Yeah, I'm cold all the time and I feel like I'm going to pass out when I either do too much or I'm standing for more than five microns. It hurts to walk and climbing stairs is like tracking down the owner of Beethoven's carriage." I waited for something genius to fall from Redblum's lips. "And there's this wretched pounding in my ears. Playing music and smoking pot drown it out, but Sisters of Mercy, when the album is done and I'm off my high, the pounding is back. My feet swell up and I can barely move. I've seen quite a few doctors, but no one can tell me what the deal is. I'm tired all the time. I get these horrendous and damn crippling back spasms that make grip the hell out of whatever I can get my hands on. Sometimes my hands cramp up and I can never seem to drink enough water. I'm tired of paying for office visits and no answers."

"Okay. I'm sending you over to the hospital for testing. When did that rash appear?" Dr. Redblum asked as he began checking my chest and back.

"It comes and goes. The one on my face itches like a bastard. Benadryl sort of works. So what do you think it is? Flu? Virus of some sort?"

"Not sure, that's why I need tests run, okay. I can tell you this with certainty. Your heart knows that you are anemic."

"Anemic?"

"Yes. That's why you can hear your heart. We will get your blood drawn and tested. You need blood. That much I know. As for the back spasms….the bone marrow is struggling to push blood through your body to keep you alive." My body went into overdrive and the bottom fell out of my drawers. I could no more make it into the bathroom fast enough than a puppy in training could. The roots of my being spewed out and down my leg even before I was off the table. There had been no warning sign. My stomach did the Herman dance, growling and cajoling a tune I had tagged as the Battle Hymn of Star Trek Enterprise. The House of Herman spilled forth the wetness between my eyes and fell down my face like a Hawaiian waterfall. Time felt as if it stood on the edge of a distant galaxy at that moment and I could do no more than bellow like an injured dog as my shit had literally been exposed to the one person that didn't need to see it. Wanda, my very own ice floe, came into the room and moved quickly to help me clean up. She told me not to worry about the mess in a hushed voice. I was so embarrassed that I couldn't even speak. Here I am, a statue trapped in Medusa's gaze, a man of age, crapping all over the place like some newborn. The room would need a hazmat unit posthaste as the entire room smelled like one of those outhouses left out in in hundred degree temperatures for a month! Quartisha handed me a set of instructions and sent me off to the hospital. I felt as though I had entered the hall of unholy and I wanted, no needed, a joint in the worst way at that moment.

I was greeted at the hospital by a man in maroon scrubs. I had been expected and my arrival was a waiting wheelchair. His blond hair was pulled back in a ponytail. Nails were well manicured and he smelled like something a ship was named after. For a moment I thought Dracula had come to my rescue but then his warm hand touched my cold arm and any ideas I had about being bitten by the master fluttered away. Scrubs man sat me down in a wheelchair and carted me off to a room where a big machine loomed overhead. He had me drink some of the most vial crap ever introduced into the human body. He had me stretch out on the table while he adjusted the parameters of the machine. The after taste lingered in my mouth like a castor oil and gasoline martini; lethal and upsetting to my stomach. The machine surveyed me, lulling me away from my misery. I was about asleep when the scrubs man came and helped me off the table. I was trying to wrap my brain about what was happening before I was taken into a hospital room and told to climb aboard.

"What did I do?" I asked the small nurse with the flower stuffed in her braided hair. The braid was neat and tidy and wrapped up in a circled bun behind her head with a flower tucked just inside of the loop.

She was quite attractive as she did her best to make me comfortable. Her perfume lingered in the room, but it did little to comfort me at that moment.

"The doctor will be in shortly to talk with you, okay Mr. Strickland." She said sweetly.

"It's Professor Strickland with a PhD. What's going on, may I ask?"

"I'm not at liberty to discuss that with you" she smiled. "Just relax. Everything will be fine." Then she left the room and silence swept in like a waltz. I sat against the pillow with fear sitting in my lap like a long lost lover. *Not at liberty? It's not like I'm asking you who signed the Declaration of Federation of Planets!* I was still trying to figure out what was going on when a doctor walked in and just looked at me as though I were newly acquired freak at the circus.

"Professor Strickland, Dr. Scotty Sheridan." He said shaking my hand.

"Would you please tell me what's going on? What did I do? Because quite frankly, you guys are freaking me the hell out." I watched the Dr. as surveyed my face, then inspected my legs, arms and felt my stomach for a moment before he spoke. I winced as he had searched my left side. It was tender and I never realized how much agony I had been in until that very moment. The full head of salt and pepper hair had been blown dry. Not a hair was out of place. His white jacket was starched and pressed and he looked to be in his mid-sixties. Maybe younger, but grey hair could be a deceitful bastard; I always thought it was the brother to Karma. He backed away a minute before he covered me up. His thick German accent filled the room. It was hard and brash, rough on the vowels, clear and yet, it was still just a bit difficult to understand at the same time.

"You didn't do anything. I suspect that you have something that we don't really see a great deal of, simply because it's harder to detect and diagnose. I can't say without certainty just yet, but it appears that you have been critically ill for at least two or three years. We are going to do a colonoscopy and an endoscopy to determine exactly what's going on. You'll spend the night here and we'll do the procedure in the morning. The nurse will give you some stuff to clean out your colon so that we can see what the scope of the problem is. You get lunch, no dinner and then around seven, you get colon cleanse." His curt manner made me dislike him.

"So how can you tell what this is already when no one else has been able to?" I asked.

"Intestinal problems are my specialty. I see many people with different symptoms. Some are harder to detect than others. I have an idea about what you have but not without certainty. You have a few things that I have not seen which makes want to take a look inside."

"So then you have an idea of what my illness is?" My stomach groaned to life.

"Not without certainty. So, I see you tomorrow okay. Don't worry. I will figure this out." Dr. Sheridan turned and left me before I could disagree with a hospital stay. He was too sterile for my likes and way too business like for a doctor. His bedside manner was about as inviting as a roach in a box of cereal. My head reeled and I was still trying to figure out what the hell was going on when the familiar face of Duke poked his head in my room.

"So you took my advice. I called Quartisha and she told me and so here I am." Duke walked over to the side of the bed and placed his hand on my shoulder. "Better you see what's going on rather than later, okay." A serious look crossed his face like a sandstorm and I was stuck dead center.

"I don't need a kid looking after me, okay. I need to call the head of the department and let them know I'm here." Duke handed me the phone. I had never taken a sick day to be in the hospital. I was to expect visitors later.....as if I needed more people in my business.

As promised, shortly after seven, a swanky looking nurse came in with a gallon of the second to most vial crap I had ever tasted. While drinking the ghastly pineapple flavored stuff (I should have said no flavoring had I'd known it would be that damaging to my taste buds, now in a coma state), a technician came in and starting sticking me as though I were a soft tomato waiting to be juiced. I freaked a bit when the tech brought out one giant knitting needle to use in my vein. The IV pole held a bag of fluid to keep me hydrated, the second bag was protein fluid, and third bag was red. I was given not one but three bags of blood in addition to all the other stuff being injected into my veins. Apparently, my engine check light was on and I was low on oil! My star ship is getting its engine adjusted.

Without warning, a gargling sign from the shit master sitting inside me sent up a flair that 'all hands better be on deck because there is a storm coming in at warp speed!' I was trying to wrangle three lines from the IV pole, the legs of the pole, and the sheet that kept me tied into bed before the first bomb dropped. For the second time that day, the bomb that had been dropped on Hiroshima had blown up on me before I ever made it to the bathroom. It ran down my legs, onto my feet and spilled out like a swamp mud around me. It was foul and I threw up even before I got to the john. I sat down hard on the toilet and the third bomb sailed right into the night. I felt like I was dying. A male nurse came in and saw me as naked as a mole rat on the pot.

"Don't worry about it." He said covering his face with a mask.

"Worry about what? The secret is already out, dude?"

"When you put it that way, yes it is!" The nurse was trying not to laugh but a small grin dented the corners of his mouth, like a too-cold Popsicle. He came back into the room with towels and laid them down on the floor and started cleaning my mess up with his feet. I cannot for the life of me imagine what he was thinking at that very moment, nor do I want to know. Had I been in his shoes I would have had a snappier comeback than what he said. I would have said *shit happens* or maybe, *"greener pastures lay in front of me"* or *"polyester is my sole mate and she's been stained by my fine fecal friend."* I watched him continue to mop up my insides while my bowels yelled meaningless curses to the depths below. After he finished, my bedside table was rolled over to the bathroom door and the nurse poured the remainder of the witches brew into cups and lined them up like a bartender.

"Well, bartender. Do you have a different flavor than vomit pineapple in that whiskey bottle? Or is vial the only flavor you have?"

"I know it's gross. We had to drink it once in nursing school so we would know what you have to go through. I don't envy you at all." He looked at me as though I was some idiot trapped in the men's room with a bad case of the flu.

"I don't envy me either." I eyed the row of plastic glasses in front me and sighed. "All of that?"

"Yes. Every last drop. And when you are clear, that's when you can go back to bed."

"Clear? My shit turns clear?"

"Like water. That lets me know that everything has been cleaned out and nothing is going to cause the doctor a problem when he does the colonoscopy."

"So what's the other thing do?"

"A tube goes down your throat and takes a look into your intestines."

"So I will have a tube going into each end? Not very subtle is he?" I stated.

"Nope. After you are all cleaned out, you can take a shower okay. I'll get you some fresh linens and a gown and then everything will be okay."

"Not okay. Wrong. You won't have tubes in your ass and mouth. Gees, it's like getting screwed in the rear and giving a blow job at the same time."

"I never heard it put quite that way before, but yes, I suppose you could say that." The nurse chuckled and left me alone to expel the rest of whatever lay hidden in my colon.

CHAPTER 13

Four hours later I was taking a long hot shower and relieved to feel clean again. I climbed into bed with my lines hanging out of my arm and pulled the sheet over me. Hospital beds are the most uncomfortable bastards on the face of the Earth. There is no single good position to lay in except on my side and to do so means I run the risk of pulling out the fucking needle in my vein. I tossed and I turned until the nurse came in and asked if I could use something to go to sleep.

"How about a joint" I asked. "Got one of those tucked away in your uniform?"

"No. But if I find one, I'll let you know." The nurse snickered handing me a small glass of water and a Benadryl.

"I don't have an allergy." I said to him.

"I know that, but this helps you sleep too." He said waiting for me to finish the water. I settled back against the pillows and waited for sleep. I had a cramp in the middle of my back that would have sent a Stone Age man over the edge. I pushed buttons until the entire bed was completely and totally flat. I turned over on my right side and sleep greeted me like a long lost friend; silent and soothing.

I was briefly awakened by two nurses after sleep took me hostage. I was transported to my new hell of ass screwing and blow jobs. I was flipped over like a pancake and some sort of instrument was placed into my mouth. The nurse said it was to hold the tube in place while it went down my throat. Probably, so I wouldn't bite off the prick stuffed into mouth. I started to rebel and the terrors in the House of Herman woke with a vengeance. Dr. Sheridan came in and damn near threatened me with an extended stay at Hotel Doom.

"I know you are scared but I cannot do this if you are going to get all fussy with me. I need you relaxed. I will cancel this procedure, and you will be sent back to your room until we can reschedule. Clear?" He towered over me like Worf with his Klingon stance and security officer garb. *Okay Lieutenant Ass-Probe, I'm cool. Filler up.* I nodded and smiled. *Time to play nice. Who gives a fuck that the House of Herman is scared? For the love of Deep Space Nine, no more fucking needles!* "Give him a few minutes to collect himself" he instructed his team. Moments later, everyone picked up where they had left off. I don't remember anything after that. I had no thoughts, no dreams, and no nightmares.

I woke up to a raging hunger. I saw a tray sitting next to my bed and when I lifted the lid, I slammed it back down. The meal was as revolting as the barf I left on the bathroom floor the night before. Later, a speckled woman in a volunteer outfit shuffled in and asked if I wanted to read the paper. I could barely keep my eyes open much less give a crap about who killed whom. She gave me some graham crackers and lemonade and I inhaled them like I hadn't eaten in years.

It seemed like an eternity before my next meal was brought in. I took the lid off the plate and surveyed the contents. I stabbed the vegetables with my fork and they split into pieces; the vegetables were so over cooked I could have used a straw. I couldn't tell what the meat was so I left it alone. The mashed potatoes was deplorable that I had to doctor them with as much pepper as I could. I drank the hot tea and the Jell-O, leaving the bulk of the meal alone. *Is this what prisoners get as a last meal?* The meal was in disastrous need of something that I was not able to give it…….flavor. And that was how my days were for the next week; blending into each other like fog and haze. I would eat breakfast with a heartiness while lunch and dinner were avoided like a bad review.

"Mr. Strickland" said a voice on the phone on afternoon of my fifth day.

"Yes."

"This is the kitchen. What do you want for your evening meal?"

"I don't know. What do you have worth eating?"

"We have chicken fried steak, meat loaf, roast beef, mashed potatoes, squash, beans, corn, pudding, orange sherbet, wheat rolls, milk, tea, and cheese soup."

"Pizza?"

"Not this week."

"How about vegetables I can eat with a fork and not suck through a straw?"

"That's how we cook them" the voice said.

"While I appreciate the fact that you are giving my teeth a vacation as well as my gums, I prefer to chew my food, not suck it through a tube. So how about a hamburger or a big fat pizza" I said without trying to sound indignant.

"We don't have those, but we do have …….." her voice trailed off into never-never-I-don't-give-a-shit-if-you-eat-or-not-land. I hung up the phone and waited for a surprise meal. I had been indoctrinated into the fabulous culinary experience of hospital food. It earned a minus 30 star review, in my opinion.

"Professor Strickland!" a male voice sang out. I was never so glad to see Duke as I was at that very moment. "Brought you a hamburger and a strawberry shake. I thought maybe you had enough hospital food by now." He said handing over the bag from Burger King. I nodded at him, grabbed the burger and grubbed. I took the shake and marveled at its taste; heaven sang along with the angels.

"Oh hell yes! This is the first decent meal I've had since I've been locked up here." Looking at Duke I realized that I appeared to be a madman eating the way I had. "Sorry. I guess I'm hungry. The food here sucks. People without teeth eat the shit they serve here." Duke laughed and from behind him, Quartisha and Jade poked their heads in.

"Hi Cousin Herman" Jade snickered. "I guess I scared you pretty bad didn't I?"

"No shit, you think? What was your first sign? My beating heart?"

"Professor, Jade told us about the rash on your face. She said it looked like something she had seen in one of her medical books. Duke suspected that you were pretty ill and told me. Don't be angry okay." Quartisha smiled.

"I'm not." A knock on the door startled me. Dr. Sheridan came in and my visitors left. He pulled up a chair and sat next to the bed. My stomach grumbled and I smiled.

"Herman" he began. "You have a disease that is very hard to diagnose. It could fall into three areas, but not without knowing for sure unless tests are done. Even though I saw the rash and read the report that Dr. Redblum sent over, I needed to make sure. First of all you do not have Irritable bowel syndrome. You don't have Ulcerative Colitis. What you have is the queen; Crohn's Disease. It's often harder to detect unless you run tests. We are doing to aggressive drugs with you to put you in remission and give you a fighting chance."

"How did I get this? What did I do wrong?"

"It's nothing you have done, it's not your life style and it's not because you smoke pot. Smoking pot has probably helped you fight the disease more than you know which is why you didn't know you were sick. Crohn's is a genetic disease that skips a generation and is caused by stress most of the time. It is usually passed down from a first cousin and can come from either one or both sides of the family. Someone in your family probably had it and wore a colostomy bag. There is no cure and there is no need to worry about writing a will because you will live a long life as long as you watch what you do and come see me for regular check-ups." Dr. Sheridan handed me a bunch of information. "Read this, it will help. I also want you to join a support group, there is one online that will help you. Since you write, and I hear you are an excellent English professor, maybe you can share you experience....start a blog and get the information out there." He got up and moved the chair. "What sort of foods do you eat?"

"Whatever I find in my fridge. Sometimes fast food. Usually I cook when I can." This was not a lie either.

"I won't put you on a special diet, you'll figure out what you can and cannot tolerate as time goes on. Continue taking the Prednisone and Azathioprine. The Flagyl you will finish here. It fights the bacterial infection that are in your intestines. Your immune system is weak so we are going to get that back up. You will need to take Iron pills to build blood. Take the iron pills twice a day until you come see me in six weeks.

Your blood will be tested again to make sure the levels are where they should be. Questions?"

"Do I have to join a support group?"

"It will help to know that you are not alone."

"What triggered it?"

"Intense stress usually and sometimes it starts without warning. It's a silent disease. It's usually not fatal."

"What about the hemorrhoid?"

"It wasn't a hemorrhoid. It's called a fissure. It's a tear in the anus caused by increased urges to defecate. I fixed that while in that area."

"Anything else you fixed while in the nether region?" I tried not to smile as I said this.

"You will be fine, Herman. Come see me in six weeks." Dr. Sheridan shook my hand and left. He ignored my sarcasm like a cat ignores 'No.'

"Guess that would be a NO, that you didn't do anything else!" I muttered to the blankets. I was angry. I vowed to hunt down the bastard or bitch that passed this genetic vermin my way, and kick their dead ass through all of space and time for the rest of whatever it is you call it after you die. I read the paperwork. Tossed them aside and stared at the ceiling. *Fucking great. There goes all hope of getting laid ever, again. Defecate: why not just say shit and get it over with. Star Fleet academy must be REAL proud of Scotty! Beam Me Up, Sheridan! I am not going to join the fucking club for Crohn's anonymous, either.* I closed my eyes and slept.

The dust had settled around me and I was back teaching my writing classes. The mounds of paper had stacked up. Duke helped me grade them as best he could. Quartisha monitored my diet. Jade made sure I was doing whatever I had to do to stay well; that included a never ending supply of weed and no stress.

`A week after I was out of the hospital, a guy showed up on my front porch looking like one of those scary-assed thugs you only see in movies. He stands about six feet or so, wears a long-assed black trench coat, has long pointed finger nails, dreadlocks to his butt crack and smells like an outhouse you'd find in one of those somewhat camp grounds after Labor Day. All the sudden I had a flashback of when my colon let one rip and explode all over the floor of my room; that smell was obnoxious as hell and made my eyes water. That was the guy on my porch, stinking like an entire trunk of fecal matter that had been collected from the hospital sewer system. There wasn't even a remote possibility of running away when the guy stood on my porch that afternoon, pulling a package out from under his coat, handing it to me and smiling with a mouth that was in dire need of a toothbrush. I was at a loss for words when I held the package. He nodded and walk back toward a waiting vehicle sitting in my drive. I was speechless. I watched him drive off and there I stood in my shorts and Grateful Dead t-shirt holding a brown package. I went to open the package and thought it would be best done so behind a closed door. I backed up against the door and opened the paper wrapping and saw the biggest score of weed I had ever seen. I looked out through the closed blinds, checking to see if I was being watched. I expected the cops to surround the house and arrest me for possession, but no one was around and I was safe.

I went through the house stashing my stash. Gulliver's Travel restocked, as well as other locations. I made sure that no one or nothing would ever find it. Jade came to the house a few hours after the outhouse tramp came by.

"That's Rock-o, Herman. He's got connections and he will make sure that you are well supplied for as long as possible." Jade explained. "He's a friend."

"But how? I mean, I don't want to seem ungrateful but I could lose my job and shit."

"You are a teacher and a writer, Herman. A wonderful guy that everyone at Metro adores. Aside from those loud and obnoxious Hawaiian shirts and shorts you wear, you aren't so bad."

"My shirts are not that loud. And I wear band t-shirts too."

"They are loud and excuse me for saying this but only students wear rock and roll t-shirts to school. You wear Hawaiian shirts that not even the locals would wear."

"The locals in Hawaii wear these shirts. I suppose those cutoffs and midriffs shirts you wear are fashionable?"

"For a college student, but not for a pre-med chick."

"Pre-med and has drug connections. Nice. And what else are you into, Jade?"

"Well, let's just say if anything happens to you, I get to work on your corpse."

"Mortician?"

"No. Forensics."

"I thought you were pursuing writing?" I gesture as Jade takes a joint and lights it.

"You haven't read my latest, have you?"

"No, but I will later." I took a long hard look at Jade. She had become responsible and mature since I had been diagnosed with Crohn's. I never read the letter from Ned, but I remembered where I put it when I was ready to read it. Jade walked out the front door and that was the last I was to see of her for a while. I located Ned's letter and opened the tri-folded sheet. The writing was neat and precise, evenly spaced black penmanship against blue paper.

Herman,

I know it's been a long while since we last talked. Life has taken its toll on everyone around me, including my daughter, Jade. About five years ago, I found out that I had a daughter. Her mother, Beth, showed up one day and told me that about the day we had been together. That was the day we conceived, a rainy afternoon after a Grateful Dead concert and Woodstock, We loved each other, we wanted to be together, but there were too many forces keeping us apart. She went to Canada to be with her parents, and I moved to England to pursue my law career. She had followed my career. Beth found out that she had cancer and that it was too progressed for anyone to do anything. She died less than a week later in a hotel room away from Jade and me. I wish I had gone with Beth all those years ago, but I didn't. Jade is a difficult girl and she has designs of doing something that I don't agree with. Forensics of all things. So Jade is coming to Colorado to attend college where you are. She may search you out, she can be pretty vulgar, but

she's a good kid. Help her and watch over her; send her
on the right path because I'm afraid that I have failed
in that.

I await your call.

Ned

I laid the letter down and sorted through the stack of student papers
until I found Jade's. Her writing was exactly like her father's. She may
one day say she has nothing in common with her father, but I could tell
that she had more in common than she realized. I read her submission.

Long Road…..

I was just a kid when my parents split up. I never knew my real dad,
but my mother said that he was a good man, he had a dream to follow
and she had to let him go. I could never understand that kind of love.
I could never understand why two people who loved each other would
ever let one another go. Then I read the letters they had written each
other over the years. Their love never died, it bloomed like the iris in the
gardens mom kept. Her gardens were always full of iris, they attracted
butterflies and bees; I never forgot the way the house felt or the way it
looked every spring. I never saw the tears in my mother's eyes when she
was told she was dying, the pain she was in, or the sorrow she would
feel when she would pass from one world to the next. My mother made
me promise that no matter what, she would help me become whatever
I wanted, for as long as she lived. But her days were getting shorter and
shorter and that's when she showed me the box of letters from my father.
She had kept a scrap book of his achievements and of yours. You may
see me as a slut, but it has helped me get where I needed to until right
now. My mother flew us to England and we found my father. Imagine
my surprise to finally meet my father, a big time lawyer in English court.
He was pompous, never married, and he was not the man my mother
had said he was. It wasn't until I found a picture of him and my mother
at Woodstock; his long hair, tie-dyed shirt, torn jeans and sandals,

sunglasses, and a mustache and beard. He didn't look anything like the man that stood before me.

My mother didn't want me giving up on my dream of being a forensic scientist, but my father wanted me to be a regular doctor. I can only hope that you, my cousin Herman, will support my dream and not try and make me into something I am not. Now that you are getting to know the real me, I hope you can appreciate who I am and that I adore you and admire all that you have done and are. I may not be like you, but I am more like your family than you will ever know.

Jade Wimberly, class of 1981

* * * * * *

Students may come and go in my life, some stand out in the crowd and the rest cower in a corner with the rest of the shadows in my life. But those closest to me know how I roll and how I rock when things get a tad bumpy. I will never be able to understand all that universe throws at me, but I know what the universe means when it says, "listen with an open heart and mind."

I listened loud and clear. When my time comes, I'm going to search all of eternity until I find the sum bitch that passed this disease on to me and I will be wearing my loud Hawaiian shirt when I put my foot up their ass repeatedly until they feel the way I do; like shit.

CHAPTER 14

Journal Entry: Every now and again, a random thought will pass through my mind as I try to find sleep, but can't. The fucking drugs have robbed me of sleep. Sleep is a five letter word that leaves me feeling robbed every single day; it deprives me of the ability to find the energy to do what I need to. To find clarity in a jumbled world of trifles and giant word-search puzzles. Before I was diagnosed with Crohn's Disease, I used to sleep like the dead without any problems. I could climb the stairs to the Statue of Liberty, climb the side of a hill, steps to the state capital, steps in the school, the single step from the street to a curb. I could swim 50 laps and laugh like there was no tomorrow. Now I can't climb one damn stair without some sort of difficulty. If I laugh, I leak from my ass...what an attractive spot that is on the back of my khakis. The disease has destroyed every joint I have in my possession and robs me of the joy I have in the climb. Now I battle a single stair as though it's the last one, the very last one in a line of stairs to reach the top. Even to climb a stair is a remarkable achievement. Crohn's disease has destroyed every major joint in my body. Fucking bitch.

To go through an entire day without racing to the nearest "head" is amazing; to even get through the day without a case of gut-busting diarrhea is a blessing. If I get through a week without using an entire package of toilet paper, it's a miracle. For whatever reason, I am afforded the opportunity to experience a disease that gives me new insight to pain. The doctors all say there is no for cure what I have. No mega amount of drugs will keep me in the clear except those prescribed, and no matter how hard I try, I will just have to deal with the shit like everything else. All the marijuana I have around keeps me sane, keeps the pain to as much as a minimum as possible, and all the weight I dropped as a result of the disease, makes me feel like I am one of those science skeletons in the science department. The sad part about all of this is that I have to make sure I know where the "head" is everywhere I go. Without that, I am screwed, glued, and once again, tattooed.

I have learned that five eggrolls will give me more than enough grief I have ever wanted. I blow up like a dead whale on the beach and I am most uncomfortable for 48 hours or until I can get the gawd-damn-shit to pass. Broccoli gives me a major gas bubble and refried beans has the same effect. Extreme amounts of gas are quite effective for revenge on certain professors who deem themselves History buffs and wear green like a fucking garden gnome. I have learned which foods will set my body into a raging gut-buster of throbbing grief, and what gives me gas equaled to or surpasses that of a dog's. Large amounts of ice cream are off limits as they make me hurl. Deep fried foods are no-no's. Green tea is my friend while coffee is not.....except Starbucks on occasion. Should I get the flu, it will be ten times worse than someone else's. I refuse flu shots as already have enough poison and crap flowing in my body to ignite a nuke; I hate needles.

The disease is embedded in my DNA code like a Trojan horse; what a surprise that turned out to be. So every few weeks or so, I experience a flair up and it makes me sicker than I ever thought possible. I miss a few days or even a few hours of work and wish to hell that I didn't. I use the time to lick my wounds and write whatever comes to mind. People pitch a fit about my illness, are indignant, feel as though I can control it. They don't understand the pain and humiliation one feels when a flair up occurs. I cannot control this damn things and I wish people would get that through their thick skulls. I try to make them understand but it's like trying to talk them about the last episode of Star Trek....only a geek would understand the term photon torpedo in the hatch.

I don't write the preverbal blog nor have I invested time in a chat session with others of the same disease. Although I did attend one and I found much to my chagrin that each of those people had been in the hospital a dozen times in a year, had their some of colons removed, and were drinking beer and eating French fries. Most don't have Crohn's Disease, they have the cousin: ulcerative colitis. I read that there is no smoking, or alcohol permitted as it makes things worse. Nothing mentioned about my friend, Mary Jane. She helps me keep fighting, helps me sleep, and she helps me keep what little sanity I still have left inside of me. The bugs in my legs, crawling around from time to time, they are part of this damn fucking disease. They will never go away, they are a part of me. Eventually things will at some point, get worse, but as long as I do what I am told to, things are relatively just peachy-keen. Thanks to the array of drugs, I've put on fifty pounds....my pants don't fit. My feet still swell up: called Edema which goes hand in hand with Crohn's.....the inflammation. It's a fucking lovely disease to have...I look up to see which book I can open to get a joint and that's when I see a fox........

* * * * * *

I awoke to another blaring of tornado sirens, shrill and screaming around me. The cramping in my body hurt like hell as I tried to find a reasonably comfortable spot to weather the storm. I peeked out from under Lady and caught a glimpse of my razor swaying back and forth in cobra style fashion. It was as though it were keeping beat with the sirens; winds swirling around the house, and the blasting hail as it smacked against the window. I ducked back under the mattress just as a huge piece of something crashed into the bathroom window. The shatter sounded like ice cracking before it exploded and collapsed. The noise was eerie and my contempt for the ensuing tornado grew. I popped a few Tylenol for my enlarged headache and dozed off. Sleep was inevitable; and hour here and there was like a captured butterfly, flirting with danger and just escaping the net.

Sleep............the only physical luxury I could no longer enjoy. My thoughts were paralyzed and the pain was a nuisance that demanded constant attention. I was an unwelcome vagrant to sleep, and my body knew it just as well as everything else did. Whoever said that you can't make up a line about how bad the shit gets, was wrong. Dead wrong. As a matter of fact, wrong enough to say that butterflies don't sit in the pit of one's stomach and rock out to Pink Floyd, when in fact they do; especially when danger is being hailed from the nether regions. Shit happens. I felt the warmth run out and around me but I was too far under the blanket of dreams and nightmares to really care.

Another long semester paraded off the campus as the first snow began falling in late September 1981. I stared at the wide-eyed class of writing students as though I was staring at the line of pins in an alley. I held the ball that would knock each of them down so that they would fly around a back wall before settling into the swell of darkness below, only to be swallowed up and reset for the next round. That's the way the semester started as each student laid his or her journal in my basket.

Their random inspirations came from dreams or from things they had experienced or felt. Originality was as alien to them as triple-decker shit in the woods. The farther they searched for a story, the worse it got. That is until Lazy Jayne, as I like to call her, waddled up and slapped her version of novel illusions in my face.

Lazy Jayne was someone you would notice in a window but never give a second thought to. She propped her glasses on her face as though she was torturing a piece of pasta between the tines of a fork before eating it. Nothing was logical about her, she didn't stand out as being someone of importance, but rather of unimportance and distant. Her waddle reminded me of an enormous duck making its way to water before finally arriving at its destination, plopping down in the middle of a puddle of water like a giant foot. The splash would overwhelm those around her like a tidal wave; daring and vicious. Her attitude was like a bee sting. She never cared who she hurt as long she got her way; maybe curl up and die somewhere, but it didn't matter. She was insensitive, and she wanted to be a nurse! The lackluster persona greeted the entirety of life as though it was a perilous journey into the unknown. She simply existed for the sake of her species with little or no hope of repopulating her kind. I tried holding a conversation with her several times, but she held herself above that level of communication and merely conveyed with her pasty, lifeless eyes that whatever I had to say, was not worthy of a response.

Her writings were more like speculations as to why she was forced to write things that were not part of her required area of study. The moment her pen would scratch the surface of the paper, Jayne was examining my face for a clue and then shake her head before continuing on. For Jayne, writing was an unforgivable torture and she was unable to extrapolate any imaginative purpose for the exercises. After three weeks of reading bland objectives formulated from her subconscious, I advised Jayne that I needed to speak with her in private regarding her assignments. Jayne arrived precisely as my last student was leaving my office.

"Professor Strickland!" She stated bouncing like a balloon into my office. "I do not appreciate giving up my afternoon for a meeting that is both pointless and futile."

"Have you ever heard of the Borg?" I asked.

"Who?" She inquired taking a seat next to my desk. A rather extended and heavy sign escaped her like a bad case of gas had built up inside her and she was trying to get rid of it.

"Never mind." I pulled out her paper. "I asked you here with the purpose of helping you to shape your writing into something more inviting rather than flat piece of kitty litter."

"So what you are saying is that I write like shit?"

"I didn't say that."

"No, but you implied it." She pointed out.

"I said it was flat and compared it to kitty litter because it's flat, lifeless, and innocuous."

"What does that mean?"

"Which part?" I asked watching Jayne.

"Are you saying I stink as a writer? Your opinions don't matter to me because you are nothing. Actually, the more I think of it you are like the patients I see lying around in the intensive care unit; they are all vegetables and pumped up on drugs, all patiently waiting to die."

"So, you are a nurse."

"No, I'm the unit secretary. I'm the one that answers the phones and takes messages, keeps the logs, and whatever else is needed." Jayne sat there as though she were the only one in the office. Her hands clasped against each other as though praying for permission to leave.

"If you don't like your job, then leave." I told her

"Leave? I like my job! It's this class that I don't like." She balked as though I had insulted her.

"Then drop it. Stop wasting my time and yours. Find something more to your liking."

"More to my liking? I have to take this class as a requirement. I don't like literature classes and this was the only thing left that stands between me and finishing my general education classes for my nursing degree."

"So you take my class looking for what? An easy A? Maybe a B but preferably an A?"

"Yes."

"Writing is an art. It's a craft that not many people perfect, but do so with lots and lots of hard work. You can't be Hemingway right out of the gate or even a Dickinson for that matter. You have to appreciate the gifts you have, the talents that are uniquely yours and refine them like you would for a diamond excavation."

"Do you always talk to your students like this or is this your polite way of saying I can do better, but I have to work at it?"

"Can't put a lamp shade on your head and stand you in a corner now can I? The sarcasm oozed out of me like lava.

"If that is your attempt at humor, you might as well join the rest of the vegetables in the hospital." Jayne whispered.

"Jayne, I believe someone has scrambled your eggs far too long for you to be this hateful. As a matter of fact, I'm quite positive that your lazy-assed attempt to slide by in my class just to meet any type of a grade has already expired. So in light of the current situation, I suggest that you redo the assignment. Reevaluate the purpose of why you decided to come to college in the first place, and start reading something more than the crossword book in my class. I know what you are doing and I don't care if you pass or fail; I'm not above failing anyone. But if I ever catch you trying to skate by without doing anything in my class, I will go to the head of the nursing department and make them aware of your antics. I sure as hell would not want you at my bedside, not even to collect my shit as it sits harboring a foulness I can't describe, inside the depths of a bedpan I would be lying on." I handed Jayne back her assignment and stared at her in the same despiteful manner she had given me. I was waiting to be hit or slapped by the heavy-handed fist of Lazy Jayne but she recanted the notion the moment she stood up and stormed out of my office like a tornado.

Silence settled into my office and I was on the verge of enjoying the moment when a voice bellowed in my ear, jarring all my muscles into fighter mode.

"I have not had all my eggs scrambled, you anal bastard. My eggs are quite fine!" Jayne yelled. The door slammed shut and I stood ready to do battle.

"Have you checked your ovaries?" I said to the closed door. I sat down and smiled. "Of course she hasn't, Professor. That's why she's as slimy as egg whites." I snickered to myself. As of late I didn't care who I offended. Because as I had discovered, a great many students were like Lazy Jayne; skating by in hopes of getting the minor stuff out of the way so they could get on with the more important studies. I reasoned that if creative writing wasn't important, then why bother me with their torturous writings.

At the same time that Lazy Jayne was considering dropping her creative writing class, Warner Washington was devoting his current afternoon to ironing out the details of his final draft of his assignment. Although Warner wasn't as talented as his classmates, he shared a passion for doing his best and providing his professor with a document that would make him proud. So while Jayne stood in line at her advisor's office, Warner was thumping down on the keys of his antique Royal typewriter; whiteout and eraser standing by just in case a mistake reared its ugly head.

Warner was the odd ball among his small circle of friends. He didn't have a computer, television, or a satellite phone. He had wall to wall books, stacked one on top of the other, from the ground up. When looking for a book, Warner would hunt for the book and then dismantle the stack as if it were Lego's in order to get to the book in question. For Warner, this was easier than ambling off to the campus library or the other libraries where a card was needed. All he had to do was search for the book among the shelves, pretend to take it to the checkout desk, and then duck behind a desk or lamp, stash the book in his bag and then pick up a random book and leave it on the table, indicating that he did not want the book. This was how Warner acquired the bulk of his library; a biblioklept in his own right.

No one was ever allowed in Warner's one-bedroom apartment unless it was someone he trusted not to violate his secrets. Warner was like one of those lost little kittens you would see in a deserted alley. He had a head of black hair, golden brown eyes, tiny glasses that hugged his face like saran wrap, a bow-shaped mouth, and long skinny neck that seemed to fit his lanky build. As Warner would walk, his feet would slap the surface like someone smacking their gum. The popping sound was expressly based on the too-big shoes Warner had donned in his earlier years. When his dad had gone off to work, leaving Warner to his own exploration of the house, he would put on the huge shoes and smack them about in the basement until his nanny told him to stop and play quietly. Growing up became a difficult task for Warner after his father died. Bounced around from relative to relative, Warner became obsessed with both books and big floppy shoes; they were the only things that never seemed to need dusting or feeding and they never talked back if ever Warner questioned their whereabouts. After his aunt passed away, leaving Warner a small fortune, he would drive to many a library and take the books he needed to fill his ever growing library of resource and adventure. No one ever stopped Warner as he would leave the library, because no one ever suspected that the six-foot something geeky looking kid was capable of theft. No one ever suspected Warner of doing anything wrong because he was straight forward and honest. That didn't mean however that Warner was incapable of deceit, not by a long shot.

After the last remaining relative died, Warner learned how to 'work the system' like the pros. Even though Warner had never been inside a prison or associated with anyone who traveled down the wrong path, Warner had devised a way to get out life exactly what he wanted, even if it meant that things were not exactly as they appeared.

So as Warner was re-reading the final draft of his paper, Lazy Jayne was getting her own rejection from her advisor, Casey Adams.

"Jayne, I've known Professor Strickland for almost twenty years and he doesn't pull punches when it comes to students. I know he's a bit rough, but he's fair and honest about what he does. Does he want you to humor him? No. Does he want you to put your best foot forward? Yes. Besides Jayne, if you drop this class, you will be three credit hours shy of graduating. You will have to take a literature class if you drop this, so your options at this juncture are limited." Casey Adams stated. Her freckles seemed to stand out brighter this afternoon as Jayne sat poised and ready to drop creative writing.

"But he's an asshole. He's too picky, he's anal, and I'm sure that he's picking on me." Jayne whined.

"Professor Strickland can be a bit overbearing at times, and he's witty, sometimes he's even cocky. Okay most of the time he's cocky, but he never picks on a student just to pick on them. Professor Strickland is awesome at what he does and he's just helping you become better at your craft."

"Writing is not my craft and neither is reading some stupid play by some idiot who wore rags and couldn't speak like the rest of us." Jayne whined again.

"Shakespeare?"

"Yes. Boring as Strickland. No one talks like that. Always using perhaps and shit like that."

"Maybe if you took the time to read what the Professor assigns, you would have a greater appreciation for the work." Casey chided.

"I doubt it. Look at my assignment! It's covered in red ink! How can I work like this?" Jayne squealed.

"Admittedly it is a bit on the red side, but think of it as a great learning experience, okay."

"I seriously doubt I am capable of learning at all in HIS class" Jayne shouted. Picking up her bag of books, Jayne took a long look at her advisor. "I don't like this. I don't like this at all and if I fail, it's because you wouldn't let me drop this disgusting class." Jayne stormed out of the office and pushed aside those standing in her way. Her only thought was to give back to Professor Strickland the same crap he had fed her; she was not going to let him get under her skin like this.

Students filed into the class the next morning with their final drafts burning their palms. Each paper laid atop the desk like flies on shit, waiting for the hit that would either send them to fly hell or off to another pile of shit. I sorted through the stack of papers as though looking for a million dollars. It was a nonsensical, irrelevant mound of horseshit that stared back at me and I was not looking forward to reading the bulk of the mess sitting in the middle of my desk.

I couldn't for the life of me remember any of the students that sat in a circle in the class, save one. Each had that lifeless look about them and they were about as interested in writing and engaging in class discussions about as much as angels in hell's dominion. Students with kinky hair interrupted the student with the pigtails, who interrupted the student with the bowtie, plaid shirt and stripped pants. About as nerdy as they came and I couldn't remember his name, but it didn't matter because he wasn't the sort that stood out among the rest of them. He might have been a character a with a minor role, or a guy you'd see walking to the geek club in a neighborhood that had a stack of books looming near him in a coffee shop. Perhaps he was the president of the chess club and he was taking a break to discuss his next strategy; a zugzwane for his chess opponent. Whatever his role or purpose, I was unaware of it until I read his paper. I'm not even sure, even now, if I would remember his name but I remember word for word the writing of the young man that crossed my path that very day.

To Have and To Hold
By Warner Walburg Washington

One starts a sentence in hopes that it will not be whittled down and asked to be revised as if it were but a mere twig lying on the ground. Should I have the nerve to gaze upon the heavens though a speckle in my father's eye I would, but alas, I cannot because he grew too old and weary to hold me in his arms. Had I come to this life a few years earlier, my father would still be here and I, just a small lad, would be upon his knee and listening to the tales he spun for all to hear. Those tales of knights and gargoyles perched in castle windows, princesses and apples forever braised with sweet delight. Dragons and royal fires sitting afoot against the night to light up the horizon for all to see. Oh the tales he would spin, how he would go on and on about the battles and wars fought in a kingdom and I but a young lad, can no longer hear of these tales because he was taken away, you see.

So one begins the task of a second sentence and paragraph with hopes of pushing forward and hoping that when the professor reads the work, that it meets with an approving eye, a nodding of the head, and a smile that can honestly show a mere delight for the task that has been wrought. How I wish for the days of yesteryear when we grew old because of labor and not because of pen and paper, shredding our dignity with a grade befitting of our genius. The days have all but flown by, but not before I share the untold secret of why I put this here and not elsewhere in the year.

As I begin paragraph three, it might appear that I have lost my wits about me, but, I assure you I have not. For in fact, I must remind you that the assignment was to share with you and not the rest of the class, a product of writing that would be, could be, or might be published at some point in my history. Narrowing down toward the end of my thoughts, I shall be thy guide into the wiles and tales I have spun, as a lad not propped upon thy father's knee but on the steeping stool of frugality. I hasten my way through thick and thin to be in your class this day, to tell you the tale you have yet to hear.

Paragraph four is a perfect stop. For I have but written nothing more than a prop, a back drop to a play darkened with decoys. I came to be one rainy afternoon, my mother but held me for a moment and then she was gone like a flint on a rock. I was moved from town to town until my father died away and no other relative would have me. I have survived the only way I know how; to write a lie to my employer and feign illness repeatedly, to forge one's signature upon a line on a check, to lie in wait to take food to fill my belly, and to whisk away fruit, meats, and cheese under my coat whilst the shopkeeper's head was turned away. I confess to you here and now, I am not proud of my crimes. I am ashamed of the way I am forced to live, but I am relieved to be telling you that this is my own work and not of some other scalawag.

Herein lies the fifth and final paragraph of the tale you see. I have sailed across the ocean once or twice, have been to Spain and Ireland, Canada and Mexico, I have flown above the clouds with the ducks and geese as they head south. Swam with the dolphins in Hawaii, met a

shark that walked the land, and took the name of no woman as my wife.
I have but seen what lies in store for me each and every day that I walk
the halls of hospitals searching for a friendly face that remembers me. I
wait for them to call me by name and greet me as their own flesh and
blood. I am but a ghost of many lives past, of lives present and some yet
unseen. I wither away each winter and bloom each spring, ruffling the
leaves in the fall, and dive in clear summer waters. I fail to recognize
each face as belonging in a book, for I have taken so many and lined
them up in my room like butterflies that I find them filled with logic
and invitation. They are my family, friends, my adventure, and all that
I yearn to be but cannot. For I, am the unknown, the malfeasance of
society and the raw product of angels that look after me. So ruined am
I that I cannot gaze upon a statue of grace and accept the fact that I
am unique and special as meant to be. For that is my tale wildly spun,
my woes exposed into the four winds as I await my fate, your royal-ness.

CHAPTER 15

I laid that paper down and thought long and hard about what I had read. I was convinced it was a confession of some sort, but as to why I wasn't sure. Was Warner playing with a full deck? Did the Joker miss the shuffle or something? My red pen was poised and ready to cut through the writing, but I couldn't place a stroke on that paper that would even begin to explain why. It was either a stroke of pure genius or the ranting of a young man doing far more weed than I had been.

Whatever this Warner Walburg Washington character had been thinking, he and I were not sharing the same page. Carefully I perused the paper again, making some small comments, but I was unable to riddle the paper with my bloody red pen. I simply left the paper alone; it stood on its own merit. For whatever it was worth, this kid was not bad and would most likely go extremely far. I saw his niche as a fantasy writer and I told him so, hoping that he would take the loot I just handed him and head for the nearest castle and start his quest.

The rest of the papers were less than amazing. I wanted to scream into the night that vampires suck better than you guy write, but decided against it just in case my neighbors were sitting in their rocking chairs drinking tea and smoking crack. What the hell did I care if the neighbors heard me; I smoke pot and no one bothers me!

* * * * * *

A loud yowling woke me from my nap. I peeked out from under Lady and saw a green cat with a tutu sitting on the ledge. I closed my eyes and opened them again. The cat with the tutu was gone but the broken glass was still there. The winds were howling like wolves and silence filled my ears.

"Shit. I'm in the cone!" I dove back under lady before the next wave of tornado sirens went off. Green had filled the window, the birds had found their own hiding spot just like the cat with the green tutu. Damned if I knew where it went, but I could only hope it was safe and away from danger. I waited for the sirens to go off, but their blaring lulled me back to sleep under the Lady I shared a space with for so long.

* * * * *

The last paper in the stack belonged to none other than Lazy Jayne. Another one pager.

"Why do they insist on writing one pagers for? Are they incapable of more?" I was impatient and annoyed. However, I decided that if Lazy Jayne's paper was as well written as Warner's, I would be fine with it. I was immediately disappointed, but not at all surprised.

It's My Way, You Sorry Bastard
By Jayne Deckers

Once upon a time, in a forest laden with shit and piss, lived a very old fat guy and his fat old dog. The dog was named Herman, and he was about as hateful as the fat old guy in these nasty Hawaiian shirts. He wore these nasty old shorts with holes in the knees, gray socks with sandals, his hair tied in a ponytail behind his head and he smelled like a wet old dog left out in the rain. I can't remember what the fat old guy said to me the other day, but its worser than usual and more badder than normal. All I remember is that he wanted me to rite better so that I could pass this nasty-assed class so that I can get my nursing degree. If that fat old guy ever finds hisself in the hospital I be working in, I am going to smash his face in with a metal bedpan and send his piss flying all over the room. And when that fat old guy starts yelling at me to stop, I'm going to shove some Vaseline in his mouth and make him choke on it. As for the dog Herman, I ran him over with the lawnmower the other day and now his ass is grass. So if that fat old guy has any cents at all, he will do his job and get me the hell out of this here class.

THE END

"Wow! Someone has an attitude. I would hate to have her as my nurse just as much as the next guy!" I said as I carved my way through her paper. I left Lazy Jayne's paper for last on purpose. I wanted to see if what Casey said was true. After all, Casey and I have been long time friends and lovers at some point and while we still don't see eye to eye on many things, we both agree that some students don't like being told NO.

"Herman" Casey had said poking her head in my office. "One of your illustrious students paid me a visit and she wasn't too happy about the fact that I wasn't going to let her drop your creative writing class."

"Really? Would that be Jayne?" I said smiling back. Casey still had a thing for me, it was the body language that gave her away.

"Oh, so you know her?" Casey smiled back.

"Yeah. One of my not so wonderful students."

"Beware of a woman scorned, okay."

"I promise not to be surprised." I smiled. Casey flipped her hair and slipped out of my office as quietly as she had arrived. I was prepared for Jayne. The bedpan scene was a bit much but it was a nice try.

I took another brief look at Lazy Jayne's paper before I gave a reply.

Jayne,

It appears that your attempt to write a fantasy piece is a failure. However, let's not rule out the fact that you could use some taming and write horror. I suspect as I have thus far, you have not done any of the readings assigned nor have you attempted to refine your work as I have asked. While I can appreciate how difficult this assignment may be for someone of your intelligence, I should direct your attention to several literature classes that will be taught during the coming semester. Perhaps one of those would be more suited to your taste. Keep in mind however, that I am one of two professors that teach these literature classes and since the other professor is on maternity leave, that leaves myself, the fat old guy and his dog

Herman, whose ass you tried to mow down but didn't because of a certain pet cemetery....had him brought back to life to teach you to become more literate than the buffoon you are. And if it behooves you to smash in every patient's head with a metal bedpan, be prepared for a stint behind bars......I hear that several prisons are in need of your bedpan experience. Also, you might want to buy a recent edition of a dictionary; you are in serious need of a spelling test.

-F

After giving the last once over to the stack of student papers on my desk, I placed them in my desk drawer and locked them up. Another red pen had been drained of its life and another sat in the cup ready to take its place.

The next day came and papers were returned to eager students whose brains would be keeling over in either happiness or hate. Either way, this fat old guy and his dog Herman didn't give a shit. The reactions were priceless and yet, I expected them as I always did.

"You gave me a minus F?" The familiar bellow stormed through the class like a thunder clap.

"G, is not a letter grade so yes, F. You earned that, Jayne."

"This is not acceptable!" Jayne yelled.

"Neither is trying to run my dog over with a lawnmower and calling his ass grass, but you did it anyway." I replied.

"But I'm supposed to graduate in a month!"

"And I don't give a shit either. If you think skating by with a bedpan under you is the answer to your prayers, think again. The wrong words were used, grammar sucked, it wasn't long enough, and I am not a fat old guy with a dog named Herman. You have an F. If you want to change it, redo the paper correctly and submit it by the end of the day. That means you have until five to get it done and in to my office. After that, the offer is null and void."

"You self-centered, cock-eating, righteous bastard!" Jayne screamed. She threw her paper at me but not before she spit at me and then waddled out of class. Unknown to me, Casey Adams was spying on my class at that moment. Thanks to her, Jayne didn't get to graduate and she didn't get back into college after that either. Sometimes the fat old guy with the dog named Herman is the one with the lawnmower who say's "Jayne, your ass is grass!"

As for Warner Walburg Washington, who knows where he ran off to...? I'd like to think that his slate is clean and that he is out in the kingdom somewhere fending off dragons and vicious gargoyles and saving damsels in distress.

* * * * * *

My buddy and pal, Crohn's disease, decided to generate one of its many flair ups on Friday the 13th. I am not a superstitious person by nature, but, superstition gets its power from belief people place in it. I chose to believe that it was time for a dance with shit on Friday the 13th. There were others however, that believed the timing of the flair up was due in part to the superstition; all things bad happen on Friday the 13th. Standing before a class of high school students one October morning, I wished I had not taken the temporary teaching gig for my friend and colleague Erick Simmons. His pleas were that no one else was qualified to take on a bunch of indigent high school kids with style. Having hemorrhoid surgery would have been easier than taking on high school kids.

It was my second time as a high school fill-in or as I like to call it, 'babysitter'. Many of them were bragging about the length of their rap sheet and others were telling stories about how jail was a cushy piece of time for those that cared to listen. I, myself, would never have talked like that growing up for fear of getting sent to the principal's office, followed by a phone call to my parents. The beating I would have sustained would have made branding cattle, child's play.

I surveyed the room with care in search of one soul member of the English class who was not involved in the gossip and drama circulating in the class. Sally Stocker sat in the back of the class, engaged in drawing on her arm and humming a tune I was familiar with.

"That's not a Pink Floyd tune you're humming is it?" I asked approaching the blooming-to-be-artist. Her head popped up like toast in a toaster; the swirl of black curls bouncing back against her forehead revealing the pale complexion of someone in dire need of sunshine.

"Yes. It's from one of their albums but I doubt that you know it, grandpa." She snorted at me. She continued with her drawing and picked up her humming from where she had left off.

"Ah, Brick In The Wall. One of my favorites. The lyrics remind me of an orphanage of boys that were left behind after the bombs dropped. Of course you can interpret what you want from it……"

"Like I care, grandpa. No one was axing you anything." She snorted again. The classroom of students grew quiet. *Had no one had ever engaged them in conversation? Not even Erick Simmons?* Students sat on top of their desks, legs swinging over the sides, cigarettes cocked behind their ears as though waiting for the moment when they can light up and feel the rush wrap them up in a velvety cloud of whispers and dreams. *Were these the throw back kids of the rocking 50's? Or were these the future thugs that would rule the planet when I was wheeling myself around a distant planet in the future?* These were thugs, vermin that parents had given birth too and wanted nothing to do with anymore.

"I see you are an artist as well as a singer. What do you like to draw? What medium?"

"Did I axe you to talk to me or are just plain dumb?" The girl chewed.

"I am asking you questions, true. But I most certainly would not want you to axe me. You don't even know me." I responded.

"I didn't say axe I said axing. So I'm axing you why are you bothering me, grandpa?"

"One should learn to speak more clearly and annunciate their words so that one doesn't get the wrong idea. I am asking you a question and you are axing me to leave you alone. The way you are speaking implies murder. So which way are we going here? Ask or axe?" I sat down on the desk top adjacent her and waited.

"What chew mean, axe or axe?"

"Chew? I think you mean you, not chew, like you would gum. Although there is the ewe version which is a rather wooly animal known as sheep."

"What the hell is your problem, grandpa? Don't chew have someone's else's to bother?"

"See, there is another one of your language fubars. Did no one bother to correct your speech while you were growing up?"

"No, why?" She stared at me at a way a predator looks at its prey just before ripping out its throat.

"Because your speech, your language, sucks. Axe implies murder and you don't know me so why would you kill me? Chew versus you, not even in the same realm yet, you are so lazy that you have managed to degrade the one universal language one can barely recognize, thereby making you look stupid. And for the record, it is and I quote, 'don't you have someone else to bother' and not 'don't chew have someone's else's to bother'? And yes I have plenty of students to bother in this classroom but, I chose you because you were drawing and I was interested to see what you were creating." I took a quick breath before finishing my sermon. "And for the record, I am not grandpa. I am Professor Strickland, young lady, and I will be here until Mr. Simmons returns from the hospital. So in light of that fact, perhaps you would enlighten myself and the rest of your classmates as to how you plan to ask me to leave you alone. Shoot for the stars because we are all dying in anticipation here." You could have heard the preverbal pin drop in that classroom. No one was staring at me. They were staring at the curly-haired girl with the blue pen stuck in the middle of a hole in her jeans. Looking around the room, the girl dropped her leg, placed her pen on the desk and sat up to face me. Clearing her throat, she opened her mouth to speak but only a squeak came out.

"Professor Strickland" she began. She noticed the writing on the chalkboard behind me and looked at me square in the face. "What does those letters after your name mean?"

"It means I have a Doctorate in Philosophy. And it's 'do not does'." I was so calm you could have skipped rocks across my surface and never seen a ripple in my Hawaiian shirt.

"So that means you are smart?"

"One would hope so." I said, generating a small chuckle out of a few students.

"So Mr. Simmons is sick?"

"Yes."

"So we have you and a not slimy substitute?"

"I think you mean, grandpa, isn't that right? Or am I not "hip" enough for you to learn anything from?"

"I'm sorry. I was being a smartass" she began. Checking her language she tried the apology again. "I was being stupid and disrespectful. I was thinking we could put one over on you and you would walk away and we would get dumped onto some other substitute's lap."

"What is your name?"

"Gangsta Sally. Um Sally Stocker, Mr. Strickland. I mean, Professor."

"Well. Ms. Stocker, perhaps you and the rest of your compadres, will do me the honor of singing "We Don't Need No Education" by Pink Floyd. And after that, then we are going to play Duck-Duck-Goose, to see which Dumbass is going to explain to Mr. Simmons how the first day went without him. Now, doesn't that sound like fun?" I watched each and every student slink down in their chairs, sitting neatly on their backsides as though they had been caught sneaking into the cookie jar. No one said a word, snickered, or smiled. Silence danced like a marionette around each student. They held their tongues, including Sally Stocker. Her days of behaving like a four-year-old evaporated. "Simply riveting, this moment has been. Does anyone care to explain why someone would want to murder me on my first day here? I can't imagine that anyone would, unless you were looking for my stash of weed I keep in my backyard, buried under the birdbath. Now that I have given away the location of where my stash is not, who wants to tell me the whereabouts of your English books because I don't see any of them anywhere." It was a race to the finish; everyone pulled out a book from a hidden backpack and placed it and a notebook on the desk.

I had forgotten why I avoided high school kids until the moment Sally wanted to axe me. They had unusual ways of communicating with the outside world; a way that was not too foreign to old folks like myself. They dressed like some cartoon nightmare, with a swag that made mouths drop wherever they walked. This was a more modern day façade kids of the day were putting up and they didn't care who they offended because it was their time in history that would be remembered. For me, it was going to be a long two weeks unless I pulled out the stops and laid some 'funk down' as Al was fond of saying. So I took a toke on a joint, prayed for a monsoon, and hopped into my daily Hawaiian gear that kids found rather entertaining. I was not the average shirt and tie guy, I was the tie-dyed grandpa with a ponytail who had a thing for proper grammar and speech. The English language had been uprooted from its origins and catapulted back into the Stone Age.

So on Friday the 13th, I opened the lid to the presser-cooker and dove in, closing the lid on any rumors that I would be a pushover. There is no angel on the face of this planet that could have prepared me for the shit factor that was gearing up deep within me. I was sweating bullets and my stomach was making noises that one hears after screaming in the face of their worst nightmare. I could no longer ignore the pleadings of my stomach no more than I could hunger pains. Before I could even assign anything, I bolted from the class and stormed the bathroom like a vulture on a carcass. Everything hit with an urgency that reminded me of how lucky I was to be crapping inside and not in an outhouse in the middle of nowhere. No Sears and Roebuck catalog to wipe my backside with, but it might as well have because that's how harsh the paper was. Fifteen minutes passed before a voice interrupted my death march.

"Professor Strickland, you okay in here?"

"I feel like a caveman doing a mud dive in the middle of a T-Rex rampage" I grunted.

"Do you need an ambulance?" Another voice said. "Or air freshener? Now I know why I don't go to the zoo! Whew!"

"Dang! It is ripe in here!" A younger voice added.

"Hey! You kids back off" a voice of authority bellowed. "Who died? Did you kids flush a skunk down the urinal?" I could hear laughter and visualizing kids bent over holding their stomachs in raging laughter. Yes, another one 'bites the dust' went through my mind.

"I'm fine." I answered.

"You don't smell fine. Do you need anything?"

"Peace and quiet without an audience. Can't a man shit in peace?" I said more to myself.

"Strickland, is that you?"

"Yes. Just cover my class for a few more minutes okay, please. I'll be in as soon as my insides retract from my anus." I busted out laughing. Another gurgling sound erupted, followed by a gaseous bubble and then dynamite lit up the bathroom once again.

"Find me some air freshener. Get the custodian fast and tell him to get a plunger, too." The voice commanded. I heard the laughter and the gust busting that pounded the halls. I knew what they were thinking. I couldn't smell what came out of me as I had grown accustomed to the stench, the disease, the rage that rattled around inside me like a battalion of angry vultures. They crept up on me in stealth mode and dropped me like I was a baby. No one knew the pain I was in, not until I yelled in agony over the announcement of a plunger. The only plunger I needed was to my oral cavity that was currently allowing gravity to deface my backside. I was humiliated and acutely aware that nearly everyone within a one mile radius of my current position could; A) hear me or B) smell me. Forget tales of a holy war or world war. Whatever god there was had just declared war on my internal organs and reduced me to a pool of sweat and puke. That god just placed a flag somewhere near the sphincter police and vowed not to give up the fort to another intruder. Another plop hit the waters below and in came the Calvary to the rescue.

"Strickland, you still alive in here?"

"Ay, captain." I sang out

"We've called an ambulance for you."

"Dandy." I breathed. I don't think I was ever so glad to have two large men knock the door down to the stall. I can't for the life of me remember much of the conversation that followed in the aftermath in the taking of Fort Strickland. For whatever it was worth, every student and teacher that either heard me or smelled me, stood guard as I was wheeled away.

To my relief, I was released from the hospital Sunday morning. I'm not one for extended stays in places that cater to people older than myself. Fortunately, Rock-o came to my aid and gave me a lift home upon receiving my release papers. He helped me into his '67 Volkswagen bus covered with peace symbols and weed décor. We drove in silence to my place. Rock-o was the silent type and I was eternally grateful for that. I was escorted to my front door and as soon as I put the key in the lock, Rock-o handed me a familiar brown package with a rubber band, patted my shoulder, and left me standing there on the stoop alone.

Stale air attacked me as soon as I opened the door. I kept the door open for a moment to let fresh air in as I walked toward the kitchen. It was comforting to know that I had not left my place in ruins, or that I had anything revolting staring at me on the floor.

"Heller?" A voice sang in the air.

"Yeah, who is it?" I answered.

"Brought yer car home. Rock-o asked me to make sure you was taken cared of. Reckon I be bidding you adios now that yer home 'n all." I saw a huge black woman standing in my doorway inspecting my home like it was for sale. She looked like Sasquatch had hooked up with some other Neanderthal; and she was in charge.

"And you are whom?" I asked the woman as I peeked out from the kitchen.

"Shasta" she smiled. Her smile was a large as she was except she had one tooth present in her smile. The rest of her teeth were gone and I made the connection immediately.

"You are Rock-o's aunt!"

"Can't put nofing over on you now can't I?" Shasta came over and gave me a bear hug that caused my ribs to crack and tossed me a kiss aside my face. *Fuck, cracked ribs. Oh fuck, don't laugh you old dog. Don't laugh.*

"You look good, Shasta!" I said grinning.

"Reckon its better 'n you right this hir moment, don't ya s'pose?"

"Yes, I suppose so." Shasta had brought over a bag of groceries and unloaded them on the coffee table. I had heard stories about Shasta from Jade and I knew that while the woman could be a genuine sweetheart, she was also capable of manslaughter as well. I was not even inclined to correct her speech for fear of having my already upset intestines removed and wrapped about my head like a turban.

"This hir is some chickin soups, and crackers. Jade said that this would helps you get well. She be by later on to check on yer. She told me to tell yer that." Shasta clasped her hands together like she was ready for a Thanksgiving get together.

"How is Jade?"

"Oh she be fine. She and Rock-o close friends. They right as rain, them two is. So you take it easy now, and gets well. I be checking on you later, son." Shasta gave me another hug and left. The front door stood open and the first flakes of the day had begun to fall. The temperature was falling fast as I placed another log on the fireplace. The warmth of the soup, crackling fire, and my old quilt wrapped around me made everything from the past few days fade away like a bad memory.

CHAPTER 16

Monday morning greeted me with five inches of snow. School buses were running an hour behind, roads were snow packed, nothing was cancelled, just delayed an hour or so. Living in Denver for as long as I had, I had grown accustomed to the cold, hard winters and the fact that sometimes I would have to put the chains on my tires just to get around town. Once I donned a pair of snowshoes and walked to work because several feet of snow had been dumped on the city over night. It was quite a workout and it made many of my colleagues envious of my stamina. While many would have cancelled class, I chose to ride out the storm and open up the brain pans of my students, filling their fresh young minds with knowledge. I sounded like a boring asshole, so full of himself that I wanted to erase that part of my personality. Unfortunately, that had become part of my genetic makeup and it merely added to the eccentric old pot head I had grown to be.

At half past nine, the first bus load of students came filing in the school. They were chilled to the bone and dying to be back home, surrounded in warmth and the sounds of television. As my students sat down, I passed out cups of hot cocoa, store bought cookies, and a sheet of paper. I was not without motives as I watched their faces. There was a look of concern as they turned over each sheet and noticed a simple title printed in the huge white space before the lines began. Only a few of the titles were different, as they pertained to being sick or dying. For some this was going to be a rough assignment since the bulk of the class had already lost a parent and lived with a relative or older sibling.

"Many of you know that I am sick. Shit happens sometimes, and in my case, it's more than you know. I have developed a sense of humor that far exceeds what many of you will ever know. So in order to handle my situation, it is that sense of humor that has caused me to become stronger than the foulness that roosts in my gut." I heard lots of snickering and I nodded that it was funny. "So, I took the liberty this morning of making a list of things that make us who we are. I comprised them into titles and I want you to create a story, good or bad, that illustrates proper grammar, punctuation, spelling, etcetera, etcetera, and have into me by the first of class tomorrow morning. This is a short story, single spaced, using both sides of the sheet I have provided. In time, you will be able to generate a longer piece. But for now, just the front and back of the sheet. I don't want any more than what I have given you. So put your creative skullcaps on, ditch the do-rags, and ball caps and put pen to scalp and ponder what you would do if faced with the title sitting in front of you." I heard wisps of agony circle the air and I saw fear in their eyes. No one, not even Simmons had forced them to face a reality that would challenge them at some point in their not so distant future.

"Can we discuss this first?" A voice whispered.

"Yeah, can we discuss it?" A second rang out.

"Why?" I asked. "Can you? Are you able of discussing anything?"

"May we please discuss this, Professor Strickland?" Sally spoke up.

"Are you axing me? Or, are you asking me for a discussion?"

"We are asking for a discussion. We degraded you and humiliated you in the way no one ever should. After we heard that you had something that was out of your control, we felt as though we couldn't deal with losing you to something as horrible as what you have. How you must have felt when your stomach acted up." Sally stated.

"That is why we are not going to discuss what I went through. I have dealt with this freaking disease the way Captain Kirk would have; kicked its ass and gave it back to the universe. It's a nasty Klingon around Uranus and it makes me crabby sometimes but I don't let it get me down. It's one of those extraterrestrial monsters with shit caked around its eyeballs that have morphed into something I can joke about simply because life is not about disappointment, but about conquering your fears and moving beyond them. For example, I don't like snakes any more than the next guy. However, as long as they are behind glass and not on my front porch, I'm fine with them. They are beautiful and amazing life forms, but if they cross my path outside the glass, I have a hoe with their name written ALL over the face of the blade. I will not hesitate to use it on them either." My students started laughing; most of them shared my dislike for snakes as it turned out. "So let thy pens rev up their engines, may you find pith and ponderings, a juxtaposition lingering a fortnight away softly embedded in the corpuses of your being, engage me thine splendor, and navigate thine way into the unknown, henceforth!" I held my hand high as if holding a sword into the clouds. There was clapping and whistling as one by one each student began to deal with the task at hand. I seriously doubt they had a clue to which I referred, but the majority of the class found their way to meeting up with Webster; a delightful encounter I'm sure.

While the scourge of writing was underway, I pulled out a vinyl of Pink Floyd and placed it on an old turntable I found in the music room. Flipping the switch on, I gently placed the needle on the track, and let the music fill the minds of those riddled with contemplation and confusion. Heads rose from their task and I saw smiles bloom on faces that otherwise were sullen and flat. The music caressed their thoughts and I could almost see their stories filter out through the room like flying cars of the future. And so began the epic turnaround of several classes of English students and the retirement of Erick Simmons. I finished my two week stint at Star Crest High on an elevated note. Each and every student begged me to stay and I chose to recant my thinking about high school students.

It was the day before Halloween when I received a call from the school principal.

"Strickland, Bob Hastings."

"Yes. What may I do for you?" I asked the man behind the voice. His pressed shirt and tie rustled against the phone like tissue paper. I could hear the heavy breathing of the overweight man sitting in the high-back chair, trying to prop his tiny feet up on a desk that his legs would never reach. Hastings was the Oompa Loompa monitoring the progress of kids and teachers that filled his school of candy land thoughts and well-wishes. I was visualizing his stoutness, his combed-over hair piece that tried to cover the ever receding bald spot, when his voice broke the stream of reflection.

"Simmons is retiring and I would like you to fill in the gap until I can find another teacher. I know you teach at the college, but we could really use your talents here at Star Crest. So what do you say?" I was about to refuse when I heard a little voice inside me say, 'go for it'. I could never refuse that voice; it was like my mother asking me to cut the lilac bushes for Mrs. Meckling, our next door neighbor that lived next to us when I was growing up. I could never refuse her, nor could I refuse the fresh apple pies she used to make. 'A gift from heaven' she would always say.

"Fine. But after this semester, I have to get back to my own realm, if that's okay with you."

"Great. See you tomorrow!" Hastings almost cheered. The click sounded like one of those bongs the Buddhist monks used. The bong sound was deafening as it veered off into silence.

Here I was back walking the halls of Star Crest High as though a tenured master of the arts. I had crafted my art so well, that students no longer made fun of my loud Hawaiian shirts, shorts, and sandals. They never chided me when the gas chamber went on high alert or the sewer system was backing up. All told, my students grew rather fond of me regardless of the nerd they found me to be or the eccentric, daffy old guy with pot stashed somewhere in my homestead. I was the cool old guy with style and a joke a plenty when the moment called for it.

"Happy Birthday, Professor Strickland!" My students sang out that cold October 31st.

"Thanks. Make way for the dropping of the ball at midnight. I fear that a demon lay rotting just below the surface." I smiled.

"Ewwww!" Everyone held their nose and started laughing.

"Grab a gas mask, it's going to be one hell of a boom!"

"Professor Strickland, do you ever wish things could be different?" A familiar voice echoed in my ear. Sally Stocker had achieved what many were still trying to grasp. I gave her points for putting her artistic pen to paper on not to jeans.

"You mean do I wish the Klingons had invaded another galaxy?"

"Yeah."

"Nah. And miss the opportunity to gross the rest of you out? Not in a million!" I said with a grin. No one would ever be able to fathom how lucky I was to be alive after surviving the misery I had been given. There was no magic wand to take away what I had inside because I had managed to make it a part of me. I had assimilated it into my collective being. I was the universe that no one could conquer, well, not yet anyway.

The last remainder of the semester flew as fast and furious as the geese flying south. Christmas break was fast approaching, a new teacher had been announced, replacing me in January. The last of the final papers sat in my basket like an invitation to a wake. I began the task of reading and marking grades on each student's sweat stained final prose. I remembered each freckle and pimple, each bead of sweat running down the side of a greasy head, the running nose, hacking, coughing and whining student. The student that slept in class and silently flipped me off under their desk for assigning yet another piece of work to create. I remember the laughter and sighs of those when I would label them a "Dumbass" for doing the unthinkable in class. For getting caught smoking in the boy's room, or in a vacant hall by the band room. I remember the pom-pom girls, the cheerleaders and the jocks, the jokers and nerds, and the occasional pothead, not including myself, that graced the spaces in my class. I would remember them long after I left this tower of education as it emerged as a beckon of commencement.

The last paper stared at me like a cat; almost purring in the hope that I would grace it with a passing grade, a pat on the head and a scratch behind the ear. I recognized the topic right away. Sally Stocker, the curly-haired, pale faced teen with braces and hallow eyes that quickly grasped the concept of proper English and excelled to the top of her class. The blooming artist that drew stick figures and graphics along her arm and on the legs of her jeans, defacing the top of her desk each Monday morning after the custodian had cleaned it with bleach the night before.

"Why are you so anal? Sally asked. I noted that she no longer wanted to axe me like a serial killer.

"I am defending my English and I am prepared to do battle with those that refuse to regard her with respect" I responded in kind. Sally's prose had become surreal and enlightening. They were assorted nightmares and figments of an imagination in dire need of psychoanalysis. I often thought there was more than one Sally sitting underneath that mop of curls, and I even speculated that she had been to see a few shrinks during the span of her sophomore year. I flipped the curled sheets of paper over and took a once over of the final writing. It would be like tracking a roach in a parfait cup. I proceeded with caution.

What Fear Has Taught Me
By Sally Stocker

Give me a stage name and I can tell you my worst fear; public speaking. It makes me as nervous as a cat covering up crap in a den full of pit bulls. It gives me the shivers and chills until I feel the life run out me and leaves me like a turd in an iceberg. I don't think fear has a future in my life, but I know it by name every time I see Professor Strickland standing before me like a geek tragedy. I can't recall the last time I felt the way he makes me feel, but I am sure if there is a scrapbook around in the group home where I live, I would find a picture of it taped next to my prison mug shot.

Fear is just a word that makes you think you are in danger when in fact you are not. Fear is that little sister you wish you had but don't have, but rather it's your alter ego banging around inside you like a tiger in a cage. Every time you visit the beast, it snarls at you, tries to rip out your eyes, but misses you each and every time. Fear is that little bubble of babble you feel when faced with why you act a certain why, speak like an ignorant humanoid, or dress like a whore on Colfax. It's just a word that eats its way into your soul like a termite does to wood. It doesn't harbor ill will or happiness, it's an emotion that evokes a reaction like a scream. It's just something you can't put a finger on because it's not a tangible thing.

It's not often that I see fear except when I look into the faces of my roommates at the home. I watch them mourn the loss of a visit with a parent, a brother or sister. I see how good behavior is rewarded and how everyone remembers the mistake you made and won't ever let you forget it. It doesn't matter that you have been on your best behavior, because in the end, it's that one little stupid stunt you pulled that folks remember. No matter how majestic I appear, or how awesome I have grown, that stupid stunt cost me my freedom to do whatever I want. My only fear is that I will be judged for the rest of my life as one that heisted a package of gum from the candy store.

So when I look in the mirror, my curly locks blocking my view and hiding me from the rest of the world, my fears are not there. I only see what I need to see and that is me. I have no fear because I faced that bitch the minute my mother walked away from me and my daddy beat the tar out of me. Fear evoked the last remaining emotion out of me, a cry, a whine, and even a slight chuckle. But it wasn't until Professor Strickland hovered over me like a deranged and twisted predator that got me to ask one last time, why me? It was because of that damned raccoon that crept into my bed one night and announced that it was going to have its litter right there. You don't know fear until you see some furry-assed thing pooping out bloody squirming things in the middle of your bed that you realize you are headed for the funny farm. Fear isn't my best friend, it's a damn raccoon with spiked hair and is something Stephen King created during one of his mushroom rides with a Walt Disney Fairy!

What does fear look like? It's a bad ride on a rollercoaster; a blood-curdling scream as you plummet down the long hill, your lungs nearly out of your mouth, your eyeballs popping out of their sockets, and the overwhelming urge to crap in your pants. In the instant that you fear all of this, you close your eyes so that they don't end up on some billboard as added imagery. You suck up the shit and you wait for it to come out the other end. Fear is the reflection I see as I ride to the bottom of that hump and start the assent to another, waiting for that endearing feeling to peel back my face and expose the skeleton underneath. All the pot I've smoked and all the bad stuff I have done are waving their arms above me and yelling like frantic nuns in a burning church.

Whenever I think that I am safe from all the shit in the world, fear sticks out its thumb and hitches a ride like toilet paper on a shoe. You never notice it, but someone always does and its creepy carrying that much fear around when you don't have too. Fear is a just a four letter that means: fiercely exterminating another roach.

I laughed heartedly and until my sides hurt.

Sally! Bravo! A
Professor Strickland

* * * * * *

Time was all I had. It ticked away like steaming tea in a teacup. Fear was not an option, but somehow it managed to catch me off guard and remind me that I was trying too hard sometimes to remember the trivial things in life. I would catch a glimpse of myself here in there, trapped in between dialogues with myself and my colleagues as though they were trinkets on a shelf. I was alone with my thoughts, endless minutes of nothingness that left me wondering what I was doing.

Fear shook me awake as I lay staring at the face of Lady piercing down on me. I felt the minor shake and disengaged myself from the bathtub. The old tales that said if you die in your dreams, you die for real also means that if you shit in your sleep, you obviously shit for real. I never believed that tale of death, but shit, well that is as a different caliber of ammunition. I was soaked from crotch to leg in the stuff and the smell was suffocating me to death. I pushed off the mattress and assessed the damage.

"Just like in the hospital, only in the tub and not all over the blasted floor." I said breathing through my nose. The tragedy had struck in my dream; the last remaining thought I had before Sally gave me her version of fear.

The howling outside had gone. I pushed the heavy mattress out of the tub and made sure that it was nowhere near my misfortunate shit factor. "Gees, Strickland, can't you wake up to take a crap?" I asked myself. I began removing my clothing with great care so that I wouldn't fling stuff all around in the tiny space. I turned the shower on full blast and waited for the water to reach the warm temperature I longed for. My muscles ached from being confined under Lady for so long. I glanced at my watch and time had moved along like five o'clock gridlock on Interstate 25. I had dozed off for another twenty minutes, and within that time I remembered people that I hadn't thought of for years.

As I finished hosing off, I made a mental note to call Simmons and see how he had faired the storm. After he had plastic surgery for a facial scar, he dropped off the face of the planet. He made a point once, that life is much like a circus and you have to be aware of the monkeys that are set free to steal your bananas. I never quite understood his point, but I got the gist of it quickly enough when the police paraded around his place searching for LSD and acid. Simmons plead guilty for possession, which cost him a teaching job. This was a guy that was as transparent as a windshield. His motive was plain but there was always a price to pay.

Exigent circumstances aside, Simmons was a pretty interesting guy, minus the stupid factor when it came to drugs and education.

"Dude, you have to lay low" Erick said to me once at barbeque he and some old college buddies were having. "The system is fucked up. It's a damn circus and those monkeys behind the bench are after all your bananas. Watch them, man. It is fucked up." Erick was so stoned that you could have used him as a doorstop. I had bailed him out of jail, and everything was cool until his court day rolled around. That's when I lost track of him; he never made it to court on time since he was higher than a hot air balloon at the time. He was arrested and did a few days in the county jail. Simmons was not the brightest star on the horizon, but when he wasn't stoned, he wasn't a bad teacher.

I found a post-it note on the icebox with Simmons' number and tried to dial the number. The phone was dead and another shake ruffled the foundation of my home. I darted into the bedroom and put on my sweat suit. The tornado sirens screamed to life and this time I took a look out the kitchen window to see if anything was nearby. It was time to hunker down again; I dragged Lady back into my bedroom and put her back on the box springs and slid under the bed. The tail of the tornado was about the size of an oil tanker as it whipped around outside. I closed my eyes and held my head tight and waited for the storm to die. Static lulled me back to sleep; it was another snippet of rest my body had been longing for.

CHAPTER 17

"I thinks I'm getting worser" a male voice blurted out. "Every time I turn my papers in, you always shred it, Professor Strickland."

"I'm sorry, what did you say?" I asked the young man whose back was to me.

"I said, I'm getting worser."

"Worser? Oh my stars in a million galaxies!" I looked at my hands after removing them from my ears. I was searching for blood. Finding none, I walked over to the young man and faced him head on. "Blshawn? Is that your name?"

"No, it's Blashon" he pronounced. "My momma made it up."

"Is that short for something?"

"No."

"Well excuse me for mispronouncing a made up name, but why did your momma name you that?"

"Cuz my daddy said he don't like no names in the baby book. My daddy is Blaine and momma is Shon. She put the two names together and I got named the mixture of the two." His dark brown eyes glared at me and dared to correct me again.

"Well, Blashon, the word is worse, not worser. Here is a recent edition of Webster's dictionary. Worser is not in here. See!" I said pointing to the 'worse' entry. Blashon searched the entire page for the word and then at me. "Furthermore, and I quote, 'he don't like no' is horrible English and is a double negative. Perhaps you should try rephrasing it."

"So you're an asshole. Big deal."

"No, you're the asshole and it is a big deal. You are in this English class for a reason; to learn. I am correcting your speech. I am doing my job and it's your job to learn" I waited for a reply.

"No, your job is to pass me to eleventh grade. It ain't to make me speak good."

"You are making my ears bleed and your language is like drinking vinegar. It's vile and offensive. You will learn to speak well, and my job is to ensure that you receive a proper education."

"You ain't my daddy."

"Thank the many Vulcan's for that!" I stood up. "What's your favorite band?"

"Why grandpa, you don't got no rhythm. You the whitest old man in here." Blashon said. The entire class laughed and I nodded in agreement.

"That may be, however, you haven't answered my question."

"Jimi Hendrix."

"Da funk he lay down, is smooth" I said sliding along the floor. "He has purple haze wrapped around him like it's the Fourth of July. He's one cool cat. You know what I'm saying, or is that not funky enough for you, brother?"

"How do you know Jimi Hendrix?" The young man with the cake cutter in his hair inquired. He looked to be in his early twenties, hitched a ride to a party and stopped at the neighborhood high school to pick up some chicks. He could have been a conman for all I knew, that escaped from jail and was keeping a low profile. For all I knew, any of those situations might have existed with him, but I looked beyond the cake cutter and the tattered jeans, boots, and Black is Right t-shirt and answered the question.

"I know lots of things. Louis Armstrong is a wonderful musician and so is Coltrane, and James Brown. The art about appreciating music is making sure you listen to everything so that you understand where they come from. Hendrix revolutionized rock and roll and he played it like he owned it. Every artist has one of the classical composers to thank for what they have accomplished. Bach, Chopin, Beethoven. The Beatles used a stream of notes from Beethoven, amped it up and rock and roll, baby. Can you dig it? I listen to the lyrics, not one of them speak the way you have. Want to test the waters again? I will correct you. You are going to listen and learn." I spun on my heels in front of them like Michael Jackson, did the iconic 'Moon Walk' and waited for the shoe to drop, but it never did. Ever.

From where I stood, that was about as blunt as an education as any of these kids was ever going to receive. I had volunteered to mentor a group of kids for the summer and help them get over the summer school hump so that they would be ready to start eleventh grade in a few short months. The moment a white old grandpa strolled in and interrupts their conversations, he is labeled as something less than an equal. I was a cracker and a grandpa. Grandpa cracker who had more funk and jive than the entire class put together. These were hardcore kids with questionable futures sitting before them; they would either remain in gangs or find themselves serving time in the coldest place on earth. Prison. The big bitch. The house of a thousand horrors that no one ever comes out of the same way they go in. In retrospect, I had been unfairly judged; I was expected to be exactly like everyone else these kids had come in contact with. I had been judged the same way they had been and I proved them wrong. I turned an English class into a lesson of music appreciation and the kids dove into that pool of learning like a bunch of skinny dippers at a Fourth of July pool party.

"Yah, know I was fitting to skip this class and just blows off the rest of high school" one of my young students said as I had turned my back.

"Who said that?" I asked. A timid hand went up, wiggling the fingers so that I would not miss them.

"Kissne, right?"

"K-i-s-s-i-n-e-c" she spelled out. *Shit, another made up name I can't pronounce.* I didn't dare ask where this one came from.

"Last name?" I was looking on the attendance roll and couldn't locate the young lady.

"Cartier" she hissed.

"Cut the attitude, Miss Cartier" I stared her down. I hadn't seen her before because she just blended in with the blackboard. She was so black that if you were to give her a ride, the oil light would go on. "Not everyone is blessed to have a name like yours. It says here that your name is 'Ruth'. That's a nice name!" I said smiling.

"That's a cracker name. Do I look white to you?" She squawked. Kissinec stood up, all six-feet-plus-of her rose out of that chair like she was blocking the basket and getting ready to steal the ball and take it down court.

"Calm down Miss Cartier. I can't pronounce your name, we see that. Don't try to push me upside the foul line for it."

"You trying too hard to be friends with all us. You jus another teacher thinking he can jus do what he want jus so he don have to deal wit us."

"For the record, it's just and don't. It's not fitting to leave this class but getting ready to leave." I walked over to Miss Cartier and pointed to her chair. "Sit."

"What you thing ima your dog or sumthin? You can't jus order me's around like that, cracker!"

"My class, my rules. You don't like my rules, then you don't pass onto whatever grade you are supposed to enter. And you can kiss all those basketball scholarships good-bye because they won't want a stupid six-foot wanna be basketball player on their team. They won't want a smartass bitch like you embarrassing the rest of the team because she can't speak well or sign her name to a contract. Nope, kiss all those dreams of riches adios because there won't be a carpe diem for you, anywhere." I folded my arms across my chest and waited for god only knew what. I was staring at her rib cage, when she bent over and sat down. "How tall are you?" I asked.

"Six foot seven."

"Holy shit. I didn't know they grew women that all!"

"Is that a joke, cracker?"

"Depends on high the shit is stacked. Apparently it's stacked fairly high at your end." I heard some snickers and a few 'oh, he got you, girl' tossed out. "So what kind of a dog did you say you were? A 'collie'? Everyone belted out an array of snickers. Miss Cartier even smiled and hid her face from view. I had managed to crack her code, and she knew it. I may not be able to pronounce whatever name she was given, but I had her number.

"You're full of jokes, aren't you?"

"Is that a question or a statement? Once again, it depends." I watched Miss Cartier with the intent of making sure she knew who the boss was in the court.

"How high is the shit stacked?" She answered.

"Higher than you know. It's so high that not even a god on Mount Olympus can reach it."

"Where did you get that loud-ass shirt you're wearing?" Miss Cartier asked.

"I believe it was a flag on a pirate ship....I seized the day and chalked one up to Crackers, the parrot of Captain Hook."

"Who?"

"You don't know who Captain Hook is? Peter Pan, Captain Hook? Fairy dust, and the Lost Boys?"

"Yo, teach, that's a cracker story, not a black one." Cake cutter kid replied.

"No, that's a story for whomever, race aside. Didn't you ever learn about this sort of thing growing up?"

"Teach, hates to breaks this to ya, but, we lives in the poor section. We grew up with drugs and gangs. Stories like the one you told us, thems for rich white kids, not us kids from the ghetto."

"And where do you think Jimi Hendrix grew up?" I asked the class. "He grew up in a home where fighting and poverty ruled. Numerous times he was sent to live with relatives in Canada, his brothers and sister were given up in adoption. Drugs caused his parents grief and they divorced. Just because someone you like isn't rich, doesn't mean they start that way. They had to come from somewhere. Even if that means the street or from a foster home. He made his mark on the world the way each of you will and can. How you do it is up to you." I finished my sermon and headed back to the front of the class. No one spoke a word for several minutes.

"So when you fixing on tell us about this Peter Pan guy?" Cake cutter guy asked.

"I will tell you as soon as we get something straight. First, it's not fixing, which implies preparing something or repairing something like your hair or clothes or car. Second, fitting doesn't work here either, it implies wearing something that fits well or doesn't fit at all. All joking aside, that cake cutter you call a pick, doesn't work well in my class so, kindly remove it." The cake cutter kid pulled out the thing in the back of his hair and placed it on the desk in front of him. "Last but not least, improper language in this class has a tendency to make me nuttier than a psyche patient trapped in an elevator with Freddy Krueger. While in this class, you will use correct English. Should you fail to do so, I will make sure that the Beach Boys play non-stop on the turntable until you 'get my drift.'" A smile broke out on my face as I heard the groans from the class. To prove that I was not bluffing, I pulled out a single, "Good Vibrations" and placed it on the turntable and let the musical vibrations filter through the room. I was in complete rapture as I watched the kids clasp their hands over their ears and boo at the music. As soon as the tune ended, everyone unclasped their ears.

"Yo, teach. You made your point. We get what you're saying." Miss Cartier winced.

"It's Mr. Strickland, or Professor. Not teach or teacher. You dig?"

"Okay, fine!" Miss Cartier hissed. I gave her a hard but stern look until she recanted. "Mr. Strickland. Gees. You're so anal!"

"I didn't realize you knew that word!"

"I nos lot of things."

"You know lots of things not, nos" I corrected.

"Yes, I do."

"Good. Show me." I challenged.

It wasn't a love story beginning that this class of kids from the ghetto showed me. It was pure agony and disrespect, which time changed over course of that summer. I never would have believed it possible, that they could reach outside their comfort zones and produce the writing style they shared with me. I asked them to show me where they came from, tell me their story the way they have never shared with anyone. What I received three days before the end of summer school was a display of horror that many inner-city kids rarely ever tell anyone outside their neighborhood. Let alone, outside their own race. Music transformed them into people that I would be honored to share a meal with and to hang-out with. They were my groupies and they hung on every word until someone on the other side of my intestinal track decided to play tuba on my lower bowels.

"Was that you, Mr. Strickland?" Ruth Cartier inquired. I had somehow managed to get away with calling Miss Cartier by her given name, but hell was paid for by those not allowed to call her Ruth.

"Seems like the battle of 1812 is about to go off." I said as I excused myself from the class. I hurried as fast as I could down the hall to the men's room. The location of the men's room had moved because it wasn't where I left it earlier that morning. "Oh dear Greek shit-mongers!" I wailed. The pain that cursed my stomach was more like Freddy Kruger carving out his next dream. I could feel the atom bomb starting to drop, the flap doors were opening as the fucking pilot that was in charge of my legs wasn't flying fast enough. "Must move faster, hold on." I chanted to myself. I staggered against the wall like a drunk, trying to hold on for dear life to the bomb that was starting to disengage itself. "Oh damn it." By the time I reached the bathroom, the damage was already done. Not only did the bomb drop, but the array of damage was monumental. I was covered in crap from groin to ankle. There was no amount of toilet paper in that stall to clean up the wrath that had lain in wait for me that day. It was if everything that was evil on the face of Earth, reached up and slapped me up side the ass and said, 'hang on tiger, this is going to get ugly.' Whatever had been unleashed, reeked. It ran out into the hallway like the Boogie Man on a mission from Santa Claus, delivering whatever jumped up and died inside me to all the bullies and gang members that dared to get in its path. You could have parted Death Valley with the smell and still come up short of smelling like roses. "Oh shit in Hanoi, these were my best shorts, too." I surveyed the lump of shit dangling around my ankles and buried my head in my hands. No one, and I mean no one, would have had the nerve to gravitate towards that stall, much less that part of the hallway. Another round of skull-binding, gut-busting pain shimmied against my stomach and I yelled out like I was woman in labor.

Tears came to my eyes, and I fought against them with everything I had, but, one tear escaped and the rest followed like sheep over a cliff. For twenty minutes I sat pinned to that toilet; my left leg went numb and flies started settling on me like I was base fly camp. Any hope I ever had of making it through the day without this mishap was erased the minute the airplane failed to get me closer to the landing zone. One could not put a degree on the amount of pain I was in or the sheer horror I was faced with as I spread my fingers and peered through the gaps at the open door of the stall. "Judas Priest." I said closing the stall door. But it was already too late. I had acquired an audience of lookie-loos and they stood as though crucified with shit nails, to the floor. The next wave of pain sent me howling like a wolf who made its first kill of the season. I hugged my stomach and I cried as another wave of pain broadcast its presence loud and clear. Twenty damn minutes went by before anyone came to my rescue.

"Herman, you okay?" A familiar voice whispered.

"Jade?" I cried.

"Yes."

"I am in so much pain, I can't begin to tell you. It shakes up a grown man, it hurts that bad." I heard Jade escort everyone out of the men's room. She closed the door and came back to where I was heaving my guts into the underworld.

"Herman, I have to get you to the hospital. But we need to get you cleaned up first, if that's alright."

"Fine. Got a joint on you, because grandpa could use a good hit right about now."

"I know. Not now, later." Jade said easing the door open. She handed me a cool cloth for the back of my neck and I started to settle down. Warm towels and a bucket were placed in front of me as I began the task of cleaning up. I put on the clean clothes Jade had picked out for me and let her lead me out of the men's room like a scared puppy on a leash. There wasn't so much as a negative word uttered, a cat call, or a rude awakening sent my way. All eyes were on the men that helped me onto the stretcher, wrapped blankets around me before taking me to the hospital.

We were escorted in silence to the waiting ambulance. Everyone gathered around like they were attending a funeral; solemn and respectful. Whatever ill will had been forged, quickly vanished into thin air. I was waiting for the ten-gun salute that would follow us, but only the scared faces that I had come to know as my Music Junkies, stared after me.

I awoke to a beeping noise near my ear. I looked over and saw an IV pole sitting next to me and a bag of fluid dripping down a tube and into my arm. I went to scratch my shoulder and found wires taped across my chest.

"They wanted to monitor your heart, Herman. Your heart knows your body is anemic. There's an irregular beat and the doctor just wants to keep tabs on you. He gave you some morphine for the pain as well." Jade said as she took my hand in hers. Her voice seemed to trail off like a score of music notes across a page.

"Groovy." I closed my eyes and fell back to sleep.

The smell of chicken both under my noise brought me back to the living. I opened my eyes and found that the curtains in my hospital room had been drawn, and a single light from the hall shown across the floor of the room. Jade had just taken the lid off the food tray as I woke up.

"Hi." Jade smiled. "You hungry?"

"Some. Is that chicken broth?"

"Yes" Jade said shaking her head. I took the cup of broth and drank it. Its warmth slid down my throat into the depths below. A gurgling erupted, Jade looked at me in an alarming manner.

"The Battle of 1812 is gearing up for another chorus." I stated. "Man your battle stations." As I struggled to get out of bed, a wave of grenades hit, blowing up everything in its wake. I never made it to the bathroom. The sphincter police had done a counter air strike and the invasion had begun. All told, the death toll in this rally was a hundred; that's how many towels and bottles of bleach it took to clear out the destruction of room 3037. I kept waiting for a hazmat team to come in their sterile white space suits and place me inside a plastic bubble until damage control had been completed. I looked for the nurses to wear gas masks and long sleeved black gloves so that they wouldn't have to touch me. I waited for some Voodoo doctor to come in and send me back to hell, but that didn't happen either. I was no more admonished for crapping on the floor than a child who didn't make it to the bathroom in time. Crohn's disease was not for pantywaists any more than it was for me or anyone else in the world. I had now become eligible for disability and could sit on my ass until death climbed up on my lap and asked for a bed time story.

Everything I knew about anything, one could fit into an extra-large teacup until it overfilled with assumptions and revelations. I was trapped inside a shit storm that superseded a sandstorm. Time to face what little facts I had in front of me; time had not run out on me, but the time between myself and the bathroom had a much shorter distance than it had before. I had to make it a point to know where each and every men's room, head, john, or outhouse was whenever I went anywhere. While I could still maintain my single-dom, it would be in my best interest to have someone check in on me from time to time, just to make sure I hadn't shit myself to death in the process. There was also the issue that I needed to keep a burn barrel handy just in case I couldn't get the retched stench out of my shorts in the event the sandstorm developed into a shit storm. I made Jade go with me to get an extra seven pairs of shorts so that every day of the week wouldn't be just an adventure, but a challenge.

I formally announced that I would not retire my post, but would hold onto my tree branch a bit longer, or at least until the tree was hacked down and I fell on my ass. Another week flew by in my life where nurses and doctors came and went. Jade and Rock-o never missed a day of seeing me, and while I was touched that Rock-o had become one of those stink bombs in my day, I would have preferred he showered before making his presence known in my room. I could smell him before I saw him. The last time he found me asleep I was curled up like a baby. I was especially touched when my Music Junkies paid me a visit the day before I was discharged from the hospital.

"Hey, Mr. Strickland! Remember us?" A chorus of voices chimed.

"My old shipmates! How ye be?"

"We are fine, Captain." They all laughed, each giving me a warm hug as they filed up to the bedside one by one to see me.

"So, you set sail for a new adventure soon, do ye?" I said, chuckling from my ungodly and uncomfortable hospital bed. I had developed a cramp in the middle of my back the size of a cow. I struggled to get comfortable as each of my students found their place in my room. "This room ain't big enough for all you pirates. One of you needs to walk the plank!" I exclaimed.

"Aye Captain, but ye have broken one of the ship's rules. Ye violated the English rule and now ye must walk yer own plank. Pirates, if you please." Blashon motioned to several of his classmates. Cake cutter guy produced the old turntable and put on the Beach Boys single. All at once, the entire class began to sing, 'Good Vibrations'. "We practiced this to let you know, we are the sailors of a new sea and we wouldn't be able to set sail had it not been for your leadership." Blashon stated, brandishing a smile as white as snow.

"Indeed." Ruth Cartier pushed past Blashon. "We owe you big time. So we all got together and wrote you our paper, seeing as how you can't grade twenty-seven of them right now. We got special permission to do a class project, since you got sick near the end of the summer."

"So Captain, we became your captive audience. You taught us more than anyone, and you cared more that any teacher ever had." Cake Cutter kid exclaimed.

"How do you pronounce your name again?" I asked looking at Cake Cutter.

"DeLe'Shene." He said, smiling through a mouth of missing teeth. It was another name that I had mispronounced multiple times and finally resorted to his nickname of Cake Cutter. He never minded the name, he always laughed, and shook his head at me as though I was an idiot. I wasn't, but I wondered what his mother was on she named him. The kid had a slight limp when he walked, and he always had toothpaste around his mouth. He was a smart kid in his own right, but he had a certain way about him that indicated that not all the bricks were in his house when the foundation was poured.

"So, pirates. What is this class project ye have grappled with and are presenting me with?" I leaned forward and looked at each of them just like Captain Hook did when he had Peter Pan cornered. Everyone laughed and then a manila folder was pulled out, exposing several sheets of paper. Each student took a turn reading their story and I sat back and listened with intent. It was a story I would remember.....wherever my ship sailed, I would remember.

CHAPTER 18

Our Pride, Our Success
By Your Summer School Music Junkies

We come from the streets, the ghetto, and the center of a world that many dare to visit. Yet, we all came together this summer to share our story with a teacher that showed us the ropes, gave us hope, and set us sailing toward our very own dreams.

I wanted to be a basketball player; the tallest woman in the league. I dreamed of bank shots, dunk shots, and cross court shots, but it took an English teacher to teach me how to dribble properly, attack with logic, and to look for those that invade my space with purpose. He taught me about respect and that I was more important than the nonsense I tried to pull over on him.

I grew up in a home with seven brothers and three sisters. I never knew that white people could be kind or could share with a brother like me. I never had a dream to be someone, not until some old white guy showed up and told me otherwise. I learned that I could be someone great; I just had to step back a moment and look at the world through music and words. Now my world is clearer and my dream is nearer as I start my final year of high school.

I didn't care much for summer school and I didn't care that boring old white people stood in front of me yelling at me to be quiet or else. All I knew was hate, hate, hate, and white this and white that. Mr. Strickland showed me that not all white people are hateful 'buffoons.' And while he may joke about his disease being no big deal, it is to me because I respect him as if he were my dad.

In my home there is lots of fighting. Sometimes we go without food because my daddy used it for heroin or my mom used it for formula for the baby. For me, being poor is just a way of life. I never knew the riches of an education until a certain summer school guy in a disgusting Hawaiian shirt, shorts, and sandals came in and proved otherwise. He changed my mind about a lot of things and now that I think of it, I will miss him more than I miss my daddy or mom, should anything ever happen to him.

In the beginning, we all gave Mr. Strickland a pretty hard time. We judged him to be like everyone else, and we were wrong. I want to tell him that I'm sorry for all the stupid shit I did before I met him. I want to tell him that I am sorry for all the stupid shit I did after I met him. Most of all, I want him to know that if I could trade places with him when I saw him peering at us through his fingers in the men's room, I would have.

My momma would always leave me in charge of my eight brothers and sisters in it's just not enough to make ends meet. None of us know who our daddies are, so we are growing up in a world that is rough and calculated. Everyone expects us to fail, to fall into drugs and gangs, to go to prison, or die somewhere on the street. But Mr. Strickland, our very own wiseass hippy, made us aware that we could make a mark on the world. A mark that would be remembered long after we are no longer here. I like that idea so I am making sure I work extra hard these next few years; I hope to be as great a teacher as the one that made his mark on my world.

After I saw Professor Strickland being carried out of the school, I realized that could be any of us. We could be shot or dead and no one would bother to look after us the way our Hawaiian Beach Man has. Here's to the best of the Beach Boys and Professor Strickland's my "Good Vibration."

I live with my auntie and uncle. They take care of me and my four sisters. My momma in prison and my daddy, he left us long time ago. I had never thought I would ever finish school or have dreams that weren't mine. But I dreamed of flying and of fairies, of seas of crystal blue, and of mountains I could climb on a clear day. Only one man made that possible this summer, and I am very lucky to have met him.

One day when the dust clears, and the fog is replaced with magic mushrooms, I'm going to make sure that my summer school English teacher, Mr. Strickland, never has to worry about pain again. (I have connections that can get me weed anytime I need it….hint, hint).

Finally, for the rest us whose lives you have touched, thank you. You're a weird old guy, but you are cool and you know your stuff. Weird is not a bad thing, it's cool and that's okay with us. You taught us that we can't rewind the past and start over, but that we can move forward and learn. So while we dream of making a dent in history, or a dent in the Earth's core, a flat on a music score, a flip on a jack, or a skip on the dance floor, we owe whatever we achieve, to you, our very own, Professor Strickland…..the crazy old guy with the loud and most dastardly Hawaiian attire ever set sail in summer school. Ahoy!

You could have knocked me over with a goose egg at that moment. I was no longer the grandpa. I was the man that won the respect out of the hardest bunch of kids I had ever met. Their backgrounds didn't make them strong, it was their desire to be great that shone brighter than any light bulb in the class. I was doing my best to fight back the tears of admiration, but that damn lead sheep stepped over the fucking cliff again and whole bloody herd fell into the ocean below. I gave each of those kids a hug and told them to keep in touch if they could. Jade watched the entire show from her chair next to the bed.

"So, they named you Captain?"

"Yes. It was a game we would play to test the speech skills and to see if anyone violated the rules." I said wiping my face off. "It was because none of them had ever heard of Peter Pan or Captain Hook. I was dubbed Captain because of the role I always played."

"I see. So I wasn't the only one having fun." Jade laughed. "I'm taking some classes close to school now and if you don't mind, I would like to set up in the guest room, just to keep an eye on you."

"I don't shit in the open, for anyone's benefit." I snickered back. "Besides, maybe I have a girl staying with me and she would object."

"Herman, Shasta already told me you live alone. So get to stepping sideways, because I'm coming over."

"Oh, that's just groovy." I said taking a swig of water. "When?"

"As soon as the warden says that you are free from the shit storm."

"Ha. Like that would ever happen. Do you have a joint on you? I need a hit….these fucking damn drugs don't do shit for me."

"Yes I have one, in my car. I was saving it for your release. So pucker up, Captain and be patient." Jade laughed one of her dumb blond laughs, threw her head back and let her hair swish around like a feather duster. "So, you tortured them with the Beach Boys?"

"Yup."

"That's wrong. You twisted old pothead. Funny, but wrong." Jade chuckled as she left the room.

* * * * * * *

Rain cascaded down the window outside my room early on the morning of my release. It was heavy and intentional. Thunder and lightning mocked each like bad comics, each joke a frenzy of commotion across the horizon.

Shortly after ten, I was released from my hospital room cell. My last meal consisted of dollar sized pancakes, two sausages, two slices of wheat toast, strawberry yogurt, scrambled eggs, two slices of bacon, a carton of milk and hot tea. That was my usual breakfast because lunch and dinner were for those with A) no palate, B) no teeth to speak of, C) blind or, D) deaf. I chose the other option, they were too old and didn't care one way or the other. Most of them hadn't been able to smell for decades and it showed when I watched patients get wheeled about stinking like a rotting corpse. I may have smelled like a sewer at times, but these people were much worse. Nothing alive smelled as foul as they did!

I got my last ride down memory lane as I left St. Joe's Hospital. I waved good-bye and fairly well to nurses and housekeepers, and I prolonged the agony of having a meaningful conversation with the volunteer that kept pestering me with questions about what I was going to do after I left. I had a general idea, but I wasn't going to reveal it until I was ready.

Jade had pulled the car up to the hospital's entrance and was waiting for me and my ever so chatty attendant. I got in the car and closed the door. I rolled down the window and said as loud as I could to the lady with the non-stop flight of conversation:

"Just so you know, I plan on smoking a bong, getting shit faced with a bag of Lay's potato chips, and then I'm going to get laid." I rolled up the window and Jade stared at me. "What? She wouldn't stop pestering me about my plans after I got home. So I shared!!" I motioned for Jade to take off. The attendant looked as though she had been touched by a demon. After a week in a place I didn't like, where all the nurses were PMSing at once, the last thing I wanted was an overly chatty volunteer in her thirties, inquiring about my home life. Jade handed me a joint. I lit up and let the drug set my aches free. The cow that had planted itself in the middle of my back had gotten bigger, so I was in no mood for back talking cousins either. Jade must have sensed this because she was quiet all the way home.

There was a minor hesitation on my part when I walked in the house. I was not prepared for surprises. Standing smack in the damn middle of my front room was Farley. The once lanky kid had managed to put on some weight. His upper body was toned and muscular now. The ever famous overalls had been replaced with jeans and it appeared that he had filled those out as well.

"Well, as I live in breathe the return of Farley, alligator hunter extraordinaire. You didn't bring anymore alligator boots, did you?" I smiled as I hugged the young man.

"No sir. While I reckon you liked 'em and all, I thought it was better to bring you this." Farley presented me with the biggest cedar box I had ever laid eyes on.

"Did you shower before you got here? You smell, ripe!"

"Shore did. Done used up all them bath things you done got me. Had to buy more. Even had enough left over to gets me a new truck! Brand new '89 Chevy, with only 50 miles on it when I took it off the lot. Paid cash so it's all mine. Even got me a camper and a boat. I done real good this season. Tagged out the day before the end of season. If I could find the line tight in the water or wrapped around a log, I knew I done had me a gator. Lots of big ones too." Farley smiled with delight.

"Really? Where did you go hunting?" I asked as I opened the box. I hadn't even finished off the last Farley joint yet. This time there were

20 of those quarter sized joints. "Damn, son! No pain in my realm!" I hugged Farley again.

"I went hunting in Marion, Homa and Pecan Island. Then finished the season in Bayou Sorrels. Found some thirteen foot gators there, paid better than I thought. One gator brought a hitch over a thousand dollars! It's mostly because he was a bull and he weighed over 900 pounds. Had a hell of a time getting him in my boat and all, but done it."

"Cool! And where is your sister/wife?" I asked.

"I figured at the last moment that it weren't the smartest thing for me to be doing. So I left her the day before we was to get married. Told her that I loved her and all, but she was my sister and I didn't want no bad looking kids running loose, if you know what I mean." Farley cocked his head and point to the box. I stuck in more this time figuring that you would need it. Reckon I was right."

"Yes. I'm glad that you made the decision not to marry your sister. Intermarriage is just wrong. I would never screw my sister, no matter how ugly she was." I snickered.

"Yeah, she is pretty ugly. She done shaved her hair all off and she got dentures. Suppose them Kentucky men find her attractive since they was always eyeing her up and all. Just didn't seem right to take her away from all those potential partners."

"Farley, whatever gator hunting did to you, it made you grow up. I'm damn proud of you." I said slapping his shoulder. "So, how long are you here for?"

"Reckon I'll stay for a few weeks to help your pretty girl look after you."

"She's my cousin, Farley."

"Oh. You won't mind if I took a hit on her, would ya?"

"Yes I would. Back the fuck off and away from her. She's already got someone." I scowled over at Jade. "Rock-o is a big sum gun that you don't want to mess with."

"Oh, she already spoken for. Okay. I gotcha." Farley acknowledged. Jade smiled, shook her dyed blond locks and left the room. I would hear about this later, but for now, she was safe. It's not that I didn't like Farley, because I did. I just don't want him being a part of Jade's life; he was the wrong kind of guy and Jade was so NOT into swamp guys that smelled like alligator guts, twenty-four-seven.

* * * * *

Jade settled up in the guest room, and Farley hung out in the front room. He replenished my groceries, and left box after empty box of cereal on the counter. I ribbed him about being a cereal killer and he said he only killed gators not cereal. I could only shake my head, smoke my pot and laugh.

The weeks fly by faster than the Aspen turned red. Before I knew it, Farley was packing up and leaving for another excursion of alligator hunting. He had rubbed off on me like moss on the north side of a cypress tree in the swamp.

"Time to head out, man. I gotta flee before I miss the next season. I'll be by again real soon." Farley announced one morning in September. "You can bank on it." Farley gave me a hug that sent a tidal wave rolling through my mid-section. Jade and I watched Farley pull away from the curb with his truck, camper, and boat in tow. He had grown up and he had learned to make his own way without any help from the system.

Later that afternoon Jade revealed that her time was up as well and that she would be leaving the following morning. I would miss her, but I still had Shasta coming by to check on me as well as Rock-o and a few students from summer school.

Sometimes it's so not much the things we are forced to live with that matter, but the caliber of people that we meet along the way that make us aware that there are others out there that are guardians of another sort. Those are the ones that the gods place on our journey for a period of time before they move on. We may never see them again, but when we do, it's because our journeys are intertwined like Twizzlers. We pick up where we left off and move forward. And for no particular reason, that's what the journey is.

Jade's departure was more nerve wracking for me. I would worry about her, albeit like a dad would, but I would be there if she ever needed me. On some scale out there in the forensic world, Jade knew that. I hoped that she would not be weighing my shit and asking for samples by mail......while that was not completely unnatural, it was however, just down right gross and I told her so. She left Sunday morning with the top of her Volkswagen bug down, her blond locks blowing in the wind, and a joint tucked between her lips as she peeled out of the driveway playing AC/DC at the loudest decibel she could find. The neighbors stood in their yards staring, while I just laughed.

I picked up my morning mail from the faculty office on Monday, sorting between the trash, bullshit news, and student work. Another semester of college students stared at me like Stonehenge. I was a relic to them as I walked down the hallway in a new Hawaiian shirt, khakis, and sandals. But, I was a cool relic and not a Twisted Sister of some forgotten bygone era. It was a new day, a new page, and a new chapter of learning for those that dared to thrash and throw pipe bombs on old Mother English.

* * * * * *

Journal Entry:

Life is pretty much like a steak; raw, medium, or well-done. For others it's burnt or so dry that an entire bottle of A-1steak sauce is needed followed by the largest glass of beer, to wash the burned meat down the gullet. Either way, it's not a very appetizing experience. There are times I wish I could hit the snooze button when the alarm goes off, and just pause life for a moment so I can catch the bastard or bitch that left me their legacy. Other times, I would like the bomb squad to come to my house and defuse the gut-wrenching terror that dwells in the House of Herman. Unfortunately, I can no more hit the rewind button any more than I can call in the bomb squad. That would be an interesting, yet amusing tabloid at the old firehouse dinner table!

"Hey Bob, I hear you got a real stinker of a call today."

"Yeah Roy. It was a stinker. It was so bad that if you breathed, you would burn your lungs and fart out the sperm to your first born."

"Bob! Really that bad? I thought it was a joke!"

"Hell no, Roy. Fact is, once you get past all the screaming, green and brown haze, the rest as we say is, for shit."

"You're kidding, Bob."

"Does this look like the face of someone that is joking, Roy? My eyes are still red and I smell like I've been trapped in a sewer of rotting eggs and Sulphur for decades instead of ten minutes. I can't get the smell out of my uniform!"

"So, Bob. How did you get rid of the stink bomb?"

"Stink bomb? Roy, it wasn't a bomb. It was sewage backup in this guy's intestines!"

Oh yes, that will be a lovely, tantalizing conversation at the old firehouse. Followed by baked beans and hot dogs! For the normal person, eating baked beans will be like walking into heaven and being able to part the Nile River with just a single loud rip. For me, it's like parting the Dead Sea and watching everything non-living, come to life and flee the area! Prehistoric sharks suddenly able to walk and the mother of all barracudas be chomping at the bit to get out of range of the stink bomb. If there weren't any extinct species prior to this, there soon will be, you can count on that!

I discover my very own personal assorted array of foods do quite an accordion rhapsody in the House of Herman. Some days it's so bad, I can feel every stroke and poke at my extremities causing pain and the most gawd-awful diarrhea that has ever passed the sphincter police in their radioactive space vehicle. If there is an alien take over, they better find a way to fix my innerds prior to entry, otherwise, they will be in for one hell of a ride in a shit storm.

There are times that I ache in every one of my joints so bad, that a hot shower, two joints, a shot of Tequila, and four Tylenol just won't cut it. Imagine a grown man crying because his hemorrhoids are the size of walnuts dangling down around his anus. They don't threaten to fall off and go by the way side. They just hang there like a worn out punching bag, exposing busted muscles, veins, and other skin that just sort of sticks around to watch the fireworks. These rips in the ass skin, are fissures that are equal to or worse than the manly hemorrhoid. The sum bitches need to be removed, of that there is no doubt. But Bloody Fucking Damn Mary, when my shorts decide to take a day hike up to see the twins, it's the World Series going off up there. The Cubs and Sox waging battle in a region where no pain should be in and there's not a bloody fucking damn thing the good old doctor can do about it. There are days when it hurts to sit or stand. Hurt to climb up and down the few steps to my house, to the school, to class, to the Bonnie Brae Tavern for a burger, malt and fries. There is no cream to fix this tear, non-fusible rip in the House of Herman. There is only the joint, bong, or empty soda can turned into makeshift bong.

My feet are failing to operate at elite capacity and I find walking barefoot is a much better cure than wearing flip flops or my sandals. I have all the symptoms of menopausal woman without the vagina and hot flashes. I have always had hair growing in the usual places, (having hair grow on my ear on the other hand, is creepy and just down right disturbing). But P.E., when you see the disease erupt, it's like a sandstorm just up and slaps me alongside the kisser and walks away without so much as a 'howdy-do, grandpa.'

The rewind button is gone and the Big Guy on Mount Olympus is doing jumping jacks in the Bermuda Triangle while I'm surfing to the bathroom in Denver. It's not fair; I give up trying to be burned up by the whole disease, I just accept it. This is one steak I can't send back to the kitchen for a redo, this is the bloody raw steak that the Big Guy tagged as mine. I am the dialectology of a disease that someone has given to me in exchange for something keen to my liking; for instance naked dancing in the middle of Washington Park. A bigger dick, perhaps, but no........I get the shit, the disease that keeps on giving.

I see this cute little lady and then the oil rig sprang a leak, leaves me with something I would not rather share. I have to wear disposable pants, P.E. just in case school is renovating the men's room and it's closed. It's not as if I can keep up the anchor. Oh no, the body has its own system of abandoning ship; the anchor is set and then it's every individual for themselves.

I hope P.E., that when the time comes for you to read this, you laugh as I have. That you remember to hold the little things in life as precious commodities, because each day is now a gift.

Chapter 19

In the distance, tornado sirens moaned to life. I remained under my bed, snuggled under the safety and away from the storm. The hail continued to pound against the house. The ground shook and the sky convulsed. I felt as though I was trapped inside a demon's body; trapped between what lie beneath and what laughed above. I curled up in a ball and went back to sleep…the only thing the storm was good for…sleep and memories.

* * * * * *

It was a bleak morning. The clouds taking their sweet time parting so that the morning fog on the glen could lift. The fog glided across the highway like a ghost. Its form more of a mass as I drove through, parting the fog with my Porsche. Its fingers reached out to latch on but I tore away and it reconnected with itself as it continued across the road. I had decided to take a much needed break from everything and everyone and just began driving. Turning off on Colorado highway 71, I headed towards the populous town of Limon. The Rockies were in my rear window waving at me to come back but I ignored them and drove towards a place I had never visited.

The town store was open and the first wave of Saturday shoppers had already begun filtering out of the store. Pushing past the desire to head back to my cozy home in Denver, I pulled into the parking lot of the Loaf 'n Jug and parked at the furthermost spot I could find. I let the engine purr a few more minutes before turning it off. I just there staring and watching the coming and going. I stared at my steering wheel. I thought about nothing but I stared. I waited for a sign from the almighty universe that things would be finer than a bullfrog on a split lily pad. I waited for that small little voice inside to tell me to get my ass moving, except that little voice was high on my road trip. The sun blasted away at my windshield and I felt the heat rising, festering, and bubbling like a bad gas bomb. A bad, bad gas bomb.

A knock on my window startled me and I saw a woman peering down at me like I was a puppy in a pet shop.

"Well, aren't you just the cutest thing since the marshmallow" she said in a squeaky-type voice. Her tied-dyed shirt hugged her body like a ribbon on a tree. Her cut-off jeans hit just at the knee exposing the toned calves of an athletic woman. She was a bronze-tanned hippie, beads thumping against her chest like wind chimes. As she spoke to me through the glass, her 70's style headband sat neatly around her head, her shoulder length hair swayed to and fro in the conversation. An invisible breeze tussled a few strands of hair up so that antennae peeked out, checking for danger. I liked her immediately and I rolled down my window.

"I'm sorry. I was in a CRS mode and dazed by your beauty." I said smiling at her.

"CRS mode. So, what can't you remember shit about?"

"Why I didn't come here sooner." I beamed. I opened the door and got out. Every mother-fucking joint screamed and it sounded like I had broken glass in my knees. Our eyes met and I found myself falling deep inside those incredible brown eyes of chocolate fondue. "I'm Herman."

"Kellie Washington." She shook my hand like a confident woman. Her hands were calloused but long and beautiful. It was a refreshing gesture. "Welcome to Limon and the one and only town grocery store. It's fully stocked just like the local fishing hole. So grab a basket and get down to business." She laughed the way my mother used to when my father said something off the wall and rather random during a conversation of great importance. He was forever tossing out random stuff that had little to do with the current topic. I caught myself sometimes doing that and found that it was for the most part an experiment in human reaction to weirdness and how fast one could think on their feet. Not many possessed such traits, but I found that my father did it on purpose sometimes because it was hard for him to get a word in edge wise. My father was the rebel. I was a better rebel which really annoyed the fuck out of him. I suppose in the end he felt that raising a rebel wasn't the worst of his faults as he lie there in peace. "Where ya staying, Herman?"

"I haven't the foggiest. I just got up this morning and decided I needed a break and headed away from Denver." I told her.

"Change of scenery is always good for the soul. It's also good for the spirit. Makes for a nice duet somewhere down the road." She winked.

"That is one way of looking at it" I agreed. "So, where's a good hole-in-the-wall room with a view and a barbeque?"

"And you cook, too. I may know of such a place you can hang up your shirt." When Kellie smiled, it was as if all the shit I had been through was flushed away and a clean slate appeared out of the heavens. It was one of those smiles that must have been hand-picked and placed on Kellie, because it was as genuine as any precious stone I had ever seen. The almighty sign from the universe has been delivered, hippie style.

"Pray tell, where is this place you speak of, malady?" I snickered.

"Is that a Shakespeare thing you got going on? If so, we have a lot to talk about at my place. Love the classics and it's relatively difficult to find an educated man out this far. I don't mind the country life, but I miss the lively conversations of intelligent men and not the worn out dismal rantings of a crazy farmer on some farm equipment that keeps breaking down every time harvest season comes along. It gets as old as PMS at seventy-five."

"You're not that old!" I challenged.

"Not just yet. But I'll be rounding that bend before you can say Billy Jo Bob broke wind." We laughed. I was smitten and I followed her like a bee into the honeycomb. Had I been a few years younger, I would have found Kellie to be one of those well-rounded women that had enough foresight to bid unwelcome company, adios. To my credit, and not the dog I had been years earlier, I had come to appreciate the females of the world a lot more than I had when I was in graduate school. These woman outside of my work environment, were visions from the inside out. They were beauties, motivated and intelligent. I had a very difficult time turning down the offer Kellie put in front of me.

"Okay, I'll take you up on your offer. I'll pick up the steaks and meet you back here in a few minutes." I played with an imaginary steering wheel as I walked into the Loaf 'n Jug. Her laughter was the medicine I had needed and I kept it close for the entire weekend.

* * * * * *

Since my last flair up, my good old doctor "Beam Me Up, Scottie" Sheridan, returned me to a regime of steroids to kick things up a notch and kept me in remission. I've been a Crohn's patient now for a little over three years. Nothings amazes me anymore. Every once in a while I may meet someone that is in a far worse health than myself; I let them vent, piss on the world, throw up whatever is eating them alive, and pretend that their shit is way worse than mine. I have the Queen of diseases. The ruler of things so foul that I can scare the wings off a fly. I would give one of my testicles to have PMS for a week just so that I wouldn't have to scour the horizon for a bathroom as the Enterprise is plummeting into planet Vulcan. My Bird of Prey is no longer a hidden vehicle of destruction......it is an obvious and deliberate beast of annihilation.....to the senses.

So here I sit in the front room of freaky, funky Kellie's place. We smoke a soda can bong full of pot in her porch swing she mounted from the rafters of her home. Rocking back and forth against the pillows in the swing I was aware of the simple joys that I had forgotten. The purity of a genuine heart and the deliberate actions of a gifted woman. I had gotten so caught up in my job, the stress of colleagues, students, and non-important crap that I followed right in the footsteps of my very own father. I fucking hated it. I enjoyed teaching but I realized that I was fed up and burned out with everything. I no more wanted to go back to the college and deal with my compadres any more than the next half-crazed idiot. Crohn's disease left me in autopilot and I was all on my own flying in unfriendly skies. I sometimes felt that those I worked with could care less that I was sick and it was a pointless venture to seek their forgiveness when I could see it in their eyes that they were only tolerating me because I am a damn-fucking great professor. I was tired of bottle-feeding English to kids who had ulterior motives. Everything I knew was worth several brief cases of cash, but not one fucking penny came my way unless I just sucked it up and struggled to be the same loving asshole prior to Crohn's.

I unearthed the edgy side of the House of Herman the weekend I spent with Kellie in her three bedroom house in Limon. I took the road less traveled. The unbeaten path and plowed a new course in my adventure. She made me reconnect the old Herman. The guy that used sarcasm the same way people put sugar in the coffee. It didn't matter if people liked me or not, that much didn't really bother me as much as it once did. Since getting sick, baring my ass to numerous doctors, my veins to technicians that left bruises the size of silver dollars on my arms, and the bitter decadence of shit in every toilet I could find, nothing mattered anymore. Not a damn thing mattered because life had changed the rules. The game was still the same but the term "LIFE" seemed to have taken a side street to 'Blow It out Your Ass'. In fact, I no longer cared if no one liked me because I wasn't their brand of tea for their teacup. I became the sandstorm. The lone particle of annoyance that one finds in the bottom of their sock and cannot seem to get rid of it. That's me......the rock in the shoe. I was also the shit storm. The factual evidence that occurs every day at the same time after a twenty-four deluge of nourishment. My digestive system was fucked. My intestines couldn't process well enough so it yelled as loud as it could until someone gave me one of those "oh shit, is that you?" looks.

And so it was Kellie with the chocolate fondue eyes, reaching into my soul and took me into her world and showed me what I had been missing. My very own album of Colorado Gold. She wasn't into the whole religion thing and like myself, had some serious problems with the cults people were into. We meditated together and it helped relieve the tension in my back. We laughed and it healed the gnawing emptiness in my heart.

> "Tact is the ability to tell someone
> To go to hell in such a way
> That they look forward to the trip."
> ----Winston Churchill

Good ole Churchill used this quote about as much as one uses the head. While he was not known for his speeches, he was known for his ability in the tact department. I admired him because of that reason. Despite the craziness of the world, I found that I didn't relish as much in politics as my counterparts did. I wasn't going to wage war on the innocent or oppressed, or even those who had a lesser brain than I did. I didn't discuss religion any more than I would my sex life. It was simply no one's business what I did in my private life. No one I worked with was even remotely aware of my intelligence. I liked that just fine. When it came to Kellie, all the shit, the illness, everything just disappeared like the Bird of Prey.

We got stoned but it did little to get me relaxed enough to sleep. I had now been up for just over 72 hours without sleep. I cursed the doctor, my sailor mouth found its home port, and I was now anchored at a pier, swearing like Swedish Viking amid battle. Forget the sand and mirth, I had grown bolder and badder in the 72 hour time period than I had been in my whole life. I could light a match head with a single glare from my eyes. Fucking drugs.

Kellie and I laughed until our bellies hurt and tears fell from our eyes. We talked about whatever was on our minds, explored several topics of sociology, our spiritual beliefs, literature, and did a recap of the crazy shit we did when we were younger. I liked Kellie so much that I didn't want unnecessary stuff coming between us and ruining a blossoming friendship. I found that I enjoyed the company so much that I didn't want to drive back to my place. I wanted to stay right where I was until I could feel no more nothingness inside me.

The bad thing about getting stoned; the aftermath of the chronic munchies that arrives like a beggar in a toga. Can't eat just one slice of pizza when there are still seven slices left. No, you eat the entire box in such a hurry that it's almost like not eating anything at all. There is an emptiness and raging hunger that ruptures like a volcano deep inside of you. Regardless of all the water you keep drinking, it's an unsatisfying constant. It persists in dehydrating you no matter what you do. The pain subsides, your mind clears and for just a few hours you are in the zone and not bothering a soul.

We embraced the mind of the other and we talked all night clear into the afternoon. Our own forensics lured us to decapitate the head of what truly annoyed us about certain stories presented in the Rocky Mountain News and Denver Post. For years, Kellie's theory was that the media was destroying the White House with marijuana brownies to get them to see the rabbit hole for what it was. I wondered how much she had smoked for her to reach that conclusion. Not that I was afraid to ask but I would have liked CAT scan of her brain for my wall. She was an amazing lady.

Kellie was an insatiable woman for knowledge and spirituality; she taught me some yoga positions to help relax me. It helped my back but not enough for me to sleep. The stretches were amazing; worked out a damn fucking cow that kept grazing in the middle of my back.

Neither of us judged the way we were, we commented on the approaches used to solve problems and how we overcame each other's calamities, failures and successes. It was a basic of needs; communication between consenting individuals. We told our stories. Told of our conquests and losses. In the end, we were more two Star Fleet officers at the academy. We were ship mates on an adventure that would last a lifetime. She could play the Alfred game and that was when I felt the first pangs of love knocking.

I had a two hour drive back to Denver. Taking Kellie in my arms, I hugged her the way I would a good friend. I didn't want to let go, but I knew that our conversations would never end as long as we stayed in touch. I promised Kellie that I would call her every week until she grew tired of me and changed her number and name.

"Like that would ever happen. I like you too much!" Kellie had said as she walked me to the car. "Let me know when you get home so that I don't worry about you like a sick dog." We kissed each other on the cheek and I got into my car before I could utter something without sounding insane.

"Kellie, I know that this may seem weird but would you do me the honor of having supper with me this coming Friday evening?" I held her hand in mine.

"My dear Herman, you know how insane my work schedule is this time of year. Castrating the spring calves, saunas in Fort Morgan, orgies in Castle Rock, blow jobs in Broomfield, highs in the Rockies, and let's not forget the annual brownie sale at the Boulder. Oh and the Rocky Mountain Oyster Fry….always the high light of my year. My social event calendar is booked solid!" She threw her head back and belted out the most insane laugh I had ever heard.

"Boulder, huh? Bring extras…we may need them for the ride back. Pick you up around six, dress casual, and be ready to talk the night away."

"My dear Herman, such a crafty old pothead. Does KISS know if THE WHO are really from KANSAS or BOSTON? Shall we ask CROSBY, STILLS, NASH, and YOUNG if the BEACH BOYS are in the house or if they've gone where all others go when THE DEVIL WENT DOWN TO GEORGIA to ask for ELO's private jet to see PINK FLOYD?

"The time for DISCO NIGHTS with THREE DOG NIGHT, is slowly upon us, my lady. I would ask that ASIA keep you safe in your JEFFERSON STARSHIP while THE CULTURE CLUB and BOY GEORGE keep THE TIJUANA BRASS on standby so that THE GRATEFUL DEAD and VAN HALEN serenade you until your Jedi Knight returns to another Star Wars soundtrack." I kissed her hand and drove away. *Holey shit, she knows the game! She plays the fucking game!*

I called Kellie every day, spending hours on the phone every night. It was that special kind of friendship one builds when reaching a certain milestone in life. She was my holy grail, the mantra in my day that motivated me to be a better person. I found that I missed her.

Our first date was spent in a neighboring town in a hole-in-the-wall diner. Those in the diner knew we were outsiders, but not too outside not to be welcomed in the place. We sat next to the window and picked up where left off in the car.

"My dearest friend, Al and I used to play the game the way you and I are." I replied looking over the menu.

"Really? Does STYX know this? Have you told QUEEN?"

"No, but I may have mentioned to THE CARS when BLONDIE was eavesdropping."

"Call THE POLICE! They will know what to do, especially if OZZY OSBOURNE has anything to do with it."

"QUEENSRYCHE knows what to do. They've got KINKS working on THE VILLAGE PEOPLE." I laughed like a school boy. Although the other patrons didn't appreciate our rowdiness, I didn't care that we were having fun and I wasn't going to apologize for enjoying my life. Gone were the days of the recliner, watching the world pass by me like it had done with my father. I wanted to park my ass in a 1955 Cadillac and cruise the streets of Denver like a complete stranger. I wanted the Dairy Queen special and an extra serving of fries that I know would cause me grief twenty-four hours later. And I wanted the bottle of Kahlua and milk so that I could feel the rush of a White Russian caress me in warmth and sleep. I needed moments like that to remind me that I was still alive and not some dried up old mushroom in a can. So if I got stoned once in a while, who cared as long as I stayed to myself and kept the good times rolling with the few friends I had kept throughout the years. I adored Kellie.

Each week we would venture out into the world and explore a new eatery. We experienced things together the way two friends do when they hook up for a date. It was a marriage made in Dante's Divine Comedy and we cradled it and protected it the way Walt Whitman did in his writings. Our own insecurities were compared to the flea on a horse's ass; it didn't matter much as long as we still had a good sturdy fly swatter to swat it aside.

Sometimes Diana Ross would speak to us the way The Supremes would when the conversation was light and mellow. Other times, it would be the classical stylings of Bach, Chopin or Beethoven. It was not unusual to be told that the restaurant was closing and we had to take our business outside. Oddly enough we didn't mind being told to leave, but it felt awkward as hell when the waiter would stand there expecting an extra tip for a lengthy stay. Since I am somewhat eccentric and twisted, I offer them my hand and I shake it firm enough for them to know that I appreciate their patience and tip them accordingly. I didn't care anymore if people didn't like me, and I sure as hell didn't care if people had a bug bite the size of Steven Hawking's brain pan. That was their problem, not mine. My pure rapture was to avoid negative sorts and search out like-minded souls like Kellie, Alfred, and whoever else was a welcome Twisted Sister in my realm.

* * * * * *

Seven months after Kellie and I had met, my life became as rich as any man could imagine. My colleagues wondered what the hell I was on most of the time, and not a day went by when I wasn't giving a lecture on how to dissect one's own work the same way an editor would. It was gratifying to learn that I was still the ever favorite among professors on campus. I didn't find it a challenge to engage in mindless conversations; I grew weary of people and their lack of proper speech and grammar. I was chomping at the almighty, bronze bit to change careers, jobs, anything to sedate the beast within.

On New Year's Eve morning, the day I was heading up to Limon to spend the week with Kellie, I received a call from the Yuma Police Department. Kellie and her adult son had been returning from Sterling, Colorado on a day trip when they were met head on by a drunk driver. Both Kellie and her son were killed instantly. The drunk driver survived. A chunk of my heart died the moment Kellie left my life. Life ceased to be what I had enjoyed it to be. I was never right after that day. At her funeral I could not look at the faces of those that spoke on her behalf, and offered words sympathy to the surviving friend. What was I supposed to do without my friend of only a few short months? What was I to do with the engagement ring I had planned to give her on our date? I withdrew the red velvet box from coat pocket and set it on the casket. I allowed my tears to fall until I was kneeling on the ground next to where my intended would be laid to rest. I bawled until the rain patted my shoulders and thunder echoed my grief.

I walked away from that moment, exiting through the door like a rejected salesman, and slammed that bitch harder than I had ever dared. I turned my back on everything bad and I refused to let anyone back in my life. Friend or not, no one was coming back. Brittany had a profound effect on Alfred when she left this world for the next. The door she had chained shut, the one she refused to acknowledge that existed between Al and I changed, when he left his beloved Brittany in the cemetery. His life was over just like mine. We weren't the preverbal peas in a pod, we were the nuts in the Almond Joy and it was disastrous some days and downright entertaining the next.

No spaceship foreign or domestic would ever come between us again. Alfred moved some of his things to my place so that he would have some place to come to and crash if he needed to. He needed the company as much as I did and we decided that being two lonely old guys wasn't so bad as long as we had each other to hang out with.

* * * * * *

One Fish
Two Fish
Three Fish,
Red, White and Blue
There Be No More Fishes in the Pet Store
Do we search High?
Or do we search Low.
Search every canal, river and stream
Find the Fishes with that uncertain pew
Cause Herman's sphincter
Is about ready to BLOW!!

CHAPTER 20

Somewhere deep in my stomach, I felt the pangs of stomach cramps unleash a vengeance I hadn't experienced in a while. I smacked my head on the underneath side of the box spring as I struggled to remove my body from my confined storm shelter. Crawling on my knees to the john was a pretty amazing feat since I was not able to pull myself up to run. My knees were slowly going downhill as the Crohn's disease had done a major demolition job on all my large joints. This was vengeance at its finest. Tears fell from eyes like memories. I brushed them aside so I could see where I was going.

I made it to the bathroom and it took everything I had to get up off that floor without falling face first into the toilet. When I sat down I felt the earth move and not in a good way either. In the midst of a tornado an earthquake jumped to life, scaring the House of Herman to its core. I knew I was safe with the tornado, but an earthquake? No fucking way. I may not live in California, but an earthquake in Denver sent me to the west side of Crazy-Ville. I screamed a high pitch yelp that may have sounded like a dog in heat. Between the Earth moving under my ass and my insides struggling to sign me up for another rodeo, I was paralyzed with fear; when the tornado sirens moaned to life, I moaned with it. Had there been an eruption under my ass, I would not have been able to survive the fallout.

Sweat pooled under my armpits as I hugged my stomach. Sweat ran down the sides of my face and gathered at the base of my chin as though collecting thoughts together for the final drop. The memory of Kellie had jarred my insides awake. The shakes came, a cold sweat ran down my back and the pain ripped through me like an axe splitting a log. If I owned a dog, it would have been in my lap trying to soothe me the best it could. But I didn't have a dog and Alfred was doing his thing in Spain. My main concern was the incredible ebb and flow of throbbing in my torso.

Stress of everything in my life had caused the flair up and the storm was a price I would have to pay. Honorable mention going to the earthquake and its demonic desperation to kick my ass back into high gear. Now I know what King Kong must have felt when those bombers attacked him, crumbling his life force between spent ammunition and strategic wings rolls. Each pass luring him over the edge until he lost his balance and fell like an anvil to the ground. These thoughts were the ones that tarried on my chin as I cried the way no man should ever have too. I hurt so bad that an Irish pint would only dim what I was dealing with. I could go from zero to jolly in twenty-five glasses and still not have enough to sedate the demon inside me.

Whatever mess had been made, was cleaned up by someone who came to check on me. Whatever food I had tried to eat came out with such force that all my clothes had been removed, and I was redressed. I rode that storm out for three complete days, liquid foods dropping inside my stomach like fish in a pond. Sometimes I would hear rock and roll music filter into my room and sometimes I could hear jazz, bluegrass, opera, symphony, and disco. The romantics of being that sick are greatly flawed and I challenge anyone to stand up to it and face it with a hidden strength. The moniker of Crohn's disease isn't that it is a death sentence but rather a sentence of one more day to do what you love and not be afraid of what others think when you shit all over yourself on the way to the bathroom. There is no "Buy Me" attached to this fucking disease. No. It's a "You're Fucked, Boy-o" tag and it was time to pay dues.

Do I feel remorseful about all the bad shit I've done in my life? Everyday. Do I feel as though I've been penalized for not tackling the quarterback at the beginning of the play? Who the fuck cares. Do I want to sit back and collect disability for something that I don't feel I'm worthy of? Fuck no. I am not dead. I have a shit more life to live. I am not done with my life and I most assuredly do not fantasize about saving mankind from Crohn's disease.

My restraint ended the moment Kellie and I conversed about our human frailties. Like Alfred, Kellie and I had unmasked each other and found that we are the people others look to for inspiration. We become their reason to make it through because no one was there to do battle for us, but ourselves. The hero of my life? Me, myself and I. I slayed the dragon and now its head is mine. Mounted the sum bitches head on my wall. For what it's worth, I still want those brief cases of cash deposited to my front door but I am through killing myself over some ridiculous individual that dresses like a retarded clown in the faculty lounge. So go ahead a shove another camera up my ass, put me back on steroids and feed me all the baloney you want about how pathetic life is. I ain't buying it and I don't subscribe to defeat.

* * * * *

"Beam Me Up, Scotty" Sheridan released me from my stay in the hospital. He was as stoic as ever and his bedside manner was in dire need of a vacation. It was a robotic conversation, all quite professional and serious. Any attempt I had at cracking a joke was like pouring salt on an open wound. It was both painful and futile. A great addition to the Borg.

I kept wondering when the last time was Sheridan had his last colonoscopy because his sphincter police were all tied up in knots. He was one loud fart away from Mount Saint Helen's eruption, in my book.

For the second time in my life, Jade had come to my rescue. The bulk of what I had left in this world would be given to her at some point. I just never really had given it much thought until that moment I saw her standing over me in the hospital. Had it not been for Jade's arrival at my house, she never would have found me. I had fallen off the can and hit my head hard enough to knock me out for a while. I never had a thought in the world until that moment when I knew that the sandstorm had thrown me back in the shit. I was one cancellation notice away from my 'employee of the month' parking space. All I had to do was dig my heels in and hold onto my tree branch with nails of steel; ride it like a freaking shock wave through time.

With a massive amount of marijuana flowing through my system, I found the depth in my soul that had been shelved without a second thought. It was time to live my life according to the House of Herman.

"Strength is not achieved because of physical capacity,
But because of indomitable will."

-----Ghandi----

* * * * * *

Journal Entry:

July 10, 2014

I find that every student I've remembered is a mirror image of myself. I used to be like them at some point, maybe even better. I would give anything to turn back the clock and redo some of the stuff I've done, but I don't think the outcome will be as monumental as it is at present. There are few regrets in my life, one being not finding my perfect woman earlier and making her the mother of my offspring.

I ask the Universe for guidance, for a sign, anything that will convince me that there is alternative plan to the madness I experience. My vision quest provides confusion and muddled answers all in an effort to enhance my otherwise tumultuous relationship with my disease. All I need to do is be open to whatever the Universe gives me. Endless possibilities; it's all I need to accept. There is hurt—it's the healing part and that is part of the quest that is as murky as a bog. I have consumed at least two cases Cadbury Chocolate Caramello bars; my sugar is all jacked up because of the fucking steroids good old Scotty has me on. The weight I gain is supposed to come off, I don't see how when I can no longer take long walks like I used to. My urge for sugar is surpassed by those of Mary Jane. When I am not up "to par", I allow myself to sleep and escape into Capote or some other classic lining my bookcases.

I no longer have any modesty; copious stints in the hospital are to blame for that turn of events. I have decided that the reason the gown opens in the back is so medical personnel can see you. I SEE YOU AT YOUR WORST, BOY-O. Therefore, the gown should be renamed to ICU. I am no longer bothered with all the numerous poking and starring at my body and up my ass.

People find my honesty refreshing and I'm okay with that. I sure as hell don't care what people think when I speak my mind. I'm not here to be a friend to a lowly fucking insect, I'm here as a teacher, a champion, and mentor to those that want to learn and if they don't like it, fuck them and the camel they rode in on. Somehow I lost my sense of Herman being sick all the time. Having a sense of humor is understated.......I am missing mine. Kellie helped me find it I buried it when she died. I miss her.

Ah, the head sphincter dictator has arrived. These people at the Walgreens pharmacy are about as inviting as the Borg. The collective working together to get my prescription of zombie fluid ready. It's time to begin the cleansing process of the colon. If I have to drink any more of this battery acid I will donate my colon to science! Colonoscopy makes its appearance: 10:00 tomorrow morning. May all my shit be as sweet smelling as freshly cut green grass! NOT!!!!!

* * * * * * *

There are only two ways to live your life.
One is as though nothing is a miracle.
The other is as though everything is a miracle.

-----Albert Einstein--

July 11, 2014

"Mr. Strickland, I need you to read over these forms, initial here and here and then remove all your clothes and put this gown on, open end in the back." The nurse said quite as she pointed out the sections I needed to look over and sign. I stood next to the hospital bed wondering how I had gotten stuck in my current registered state. The nurse had all the personality of a moray eel and an underwater sea witch.

"Is there is a please anywhere in that phrase?" I asked the petite blond as she stared at me over her glasses.

"Can you have a please?" She stared at me with a hatred and horror that one sees when they find a dead body lining the interior of a bathtub. Her zombie like stare caused me to clear my throat and grin.

"Just as a common courteous manner, of course." I tried smiling at the short nurse but I felt as though it was more of a grimace, a forced Herman sort of smile that drove one to question my intent. *Bitch, please.*

"Please read over these forms and then please remove your clothing. Is that better?" She asked mocking me. There was a curtsey shadowing her mannerisms but I discounted it long enough to answer her with a retaliatory comment.

"No. Don't patronize me. Act like you're semi-excited to be here while I spread my cheeks to the world for inspection." My tone was flat and the forced grimace stayed on my face long enough for the nurse to admonish me one last time before she left me alone. "Would it kill you to be nice?"

"I see people like you in here every day. Just do what you're told and then we can get the process going. This is not the circus."

"Said the ring master to the elephant." I muttered.

"What?"

"I was just admiring how freaky you must be in the bedroom. Frigid and pruned." The nurse left the room. She yanked the curtain behind her and left me in the smallest room I had ever seen. Only a sink and a pair of chairs separated me from the outer realm of my prison. An adjustable table was positioned at the end of the bed with its buddy the IV pole on standby. I surveyed the entire room memorizing the placement of equipment. It was as cold and calculating as the nurse with the attitude. There was a genuine lack of kindness present and I shivered. So this was the outpatient venue; no wonder no one wanted to talk about it. Depressing place and about as cheerful as a pimple on my ass. *I've entered a new level of hell. Fuck me sideways and call me a jelly-filled doughnut.* As I started reading the mound of paperwork sitting in my hand, Nurse Piss-me-off, stood outside my room whispering about my attitude. "Ah Princess Buttercup at my service." I whispered. "Besides the tartness of your bedside manner, you have the same chance of winning the love of a Great White Shark." I shook my head and read over the forms. It was a daunting task and each line blurred into the next. I was aware that there was an urgency to head to the bathroom. It was an urge to unleash the wet monster before Sheridan drilled for oil. After removing my clothing and placing it in the bag provided, I called for Princess Buttercup.

"What do you want?" Her tone was sharp and toxic.

"It would appear that I need to use the bathroom." She stared at me over her glasses. If I had a fly swatter at that moment, I would have hit her with it multiple times to just make sure she was dead and would never bother me or anyone else ever again. *Look out for the Great White….. she's coming around the mountain!* I often wondered why people got into the health care profession in the first place and why they chose a particular field. Certainly it was not because they really wanted to "care or help people" but because the pay was good and they could get free drugs when they needed them. Maybe it was an option that just addressed them one day and said, 'hey, you aren't doing anything of importance… let's clean up sick people and make them feel like shit for a week. What's that worth to you?' Princess Buttercup got into health care for a reason that alluded me; maybe it was the lure of a free colonoscopy whenever she wished. Her bedside manner left a bad taste in my mouth like stale crackers and old peanut butter…..downright nasty.

I returned to my luxurious, unmistakable, sterile garden floor cell in outpatient central when this guy shows up and announces he's the IV guy. He's not a talker. He's a poker and a pincer. I turned my head when he brought out that needle. I felt that needle and the moment it punctured my left hand, the moment of truth was a lot clearer. I didn't want to create a scene on top of one that was already in motion. The House of Herman was scared shitless. I'm not the guy that cries at weddings or anniversaries, puppies or dead guppies lying upside down in a bowl. I'm not the guy that cries if I stub my toe or bangs my head on the side of the dresser (that actually happened and it left me with a black eye…..so much for wandering around in the dark!) I'm the sort of guy that accepts things and moves on, but I was in a real sticky spot and when that first tear fell over the cliff, the rest of the motherflockingassholesheepleader and all of its neighbors came with it.

Princess Buttercup didn't walk through the curtain, but her replacement did and she saw those tears, the look of fear on my face, and the terror that awaited me.

"You okay?" She asked. The hospital identification badge showed a younger version of the one standing before me. Janee, was a smidge older than Princess Buttercup and her bedside manner was similar to being aboard the Enterprise. She could have been Dr. Crusher for all I cared at that moment, but she saw the House of Herman coming apart and she did her best to rescue the foundation before it toppled over.

"Not exactly stoic here." I sniffed. "I am not a fan of hospitals and visiting someone that is here versus being a patient in one is vastly different. There is a fine line distinction there, you know that?" I stated brushing aside a few tears. *As many times as I have been in the hospital, you'd think I be used to by now but I'm not. The House of Herman isn't stoic….it just plain doesn't like fucking hospitals and unfriendly custodians of sick!*

"Yes there is. If you were a fan of being in a hospital I would have concerns." She smiled. Janee pulled out a stack of paperwork and went over it with me. "So, do you know what we are going to do today?"

"A colonoscopy." I said a little too flat.

"Well, most people don't really understand that term so we don't encourage them to write that down. What we are going to do is scan your colon."

"If we aren't supposed to use the word, colonoscopy, then why did you ask for?"

"I just need to know if you understand what we are going to do."

"Of course."

"So what are we doing?" Her look was priceless. I must admit, I was going to play this one. *What did I have to lose? Not a fucking thing, boy-o.*

"A colonoscopy." I couldn't resist. I smiled.

"No." She growled.

"No? Then why the hell am I here for if you aren't going to be up my ass, checking out the goods?" I was struggling not to laugh. She glared.

"So on this line, you need to write down what it is that we are going to do to you." Janee looked at me as though I was one of those sick dogs you find in the pound. Euthanasia….quick, painless, and be done with it. She kept her finger on the line for me to write.

"Ok." I took the pen and started to write on the line. "Today, the sphincter police are being interrogated for information." The pen was poised over the line like a ballet dancer.

"No. Just write down scope the colon."

"How about the sphincter police are surrendering and you're going to pry sensitive information from them."

"No."

"The FBI heard the rectum was involved in a hit and run?"

"No."

"You've got the cuffs on and the sphincter police aren't cooperating."

"No."

"Well shit, guess the colon is holing out again."

"No. Just write we are scoping your colon." Janee was restraining the urge t to choke me. I could see her jaw muscles tensing up and down. Back and forth.

"I didn't hear please." I said in a mocking tone. *She is so pissed. She reeks of pissy-dom. C'mon pissy, wanna play? Here pissy, pissy, pissy. It's a brand new galaxy down there, I'm telling you!*

"Please, just write down what I asked you to." She snipped at me.

"Fine. But just so you know, colon is siding with the rectum on this one and sphincter is liable to turn like a bad fart later. They are in colon-hoots you know." I handed Janee the stack of papers; she glanced over the blank I filled in and glared at me. *Yup…..it's a winner! Penned especially for you….a Sphincter assassination.* Shaking her head she walked off and admonished me for my lack of seriousness. "Observation number two: nurses that work in this field are about as happy and carefree as a fart on hiatus." Janee took one last look at me and left. I may have thought I lost my sense of humor, but apparently a sense of humor is not needed in the colon business!

"Mr. Strickland, is someone coming to pick you up after the procedure?" Janee said coming back into the room.

"Yes. I've called for my space shit. It's circling Uranus right now. Apparently the Klingons and Vulcan's are playing hide and go seek. Seems someone hid the rings of Saturn near Pluto's vaginal enclave." I folded my hands in my lap and waited. Janee did not return. I'm not sure what the hell these nurses were on this morning, but they all lacked a sense of "funky and spunky". I heard once that a sense of humor is the best medicine in the world and if you don't possess it, you will lead a very sad life. A sense of humor is not a deflection of what is serious, it's about taking a serious moment and recycling it to ease the tension. That's how the House of Herman rolls; straight up sense of humor in every bowl.

Princess Buttercup returned to take me to operation Sphincter Talk. Even though I joke about the rectum and its sidekick sphincter, this is an area that no one laughs about. Our flatulence is not a laughing matter because it stinks and the amount of buildup in the intestines in similar to tooth decay. We go to have our teeth cleaned and fill in cavities in hopes of a clean bill of health. In a colonoscopy, we clean the colon and scope out defects......a different bill altogether. The only difference is we don't have a dentist scraping our asshole, we have a rectal dude scoping out our problem, collecting polyps for scrutiny and determining if cancer is present or not. We aren't supposed to joke about cancer, we aren't even supposed to tell jokes about it, or even make light of it because it offends people. In my realm the only thing that offends me is not seeing the lighter, more positive side of life. Damn it to hell I am not going to die being serious and boring. That's not what life is about. Life is about living it each and every day, good, bad, or fucking indifferent. Live it with no regrets, not this "we can't joke about it because it's serious" shit!

I get into operation room 3 and I am surrounded by more techs, equipment, lights, counters and gadgets than an NCIS forensics scene. The most amazing thing about this area is the genuine pleasure I feel in the presence of these people. After I am instructed to roll on my side, a drug is sent pumping through my body. Dr. Sheridan comes in and then................. I was out like a photon torpedo in a starburst. The Klingons could have stormed Earth and I wouldn't have cared. By the time I came too, I had an appetite of someone that had been stranded on a deserted island for an ungodly length of time.

Tucked in the recesses of my mind, a foggy memory latched onto my conscious awakening; beckoning me to explore the new day around me. There was inflammation, some samples were taken to see if they were cancerous. The bugs in my legs will be permanent residents and something about my sphincter being assassinated made everyone snicker during the procedure. The whole conversation was a bit fuzzy but I got the gist of what Scotty, the butt inspector said. Jade and Alfred helped me get dressed while Rock-o brought the car around. The minute I sat in that wheel chair, I felt a deep and dire urge to crap myself. I was not prepared for what was coming. Whatever had lain dormant during the duration of Agent Rectum Scare-em's interrogation, was seeping out faster than Rock-o was driving. Every bump and brake was like pulling out a plug in an otherwise stopped up toilet. I was bloated up like a dead whale on a beach, and the very thought of exploding before I got to the privacy of my own bathroom really bothered me. *Walk it off, who said that?* Walking was not going to help me in my present condition. A landmine could be deployed here and the fallout and deadly fumes would destroy the surrounding buildings and people within. It was an evil that would indeed result in injury to the senses.

As soon as the key turned the lock in the front door, the drifters from the other end had begun to escape the prison camp. Their lines could be felt running down my leg and into my sandals. Slimy rectum trails left untended by the sphincter police followed me down the hall to the bathroom and the moment I planted my sore backend on the signature bathroom of dreams, all hell broke loose. The stench was so bad that even I had to cover my face with a towel. The nostril bomb slid like a page turner under the door and rippled through the house like an invisible guest. It was suddenly a toga party in the house, no sheet left un-tucked as it whipped through each corner and overpowered the Glade scent dispensers. I heard the squirts of air freshener being let free from the other side of the bathroom door. Alfred was hacking, Jade was laughing, and I'm quite certain that Rock-o was standing outside on the front stoop catching a good breath of fresh air. After the H-bomb dropped in my bathroom, I cooled off in the shower and then dressed in my shorts and Rob Zombie t-shirt. I didn't care about food. I wanted a nap, to sleep on my left side and be alone until the urge to fucking kill Sheridan left me. I wasn't just a beached whale, I was an overly bloated beached gray whale with a cataclysmic shit storm on standby. The sandstorm doth move in.

After a few hours or so, both Alfred and Jade accompanied me to dinner and made sure that I was not allowed to be left alone for one minute. The smallest miracles are the ones we overlook because we are waiting for the bigger one. The miracle is that I didn't kill Sheridan or his team of colon assassins. Miracle number two: I can still walk. Miracle number three: Uranus is not in control, I am, thank you very much.

Gawd Farley, I need one of your joints!

CHAPTER 21

My return to the classroom was like walking into the aftermath of a sandstorm. Everything was an earth-shaking-deafening quiet, hassle free with clean chalkboards greeting me with divine grandeur; no more attempts at trying to write over a glossy residue that hid the real beauty of blackness and the words transforming the barren wasteland of the board into a platform of splendor.

The janitor had finally gotten the message to clean my blackboard. The fresh blackness stared at me like a blank page, exposing no fear but the writing on the wall. I arrived ahead of schedule and took a seat at the rear of the class and waited for the first students to enter. My head was buried in Blake when the door opened and several blurry eyed students walked in, plopping their belongings on the floor. I glanced up for a second before taking note. *Interesting term ahead.* My head was wrapped around the spiritual realm as more students came in and took their seats. They talked among themselves and I watched for the mutiny that was about to take place. No one paid any attention to me because to them I was just an older student cramming my head with unknown authors.

My only desire was to not draw attention to myself but to observe those that chose not to ask where the professor was. Several students decided that if professor was a no-show, they would be long gone. I waited twelve minutes before putting my book down on the desk. Another minute passed and I got up ever so quiet and stood against the back wall like a Greek statue. Another minute ticked by and students started picking up their belongings and were ready to bolt. At fourteen minutes and fifty-nine seconds I picked up my bag and walked up to the front of the class and everyone else followed. I stopped at the desk and turned around. The looks were priceless; shock and disbelief to 'are you shitting me?'

"Good morning Earthlings. I am Professor Herman Strickland and this has been a test of your creative side. So grab a seat, make a circle, and get busy with creative flows and address what you would have done had I not been here. Then I want you to discuss what you felt as you started to follow me out and discovered I was your leader on this journey. Spare me the bullshit, keep it real." Never in the history of my career had I ever done that. It was good to be back. "I am familiar with the word fear. It means, 'forget everything and rise.' Don't gravitate toward the fear, rise up and meet it straight on. Challenge it and find out what sort of stuff you are really made of."

My students took out their assorted spirals notebooks and began to write with fury. Every so often I would throw out a phrase that would need to be integrated into the writing. The groans were minimal but they were making progress.

I did this every day for an entire semester, encouraging my students both talented and struggling to redefine their craft and learn how to become better writers. The challenge to creative writing is to write what you know, not what you don't. So when I read the entries of my students, I am amazed by the complex bullshit they create in order to scathe by without so much as a lesion sitting on their ass.

"Okay, kids. Its pucker time. I'm going to piss you off and you are going to suck it up. Because as of now, Buttercups, those that think the English language is a joke, that creative writing is an easy A, or any other scenarios you care to invent, are not okay in this class. I asked you to create and all you give me are excuses as to why you can't. So here is your challenge: each and every one of you are failing my class. In order to redeem yourselves you must tell me something that has shaped you into the vial pieces of crap you are right now. I want you to roll up your sleeves and get in the shit, so to speak. Don't be afraid to get dirty because whatever you write, will be awarded a letter grade that I deem appropriate. Your writing is for shit. Tear out everything you have thus far and toss it on the floor. Just rip out those deplorable pages and let them fly to the floor. The age of pith may immobilize you but I assure you that buried in the recesses of your mind are particles of danger and

I want you to release them into the wind like feral animals." The class stared at me as though I had lost my ever loving marble sack. I didn't care. They wrote like shit and we were going to start over.

I picked up every sheet of paper and scrambled them up and put them in a nice neat stack. I sat back on the desk and started reading the mess of writings in my hands. It was actually quite horrific and amusing at the same time. I read out loud what I held and the class stopped for a moment to listen.

"Today I got fired from my job. I had been caught coming in drunk. It was the only way I could face the fear of staying in someplace I hated. I dove into that pool of toxic waste like it was a bowl of Fruit Loops, licking the rim every time I splashed the edge with the sewage of my mind." I looked up at my students, their upturned faces were watching me with intent as though it were a surrealistic flashback from the 70's. "So what the hell are you guys smoking? This isn't half bad! This is what I need from you….write it, own it, and make it scream your name." Their laughter broke the silence and I witnessed many a pen sail across the pages of those books. "For the record, I made that shit up. Herman Strickland =1, class = 0."

There were groans aplenty and I could see lines of frustration making camp on numerous craniums. In the House of Herman, fucking with a young mind is the most awesome thing in the world. They need to think and express what lies underneath their surface. I was still making my mark in life, and I wanted them to do the same. I had tried everything imaginable that I could think of to get kids to think outside the box. Each time I found someone moving outside their comfort zone, I was elated. Funny how a colonoscopy and a round of pathetic nursing staff can kick things up a notch.

* * * * * * *

It has been six weeks since the sphincter police had mortally weathered my colon. Dr. Sheridan and I shook hands and settled in for the usual patient and doctor update-chat.

"How are you feeling, Herman?"

"Right as an angle." I smiled. I had pondered a witty reply; I decided to save it.

"Any problems? Blood in stool? Stomach cramps?"

"Let me think. I have heartburn so I need some more of those little pills. I have a garden gnome at the college that could use some of your technical work, if you know what I mean." No reaction. *Bastard.* "No. No. And still no blood of any sort on or near my throne."

"Good. I will get you some same samples for the heartburn."

"There is one thing, doc. I can't sleep for shit. I get three maybe four hours of sleep and then I'm wide awake. I've gained weight and I feel like a blow-up doll."

"It's the prednisone. It interferes with sleep and causes weight gain."

"Nice. I suppose the freaky sugar cravings I have are part of that?"

"Yes. But once you come of the steroids, the weight will come off and the sugar cravings will stop."

"Groovy. I was beginning to wonder if I needed to upgrade to the ugly Hawaiian shirts I've seen." I laughed. Dr. Sheridan smiled and shook his head. To him, all Hawaiian shirts were a subtle way of hiding from reality; everyone lives in a fantasy of flowers and jungle weeds. That's where I live; no exception is to obscure for me! *The gods have blessed me with good weed!*

"I'm going to put you on a new drug that will keep you in remission from the Crohn's. Humira works very well with Crohn's patients. It's an anti-inflammatory drug that helps with all the joint pain that comes with the Crohn's. You get injections twice a month, we'll set you up with the pen, and your insurance will cover all of it but the co-pay portion. Shouldn't be too much. Michalea will help you through the process and get everything done. I want to see you in a few months as a follow-up." He said in his quite frank manner. Everything was always so matter-of-fact-this-is-not-a-problem for "Beam-me Up Scotty" Sheridan. His typical bedside manner was like staring into the toilet after I just poured a half bottle of bleach into the bowl. I would watch the ooze fizz to the surface and lay dormant until it was time to scrub-a-dub-dub before flushing away the scum left behind from my intestinal release. Being in the presence of Dr. Sheridan does that to me; always wanting to flush his mannerisms away like a bad case of shit before another flair up crops up.

Dr. Sheridan was a great doctor; just needed to have to stick removed from his ass more often.

"Sure, whatever you say" I hopped off the table and followed my "Enterprise" Doctor to the head nurse's office. Hey Doc. Do you ever smile or joke around or anything?"

"No."

"Why?"

"Because colons are serious business."

"Have you ever tried out for the role of Spock? I think you would be perfect. Also, the Borg are looking for more to incorporate into the collective." Sheridan eye-balled me, nodded with his usual curtness and left. "Maybe you need a colonoscopy...lighten your load." I muttered.

Michalea was the exact opposite of her boss. A chubby minion with short cropped hair, glasses perched on her head like a head band, pencil stuck behind each ear, and four incoming lines placed on hold with one on the speaker. Her voice was the kind that you hear over the speaker at McDonald's. The kind that begs you to get the extra-large order of fries to go with the double dose of stomach acid you will have later because of it. I waited until she was off the phone before we attended to my medications.

"So how you doing, Herman?" She asks me as she begins the computer work sitting in front of her. "I love this new system; two screens and I can print and fax at the same time to the pharmacy. It's really a great system. So glad we got the upgrade."

"Yes, technology is a splendid thing. I hate it. I'm rather retarded in that area. Thank the tech minions on campus for helping to fix my retard-ness in that area. I'm getting crash courses every time I manage to break my office system."

"You are so funny!" She said snickering behind her computer screen. "Okay, I've gotten all your insurance information on this form. I just need you to sign it and then we will get you hooked up with the Humira." I listened to her ramble on and on before I got the appointment card and when to expect my first shipment of injectables. While the process seemed harmless, I had a feeling that something was being left out.

"So how much does this medication cost anyway?" I ask.

"Depends on the pharmacy. Usually it's around $600 per injection. The insurance gets a bill for about seven grand. We have you set up on a program to help with the bulk of the bill through a grant program by AbbVie labs. It's the Humira Patient Assistant Program. It's really neat." She stated.

Are you fucking insane? This is shit is expensive! We need to find another avenue Boy-O. Going to bleed the insurance people dry and not leave any for the druggies in rehab! I was not liking this.

Michalea took me into another part of the office where she pulled out a water cushion and taught me how to give myself injections with the eppi-pen that had been ordered. Practicing on a water dummy is easy. I was a pro as long as the needle didn't touch me I was good. I assured Michalea that I would be able to handle the procedure like a kid taking his first ride down a snow covered hill on the sled he got for Christmas. I assured her that I could do the tiny needle as long as I had someone standing there to deflect and refocus my attention away from the needle. I told Michalea that I would be fine. It was after all, a shot in the thigh not in my groin or ass. I could do this. I convinced the minion but I really hadn't convinced myself of the proposition.

That afternoon the pharmacy called to confirm my information and to let me know that the FEDEX guy would be on my door step between 8:30 a.m. and 4:30 p.m. the following day.

"I have a request. Is it possible for the delivery to be at 8:30 a.m. on the nose? Otherwise, the stuff is going to sit outside until I get back home from the university."

"Mr. Strickland, someone has to be there to sign for it. I can't guarantee it, but I'll see what I can do." The girl on the other end of the line said. Her flirtatious manner was more of an annoyance than a turn on. I felt like a fish in a bowl and now the whole world was checking in on me to make sure that I wasn't going end up floating belly up or leaping out of the bowl like Nemo had.

"Crap in a hat box" I muttered under my breath as I hung up the phone. "Why does everything have to be so fucking out of whack? I want my normal life back!" I yelled into the silence. A door squeaked behind me and a picture suddenly fell lopsided on its nail. "Swell. Now I've got fucking ghosts living with me." I settled down in the chair next to coffee table and lit a joint. I started to relax.

The next morning arrived like a typhoon on the high seas. The FEDEX guy showed up promptly at 8:30 with a box big enough to have ten pounds of cannabis stuck inside. The contents were packed in dry ice and I was beginning to wonder what sort of drug I was getting to warrant fifteen dry ice packs. I reached the bottom of the container to find a plastic Ziploc bag with three large boxes of Humira. I placed two of the three boxes in the refrigerator and took the other with me to the university. I had a brief lesson on how to give myself the injection with the pen I would be receiving. Nothing prepared me for what I was going to find once I opened the box.

After my last morning class, I went to the faculty lounge and took out my box of drugs. I had a smug look of satisfaction knowing that I was the only one keeping my narcotics in the teacher's refrigerator and not being scrutinized for it. Part of me wanted to dance a happy random dance and the other part wanted to take a poke at the schmuck that ate my tuna sandwich from the day before. None of that seemed to matter once I opened that box in my hand and pulled out the contents and turned them over so that I could see my new life-line to remission. I froze. Had there been any compassion anywhere in my being at that moment, it most certainly fled at warp speed…I was scared shitless. I stood in front of the open refrigerator with a package large enough to stifle a druggie for days. I was not seeing the almighty pen that Michalea ordered for me, or the pen that I had practiced with on the water dummy that was supposed to be my thigh. What I was holding was nothing short of a heart attack sitting in the realm of Herman's House of greatest hits. I am not the guy that cries at weddings or even funerals. I don't cry when I see a dead cat in the middle of the road or a dog lying in a ditch. I am not particularly fond of snakes unless they are behind glass and I think spiders are one of the greatest creations ever designed; eight legs or not, they make webbing an art form on my front porch every morning. But the caption under my little cartoon at that very moment should have read "Dude, Freddy's back!" If that was the almighty pen I was holding in my hand, then my idea of a pen was infinitely different than Michaela's.

I began to hyperventilate, and I was sweating bullets just standing in front of the open refrigerator. I wobbled a bit as I found a chair to sit down in and access the situation. I started to cry like a damn two-year old who has just discovered that his toy GI JOE doll has been eaten by a very disturbed dog. I held that package with such disbelief that I didn't care who saw me reacting to it. Twenty-five minutes went by before I was able to pull myself together and find a way to break the bad news to the rest of my being.

"Well shit. Isn't this a fine day for a rotten, moronic, dazzling array of comical cliché's that I can't think of?" I sat there speechless for another ten minutes before I pulled myself out of the chair and left the faculty lounge. My brain was thinking and guiding my body long before I knew where the rest of me was headed. I suddenly found myself walking through the entrance of the emergency room at Denver General Hospital with my car keys in one hand and the Trojan horse in the other. Tears were streaming down my face and the fear factor was so apparent on my face that I had trouble breathing. A kind nurse rounded the reception desk and asked me what happened.

"I think the pharmacy made a mistake." I handed the nurse the box. "I don't do needles." I babbled in coherently. She took me to a triage room and sat me down while she phoned Dr. Sheridan's office. Another nurse came in and did her best to get me to settle down and relax while the other nurse was talking to Michalea.

"Herman" the first nurse said in a soothing voice. "Your doctor's office said that you should have gotten the pens not the syringes. She is going to call the pharmacy and get that fixed for you. In the meantime, however, you will need to have someone give you the syringe twice a month." I shook my head and waited for the other shoe to drop. "Where are you supposed to get your injection?"

"Thigh." I said rolling up the cuff of my khaki shorts. The nurse took out the first syringe and I about passed out. The needle could have been the length of a dolphin's dick at that point and I still would have fallen over and passed out. A needle was needle. I didn't care what size it was. It was enough to make Typhoon Mary spray my face with salt water. I turned my head away from the nurse and I jumped when the prick hit my leg.

"Sorry. There's going to be a slight poke" she said as she pricked my leg again. No matter how hard I try to rewind that play by play, it still does not erase the emotional aspect of the moment. I could have double dubbed that and still not have been able to reproduce that raw, genuine emotion that filtered through my body and out the tear ducts. I sat there for a moment with the partial box in my hand and a throbbing thigh beating somewhere around me. I cried the way a brand new baby does when it wakes hungry; cried the way a three year old does when it walks into a wall while chasing the family dog into the kitchen, cried like a water fixture stuck in the middle of a tidal wave. There is absolutely no comparison to how a single, solitary needle can trigger so much fear in just one individual, the way that syringe did. At some point I realized as I limped out of the emergency room with my pride tucked in my pockets that I would have to do this five more times before I could get a corrected shipment of medication. Five more times of needles that were enough to the scare the Skittles out of a grown man and never leave a rainbow of fun for him to follow later.

I took the rest of the day off. My thigh was sore and standing on my leg was giving me more grief than I needed. Between the shock of the needle and a trip to the emergency room, the House of Herman was in Dire Straits.

CHAPTER 22

"Why didn't you tell me you are scared of needles?" Alfred asks as he hands me a beer.

"Why didn't you tell me that you own three sets of the same clothes?" I answer, taking a swig of beer before belching.

"You have a needle phobia. It takes a great deal of courage to do what you did today."

"Thanks for pointing out the obvious, Spock. Oh yeah, so brave I am. Crying like an ankle bitter in the midst of adults that make a point of needling you while in their presence."

"At least you haven't lost your sense of humor. A lot of bravery to do what you did, driving to the emergency room with that box in your hand. The real courage is letting people see you cry, letting them see the real authentic Herman and not the suave, sophisticated, sarcastic asshole that you are most days."

"Suave? What the fuck are you drinking in that Miller?"

"Just beer."

"Just beer, my ass. I am not suave and don't you go starting anything either."

"And give you the opportunity to rob me of my Glory Days? Never." Alfred sits next to me as I rub my leg. "She could have at least rubbed your thigh for you after sticking you with that shit."

"Bitch. It's already leaving a damn bruise!" I rub my leg placing the cold beer on the spot where I had been shot. The bruise is a new thing, an afterthought on an otherwise rotten day. "It's sore as hell and I bet by tomorrow it will be worse. I hope to hell I find someone other than an ER nurse to give me my next injection. Otherwise, I will just have to drive to the doctor and have good old Michalea give it to me."

"That should be interesting. Can I watch?" Alfred is doing his level best to cheer me up and so far, I am not drunk enough or high enough to be even amused.

"No, you dried up old fossil, you may not watch. One look at my leg and you'd probably get jealous or something."

"Listen here you ancient pothead, I've seen your leg before and it's nothing to brag about. Matter of fact, DiVinci and DE Goya are rolling in their graves. Your tattoo of a fish and cross bones looks like a wrinkling nightmare…..with a twist."

"Skull and crossbones, not a fish you dried up old prune."

"Funny, it looks like a fish with a black eye!" Alfred leaps off the couch before I can punch him. I take another swig of beer and sit back against the cushions with the beer hugging my leg. I am ever so grateful for the presence of my dear old friend Alfred and his bag of beer and boxes of Little Cesar's pizza. One thing that is an absolute constant Al; impeccable timing. He wears the same freshly pressed black slacks, mauve colored Ralph Lauren Polo with sandals and socks. I shake my head, bite into a slice of Super Supreme gooeyness and watch Alfred as he pours out a beer into a glass and proceeds to blow a bottle tune.

"You're a strange little man, Alfred P. Handleman" I chuckle.

"Look who's talking Herman. 'Just Call Me Herm' Strickland. No snappy comebacks?" He asks as he continues to serenade me with Row-Row-Row-Your-Boat.

"Sorry, my man. But Snappy and his Ghetto busters are lying low. You already swallow the comeback." I watch Alfred for a moment and realize that he does not get the slip I slid across his lap.

"You want to catch a movie? I can go to Blockbuster or something and get one."

"Dude, what Stone Age time period are you still living in? Blockbuster? They are long gone….like you will be if I have to see another sandal with a sock on your foot."

"What's wrong with my socks? They match!"

"Matching is not the problem, Al. I can see your toes through them."

"I'm wearing sandals."

"I know. I see that. It's the whole toe thing I'm referring to. Look." Alfred scoots over to the edge of the couch before seeing his feet. His stomach grew; travel, rich foods, and hotel beds. His Ken doll sleekness, gone.

"It is a no toe-holds barred moment." He says laughing at the hole in his socks. "That's just pitiful. All that money you have and you wear holey socks to my place. Nice."

"Yeah, all that money....no wife, no kids, no girlie friend, just you."

"Meaning what, exactly?"

"Nothing. Just saying that I find out you are sick and you need watching. "Maybe it's time I stay closer to home and look after you."

"Look after me like what? Ripening fruit on a vine? Or like an old prune sitting in a bowl waiting for a rainstorm?"

"Like an old pot plant in the Sahara desert."

"Call the Beach Boys. You're stealing their California Girls again!" I smile.

Alfred sits back against the couch and laughs. I can see every wrinkle on my friends' face the way one sees a ripple on a pond. He is the ripple effect in my pond, the one that keeps me moving toward bigger and grander ripples. I rub my leg where I had been shot, hoping the effect of the alcohol will numb the pain enough so that I can sleep.

Al leaves the couch and walks over to stand in front of one of my many bookshelves. He scans the titles, fingers the spines of each book until he finds a book that catches his interest. I recognize the book immediately. I wish I had that book elsewhere.

"You've got to be joking!" He snickers as he turns around to face me. "Is this for real?"

"Is what for real?" I ask innocently.

"This inscription. 'To my beloved grandson, Herman Munster Strickland. May you always have a yearning for learning and a screaming for your dream, Love, Grandma Ida Munster'?"

"Oh that one. Yes. My grandmother was a real card. She was the queen of the jokers."

"Your middle name is Munster?"

"Yes."

"Like Herman Munster, of the Munsters?"

"Uh huh."

"The Frankenstein Munster!" Alfred props himself against the bookshelf, holds his stomach with one hand and the book with the other.

"Uh huh. Put it back, Alfred, before you spill beer all over it." If I could morph into a Klingon right now, I would be the almighty warrior. With Al keeping me company that was not possible. Humility overtakes me and I cock my head, watching him enjoy the moment of discovery.

"Moby Dick. She wrote that in Moby Dick!"

"Yes, Herman Melville's Moby Dick." I try not to laugh at Alfred who is holding on for dear life to a long held secret I no longer have secreted away.

"They could have named you Moby Dick!" Alfred is bent over laughing so hard I'm afraid he will barf up beer and pizza cocktails.

"They could've named me Herman Dick and then we really would be a pair of dicks. But they didn't!"

"So now I know who to leave all my money too. Herman Munster. The grandest old pothead around!"

"When you put it that way, won't your kids want a piece of the action?"

"Fuck the kids. They have their own money. What the hell are they going to do with mine? I have Herman Munster in the house!" Alfred rarely swears and I am somewhat surprised. He continues his barrage of laughter until he collapses in the arm chair at the far end of the room. The very same chair that Grandma Munster used when she wrote in Moby Dick. I would listen to her stories. The way she grunted like an old man, whined like a horse and changed her voice to mimic the characters. The way she told her told her stories I felt I was right there, seeing with my own two eyes the miracle of fantasy and horror. Grandma was the greatest story teller and the reason I became who I am today. I owe all I have to my grandmother…the inspiration for reading and discovery. Grandma Munster in her up-do of lavender gray hair, tiny glasses, and smelling of lilac and menthol rub. I can still remember her hugging me after writing in Moby Dick. Her tiny but dainty handwriting was flawless as it swam across the page with the fountain pen she always carried with her. It had been her favorite pen up until she passed away. Now it sits in the ink well in my office waiting for her to pen a 'hello' if ever she comes by for a visit. I take Moby Dick away from Alfred's shaking hands, giggling the same way I had when my grandmother called me Herman Munster's baby. "You really are named after a classic, Herman, my man!"

"Yes, but at least I don't have a Peter in my name." I grin.

"Touché!" He swirls an imaginary sword in the air. "Your secret is safe."

"I doubt that. After all, you now know two secrets of mine which means I am compromised and you could end up, you know, disappeared."

"Really? How? I can't seem to remember a damn thing! Too much weed or something." He winks.

"A toast, Alfred P. Handleman. May the force always be with, us!"

"May shit never fly any lower than the toilet" Alfred yells. We both laugh like school kids.

* * * * * *

Journal entry:

I remember each every student I ever had; from their freckles to their pimples. The days they slip in and out of consciousness in class to asking for help. Each kid that crossed the barrier of my office regardless of where my office found itself, I remember those kids.

Years back a little girl with a busted lip and black eye walked into my office. She had visions of being a writer. Someone wanted to be truly great. P.E. before I even got the opportunity to help that little girl, she was yanked out of school and my class. I was fucking scared that something bad happened to her the way bad things happen to bad people. She was not a bad kid. She was a spark whose light got snuffed out before it got going. Or so I believed.

Today a young woman, Marion Dressler, formerly known as Marion Clemson, the geeky ninth grader from years long ago, shows up in my office. I never forgave myself for not doing what I should have done all those years ago. So here she is, an attractive woman, married, productive, and a full time editor and writer. She came to thank me for guiding her safely on a journey I never knew she had taken. She found me through the usual channels that teachers use when hunting for inspirational purposes.

You see P.E., Herman Munster is not just a secret, but a legacy that I leave to others to follow, you included. I chose to remember Marion the way I remember Kellie; gentle souls with a great deal of life yet to explore. I shower my students like Marion with praise and then I let them walk away, free as a rabbit in a teacup. No shit storms accompany them, No sand storm to upset the balance. Just a casual walk in the park on a clear summer day.

* * * * * *

"YELLO! Your shirt is on backward again, Herman. Do I need to hire a nanny to dress you?" Alfred asks pouring another cup of tea.

"You would do that for me?"

"How nuts do you think I am, Herman?"

"Well, on a scale of one to who gives a shit, I will have to say, and who gives a shit how I dress, as long as I am dressed before I leave the house each day." I peer out the window and the unremarkable cloud covering lowering itself down around the Rockies.

"Pot Head." Alfred hisses at me.

"You know there isn't a Green Day that passes by in my life without your snippy little fly-in-the-tea comebacks. You should probably head over to Linkin Park and ask for your money back because you got Motley Crue-d. Furthermore, one of the Funky Kings is looking for you. Seems you were seen red handed dissecting the muffins again....really? Pulling off the tops and rolling them up into balls of goo and stuffing them in your mouth?"

"Funny. It wasn't the muffin tops I was picking off. It was the Bee Gees and their fat hair! The game is afoot old man.....pack your bags Manfred Mann, we're going to jazz things up a bit and get the Coltrane out of here." Al burped.

"Do the Kinks know you've been tampering in their George Strait, again? If so, I'm guessing that Three Doors Down are collecting a little Alice in Chains long before the Sisters of Mercy get a chance to sing your ass a lullaby."

"Just leave the collecting to the professionals, Herman. From where I sit Journey is about to take a sudden turn and land you in Alabama. On the other hand, The Black-eyed Peas…they are itching to redress you. I am cheering for Simon and Garfunkel's Bridge over Troubled Waters. You're going to need it." Alfred snickers in his teacup. He sputters out tea from the sides of his mouth until it sprays out all over the front of his silk tie. "Shit. This is my favorite tie too."

"I had one of those once."

"When have you ever worn a tie? Never. Not since I've know you."

"Well I used to have a tie, when I wasn't around Bad Company."

"And when was this supposed time, old wise pothead?"

"When it was holding up an old pair of shorts I used to wear a long time ago."

"What tie was that?"

"The drawstring kind. I had to burn the tie with the shorts….it was a package deal." I snicker.

"Why burn your shorts?"

"I shit in them and the stench did a dye job in the crotch!" I rush to the bathroom. It is going to be close.

"Damn! Remind me not to ask for an Usher to your funeral! You'll be able to float into your grave without any assistance you fermented old pothead! Whew! You are fucking rank!" Alfred shouts after me.

"Wrinkled up mushroom fart!" I yell back.

"What the fuck is that horrid smell? Did you eat beans again? You know you aren't to have those. Did you die in there?"

"Not yet. That's a kiss from my ass to you!" I laugh so hard that my bowels lose control. Fresh air blows in the house like Storm Troopers. Alfred is hacking up a lung. I am accustomed to the old man smell, and the putrid nastiness that goes with Crohn's disease. I never let it get the best of me.

"Are you quite through stinking up the place? Shit! If I was a cyborg, I would be turning off my smell receptors right now!" Alfred yells through the front door.

"I don't smell anything." I snicker to myself innocently.

"That's because you are used to smelling like a rotting corpse in a shit sewer! How the hell can you live with yourself smelling like this?"

"It's easy, I have a picture of you taped to my medicine cabinet and every time I see your face, I think of you tossing up your cookies and clinging to the last remaining shred of fresh air in your gas mask." I yell out from my post.

"You demented old pothead!" Alfred gags again. I am pretty sure the neighbors wonder why Alfred is yelling at me through the door. Not that we care but I would give anything at this particular instant to be a fly in their bonnets and to hear the reactions. My imagination gets the better of me and I laugh it all off. Al is standing in the entrance to the bathroom when I look up.

"Don't you knock, you old fart?"

"When I hear you laugh like a deranged hyena with a pipe bomb up your ass, I forgo the knocking and check out what's going on. Glad to see you are still among the living, you gnarly Funky Kings. I can't imagine for the life of me why you don't send up a warning flare when your sewer system goes on the fritz."

"Flares are for people that are lost and I am not lost. I am in the right room."

"Sarcasm should have been your first name, you know that?"

"Sarcasm is just something I crap out multiple times a day. Others have to work at it. And for the record Al, old buddy, you can't use the same rock group I just did. Game rules. And for another record hit, when I get out of here, I am going to pass you the biggest joint you've ever seen. A very successful alligator student of mine gave a box of them to me a few years back. I save them for special occasions, just like the one we are going to have momentarily. We are going to light up one of those babies, order out pizza, and get chipped faced. There are two pints of chocolate chip ice cream in the freezer just for such an occasion." Alfred shakes his head, snorts a laugh, belts out another laugh and then leaves me in silence. *Why is it that I am not able to go to the head and shit like everyone else in private? Why do I keep having an audience? Am I that damn entertaining?*

* * * * * * *

Journal Entry:

A truly incredible afternoon by far. We smoke multiple joints, order pizza (P.E. dissects his pizza like it is a science project in a high

214

school biology lab), get chipped faced (P.E. takes out all the chocolate chips and collects them like they are molten lava chips. For some weird reason he thinks they are burning the lid to the ice cream and when he tries to eat one of them he manages to eat his tie instead and announces that the Trail Dust Steak House can no longer have his tie….gag, like who would?! I didn't have the heart to tell him that he kept setting his tie on fire so he could watch the chocolate chips melt), and then pass out in our own spots across from each other.

I sleep for a few hours. Wake up, pop a few Benadryl and try to go back to sleep. This is my constant; popping sleeping pills, Benadryl and smoking pot. Sleep alludes me like silent footsteps in the dark.

It is still early; 1:30 in the morning. I can still get six hours of sleep in before Alfred the Fearless (AKA P.E.) rises for his morning constitutional. I feel a certain gas build up brewing in the nether regions. I may never be able to run a marathon or ski in Winter Park without worrying about the almighty shit factor. I count my blessings every day and thank the universe for its twisted and ever so demented sense of humor. The brutality of Crohn's disease is not that is an end of a life but a beginning to new possibilities. I am not going to sit here and give you advice on how to take care of me P.E. I want you to know that if there any alien lifeforms orbiting Earth and they are looking for volunteers….beam me up. I have a squadron of toxic waste just waiting to blow the mother-fuckers up.

And I promise to keep the Klingons off Uranus.

BE BRAVE WITH YOUR LIFE

ACKNOWLEDGEMENTS

A very special and heart felt THANK YOU to my three wonderful, amazing, and stellar children; Jeremiah, Anastasia, and Harrison. Had it not been for the jokes you cracked when crap was flowing, LITERALLY, I would not have been able to row myself out of it and become the Death Star Bomb of our house.

To my best friends Faye Flick, Lisa Ivey, Bob Kahn, Julie Quinn, and Bobbi Brooks.........you wouldn't let me give up.

For Djamel Guenifi and his jokes about milking male camels (don't ask).

And to My Aunt Ginny for believing that something good always comes from poop.

Printed in the United States
By Bookmasters